DETOUR
Book #2, The Mac 'n' Ivy Mysteries
By
Lorena McCourtney

Chapter 1

IVY

By now we should be in Arizona, romantic newlyweds lazing around a sunlit pool at some nice RV park, holding hands and sipping something cold and fizzy. Instead, here we were, somewhere on the rugged coast of Northern California, peering through an Ark-worthy downpour at a monster in the middle of a parking lot.

"What *is* that?" I asked.

"I think it's a triceratops," Mac said.

The tank-sized creature had a bony ruff around the neck, two enormous horns above the eyes, and another horn on the snout. A nearby sign read GHOST GOAT DINOSAUR PARK. Below, in smaller print, Come See Ferocious Beasts of the Past Up Close!

No doubt this parking-lot creature was meant to be intimidating, and in size it certainly was. But, as Mac pulled our motorhome closer, it looked more morose than ferocious, as if it were having a really bad dinosaur day. Maybe having the tip missing from a horn, two plastic bags plastered to your side, and three of your feet in a puddle will do that to you.

A rough hillside loomed beyond a high chain-link fence, and another dinosaur head on a long neck peered at us from above a forest of tangled foliage. This one too, in spite of its height, came across as somewhat less than ferocious. A windblown, broken branch drooped over one eye, like some attempt at dinosaur fashion gone awry.

BoBandy jumped up on the console between Mac and me. No friendly wave of his reddish-brown tail for the dinosaurs. He looked out at the creatures and decided they warranted a semi-growl. BoBandy is only a mid-sized dog, but he's very protective. Orange-colored Koop, his stubby-tailed body curled in my lap, opened his one good eye and then shut it again. Koop couldn't care less about dinosaurs unless they came packed in a cat-food can.

"That long-necked one may be a brontosaurus," Mac said.

"How come you know so much about dinosaurs?"

"I was really interested in them when I was a kid. But I've probably forgotten a lot of things. This one might be a brachiosaurus instead of a brontosaurus."

Which made me realize again that even though we'd known each other for several years before we married a few weeks ago in October, there was probably still a lot I didn't know about my new husband. Who'd have thought Mac knew anything about dinosaurs? It was exciting to think we had the rest of our lives to explore and learn all these surprises about each other. Including the not-world-shaking but interesting puzzle of that blue motorcycle tattooed on Mac's forearm, a tattoo that he's always been reluctant to talk about. I've not yet asked a direct question about it, but I've been curious about it since the first time we met.

I wasn't thrilled with this unexpected detour into dinosaur world. Neither was Mac, but just before we were ready to leave on our honeymoon, he'd received a frantic phone call from the editor of a magazine that has published a number of his travel articles. The magazine had scheduled an article about a big dinosaur theme park somewhere back East for next month's issue, but the writer had come down with shingles and couldn't get the article done. Now the editor was desperate for something to fill the space. He'd suggested we make a quick detour to visit this Ghost Goat Dinosaur Park.

That's one of the things I love about Mac. He's always willing to help someone in need, even an editor who thinks Northern California is a "quick" detour between Montana and Arizona. So I'm not going to let a detour, bad weather, and

2

some deteriorating dinosaurs dampen my enthusiasm for our new married life together. Although the place did look like an excellent spot for hiding dead bodies, which have a troubling tendency to turn up in my life. Hopefully, marriage will change that.

"Do the owners know we're coming?" I asked. The one-story building to the left, with a TV satellite dish on one corner of the roof, had "Gift Shop" in faded rainbow letters across the top, but a Closed sign blocked the door.

"The dinosaur park isn't open during the late fall and winter months, but there's supposed to be a manager or caretaker living here all year who will show us around."

"The dinosaur business doesn't look too profitable."

Potholes dotted the parking area, and I noticed now that the triceratops also had a toe missing on the one foot that wasn't in a puddle. A fanciful imagination might suggest the dinosaurs came to life and fought epic battles in the night. I figured a more pragmatic explanation was that time and the elements were gradually weathering the triceratops into an amorphous mass. Rather like time has aged me, if not yet into an amorphous mass, at least into a state often close to invisible. An invisible Little Old Lady, otherwise known as an LOL. Although I'm pleased to say that invisibility can sometimes be a handy asset.

"I think people expect more than statues just standing around these days. They want *Jurassic Park* type action. Leaps and roars and snapping teeth. Maybe a stomach-churning ride or two." Mac peered at the trees and vines crowding the fence and thrusting green tentacles into the parking area. The dinosaurs were lifeless statues, but the dark labyrinth beyond the chain-link fence looked as if it might hide anything from otherworldly beasts to man-eating fungi.

"This also isn't the most accessible location," I noted. We were several miles off Highway 101, the main route along the

3

California coast. There was a sign about the dinosaur park out on the highway, but this wasn't a place kids would see from the car and instantly clamor to stop.

"Well, let's go see if we can find Brian Morrison. Maybe I can wrap this up in a day or two."

I followed Mac out of the motorhome. We take turns driving, but my bones felt stiff and creaky, and I needed to move around after sitting most of the day. Shades blocked windows in the gift shop, so we circled around back, gusting wind driving rain at us as if it had a personal vendetta against us. A carport attached to the building stood empty, but an older green Honda was parked behind the building. A travel trailer and a blue pickup stood in a cleared space back in the trees. None of this suggested any greater prosperity in the dinosaur business than did the morose triceratops in the parking lot.

A sign on a back door of the gift shop building read Private Residence, and Mac knocked there. I stepped up beside him to get under the shelter of the overhanging roof.

No response to his knock. Another knock. Another nonresponse.

Nothing peculiar about this, of course. Brian Morrison didn't know what day we'd arrive, so he wouldn't be sitting around waiting for us. My nerves skittered anyway. Little Old Lady intuition telling me all was not right here?

Then a woman's voice came through the door. "I'm sorry. We're closed for the winter."

Sometimes my LOL intuition is as spot-on as a laser beam. Sometimes it's about as accurate as a fortune cookie. This time it was apparently spinning in cookie world because the woman's voice sounded, if not welcoming, at least normal.

"I'm here to do an article on the dinosaur park for *Fun on the Road* magazine," Mac said. "I'm looking for Brian Morrison?"

"Brian went into Eureka for the afternoon, and I'm kind of . . . busy."

What was she so busy at that she could come to the door but couldn't open it? It could be something unpleasant but mundane, of course. Scrubbing the toilet or oven. Cleaning moldy gunk out of the refrigerator. Been there, done that. But, considering my experiences in recent years, other possibilities loomed: maybe she was cleaning up blood puddled on the kitchen floor. Dismembering a body in the bathroom tub. Hiding a corpse under the floor in a closet. Or maybe she was being held prisoner, with a gun at her head and a murderer/kidnapper telling her to get rid of us?

No such ominous possibilities apparently occurred to Mac, however. He simply said, "Okay, thanks. We'll wait out here for Mr. Morrison."

I didn't mention my thoughts to Mac. He never disparages my thoughts, even the far-out ones, but I had to admit these were probably circling the drain. Find an occasional dead body and you start imagining one in every dark corner or unanswered knock. But still . . .

Mac turned and started back through the rain to the motorhome, but I leaned toward the door. "Are you all right? Do you need help or anything?"

The dead bolt unexpectedly clicked and the door flew open. The plumpish woman standing there had a towel flung around her shoulders and a plastic cap over her head. A few stray rivulets of reddish-brown color dribbled down her cheek. She swiped at them with a corner of the towel.

"That's so nice of you to ask. I could have been in here in an 'I've fallen and can't get up' state of distress, couldn't I? Thanks." She smiled. "Come on in. You don't have to wait out there in the cold."

Mac turned and looked at her as if she were some sort of two-legged dinosaur, and I was mildly annoyed with him.

5

Hadn't he ever seen a woman coloring her hair? Of course she didn't want to come to the door. My next and quite unexpected thought made me squint at her. *Hey, don't I know her from somewhere?*

"Come on in," she repeated. "Brian should be home before long. He's looking at some local properties for investment." She lowered her voice, as if we were in a small conspiracy together. "Just don't tell him you caught me improving on the hair color nature gave me."

I smiled back and joined the conspiracy. "Everybody colors their hair," I whispered. "It's practically un-American not to."

She eyed my hair. Was she wondering if some company actually sold possum-gray hair coloring? I've tried changing the color, but after disastrous results a few years ago—think volcanic eruption of neon orange—I let nature have its way. Unfortunately, nature seems stuck on possum gray.

"You're welcome to wait for Brian in here. I'll make coffee or tea as soon as I rinse out my hair."

I motioned Mac back, and we stepped inside. Again I had that definite sense of familiarity. She was midfifties or thereabouts. She probably bemoaned her weight—I could see a carton of Slim Fast on a kitchen counter—but plump looked good on her. No wrinkles marred the smooth glow of her skin, and her blue eyes had an energetic sparkle.

Yes, I knew her from somewhere. I was sure of it. But I've traveled all over the country in the last few years, avoiding the clutches of the murderous Braxtons, so it could have been anywhere. I didn't see any echo of recognition from her, but I asked anyway.

"Haven't we met somewhere before?"

Her head jerked as if I'd poked her with a hot curling iron. A few reddish-brown dribbles flew as she shook her head with unexpected vigor. "No, I don't think so."

"Colorado, perhaps? A little town in the mountains called

Hello? Were you in the chorus line at that town celebration there?"

"I've never been to Colorado. Or in a chorus line anywhere." She wiped a streak running down her neck. "But I do remember now that Brian said someone was coming to write about Ghost Goat Dinosaurs for a magazine. So that must be you."

"Yes. I'm Mac MacPherson and—" Mac motioned to me. "This is my wife, Ivy."

She held out a hand and smiled. "Kathy Morrison."

Mac supplied information about the magazine and the article he planned to write. Tactfully not including the information that Ghost Goat Dinosaur Park was a second-choice replacement for a larger and more important dinosaur theme park. He didn't show any sign of recognition as he was talking to her, and I had to pause for a moment in my efforts to place her anyway. Hearing myself identified as Mac's wife does that to me. I'm now Ivy *MacPherson*! That giddiness will no doubt wear off eventually, but right now I get this tingle of delight.

"I'm curious about the name Ghost Goat Dinosaur Park," Mac said. "Do you know any history on that?"

"No, but Brian probably does. I love it here, but sometimes I think a more dinosaur-ish name would be better."

Dinosaur-ish. My kind of word. I liked Kathy Morrison. Maybe a rekindling of liking her from some time in the past when I'd known her before? Not unusual that she didn't remember me, of course. Being non-memorable runs parallel with invisibility.

"Perhaps, to save time, you could give us a little more information before Mr. Morrison returns?" Mac suggested. "You can probably tell me much of what I need to know."

She took a step back. "I'm really not out and about in the park much. Brian takes care of everything out there, and I just

7

run the gift shop. But we have some pamphlets—" A buzzer sounded somewhere beyond the living room. She grabbed at the plastic cap again, as if the buzzer might signal imminent hair explosion. "Would you excuse me for a minute? My hair's done. Do sit down."

"Okay if I go outside and look around?" Mac asked. "I think the rain has let up."

Hand on top her head to hold the plastic cap in place, she reached toward a hook beside the front door. "I'll give you a key to the gate so you can— Oh, dear, it isn't here. Brian must have stuck it in his pocket. He makes a quick tour through the park every few days to, you know, check it out."

"To see if any dinosaurs escaped in the night?" Mac suggested.

"Or if any new ones sneaked in to join them." A friendly smile replaced that hint of uneasiness when I'd suggested we'd met before.

Mac has that ability to set strangers at ease. But I still thought I knew her from somewhere. Maybe that little town in Arkansas where I'd stayed with my niece and her family for a while? The place where the Braxtons had tried to blow up my old Thunderbird?

She waved at a sofa and disappeared down the hall. I looked around the cozily cluttered living room. Bright pillows and throws swamped the blue sofa. A pair of blue recliners faced a flat-screen TV. A door on the far wall apparently led from the apartment to the gift shop. Tucked in a corner, partly concealed by a folding screen, a laptop computer sat on a small desk, a printer on the floor beside it.

Pamphlets and booklets covered an end table by the sofa. I picked one up, thinking it was something about Ghost Goat Dinosaur Park, but these were pamphlets from various other dinosaur parks around the country. The picture on the cover of the one I'd picked up showed a merry-go-round with kids

8

riding dinosaur figures. Stuck inside was a sketch of a big-toothed, walking dinosaur with a carrier basket on its back.

Vigorous green plants overflowed hanging baskets around a window. Knickknacks, elves and fairies and angels, covered the glass shelves. No dinosaurs, I noted. No photos of grandchildren, either, which surprised me. I'd have tagged Kathy as a woman who'd plaster her walls with pictures of grandchildren.

We heard the sound of a car outside, and Mac stepped to the window. His head gave a little jerk of surprise, and I peered out the window beside him. I'm not all that great at car recognition, but even I could see this was an expensive vehicle pulling into the carport. Red, low-slung, and classy. It looked as if 90 mph might be its natural cruising speed.

"What is it?" I asked.

"Porsche. Maybe the dinosaur business is more profitable than we thought."

The man who got out of the car carrying a grocery sack had dark hair, mustache, and beard. He was on the heavy side—maybe they shared that SlimFast—but he walked with a rakish swagger. Mac stepped up to tell him who we were when he opened the door.

"Brian Morrison," he responded with a smile. He held out a hand. Do men ever get a little help with beard coloring from a bottle? Mac doesn't. His beard is elegantly silvery white, but Brian may have, as his wife put it about herself, improved on nature.

"Good to see you got here okay," he added, and we all shook hands. "I hope you had a good trip?"

"Yes, great trip. If you have time, perhaps you could give me a quick tour through the park before the rain starts again?"

"Sure. I'll take Duke's almond milk over to him later." He took the sack to the kitchen, set it on a counter, and turned back to us. "Although I have to admit I'm surprised a magazine

9

such as *Fun on the Road* is interested in our little dinosaur park. We're not exactly a star among the dinosaur parks around the country."

"I think the editor had some fond memories of coming here as a boy."

Mac asked if I wanted to come along for the tour, but I said I'd see the dinosaurs later.

At the moment I had something else in mind. I knew Kathy from somewhere even if she didn't remember me, and I wanted to dig a little deeper.

Although I had the odd feeling it might be more that she didn't *want* to remember me.

Chapter 2

IVY

Kathy had put on glasses and changed into leggings and a tunic decorated with somersaulting kitties when she returned to the living room. She was toweling her hair dry, and the swingy auburn bob had a nice shine. If I'd had that kind of result with hair coloring, maybe I'd be tempestuous titian instead of possum gray.

"Brian knows I color my hair, of course, but I always take care of the actual process while he's not around." Kathy laughed. "It's like when I make smoothies for him. I never let him see me put in the kale. He hates kale. But it's good for him, and he never realizes it's there. Coffee or tea? It's no bother," she added quickly, as if anticipating my response.

"Tea would be nice." I went into the kitchen to join her.

Kathy put the almond milk in the refrigerator and pulled several cartons of tea from a cupboard. "Is this a full-time job with you and your husband, traveling around doing articles about interesting places?" she asked as she filled a copper kettle and put it on the stove.

"Mac started doing it mostly because it was a good reason to keep traveling all around the country. He's also very good at it and enjoys it."

"Isn't it wonderful to have a competent husband? Brian has such creative ideas and big-thinking concepts. He knows so much about computers and can do so much with them. He opened ours up and fixed something inside last week." She frowned. "But luck does seem to play such an unfair part in so many situations."

I wondered what that meant. "Creative ideas" and "big-thinking concepts" didn't seem necessary to manage what appeared to be a rather run-down dinosaur park. Was that part of the unfairness of luck? Or maybe the stack of pamphlets from other parks and that sketch of a dinosaur with a basket for riders meant Brian had bigger things in mind for the park?

"Actually, right now we're looking for a good place to settle down and live," I said.

"What kind of place?"

I told her what Mac and I had already discussed. "Not too big but not too small. Not too cold but not too hot." I didn't mention another requirement. No murders or dead bodies. "Just some place comfortable and friendly, with nice weather."

"I love it here. But I guess I mentioned that, didn't I? We're not far from the beach, and I like to go over there and pick up shells and rocks. There are awesome flowers out in the park in the spring."

"Some people might think you're rather isolated here. No close neighbors at all."

"That's true. But I'm not into gossipy clubs and playing bridge and all that, so it's fine with me."

"Have you been here long?"

"A year or so."

"You mentioned you don't go out in the park much—?"

"Well . . . I don't." She took an almost furtive peek out the kitchen window and then laughed. "I know it sounds foolish, but the dinosaurs and even some of the huge plants out there feel so . . . hostile. Once I even thought I saw one of the ghost goats. A mean-looking old billy goat with big horns staring at me out of the brush. And there's a cliff on the far side of the park. The only time I was up there I kept thinking that old goat might shove me right off the cliff." She laughed and twirled a finger against her head to suggest her mind might be a little wonky with such thoughts. "But don't mention any of this to your husband, okay? I wouldn't want anything about aggressive ghost goats in his article for the magazine. Brian thinks I'm ridiculous." She laughed. "Just wait until one of them butts *him*

12

and I'm saying, 'See? I told you so.' I think his attachment to the Porsche is a little ridiculous too. It's just four wheels and expensive insurance, but he waxes and polishes that thing more often than I color my hair." She laughed again, but I had the feeling this might be a point of real contention between them.

"Do you enjoy working in the gift shop?"

"Oh yes, that's fun. I have a Dolly Dinosaur costume with a frilly apron and a horn that makes a foghorn beeping sound. The kids love it. I still have some of my ghost goat and dinosaur cupcakes in the freezer. Would you like one with your tea?"

"That would be great."

She pulled a plastic-wrapped carton of cupcakes out of a chest-type freezer under a kitchen window. "They're popular with our gift shop customers in the summer."

The cupcakes were delightful, each one topped with a frosting figure of a dinosaur or goat. I pointed to a purple one with a thick tail. "That looks good."

She put my cupcake on a plate and popped it in the microwave for thawing and warming.

"You're not having one?"

She planted a hand on a generously padded hip. "Do I look as if I need a dinosaur on my hip? I have been on—and off— every diet known to womankind since I was a teenager. Although if you know of a good new one, I'm always open to suggestions." Her eyebrows lifted hopefully.

I've always been on the petite side (well, okay, to be technical, more like scrawny) and never needed to diet, but, since I popped a seam on my wedding dress, perhaps I'll soon have to start thinking about one.

I dismissed the subject of weight and diets. Kathy looked healthy and energetic, although I noticed a string of prescription medications lined up at the back of the kitchen counter. Hers or Brian's? I studied her again. "You know, you do look so familiar. I'm sure we know each other from somewhere."

She didn't ask questions or offer suggestions about where that may have been. She simply rejected any possibility with another shake of head. "I have one of those ordinary faces and overweight bodies you see everywhere," she declared. "Crowds are full of us. A few weeks ago I was approached by a teenage girl in Eureka who thought I was an aunt she hadn't seen for a while."

"Where did you and Brian live before you came to the dinosaur park?"

"Oh, here and there. Texas. Southern California. Actually, we haven't been married all that long."

"Really? I'd have taken you for a long-married couple."

"No, just a few years."

I was curious that she wasn't more specific. What woman isn't proudly aware of exactly how many years she's been married? And the anniversary date as well.

"How about you and Mac?" she asked. "Have you had your fiftieth anniversary yet?"

I was flattered that we looked like a couple wed fifty years, but I had to admit we were somewhat short of that. "Actually, we're newlyweds. We haven't even had a one-month anniversary yet."

She gave me a surprised inspection. "Really? Congratulations! So how come you're here instead of honeymooning in some place moonlit and romantic?" She sounded mildly indignant.

"Honeymoon is a state of mind, not a place." It was a spur-of-the-moment thought, not some noble philosophy I'd arrived at after deep consideration. But I decided I should keep reminding myself of the thought on this dinosaur detour.

"I like that. But we did have the most marvelous honeymoon in Tahiti." She touched her fingertips together, and her smile was almost rhapsodic. "Brian's idea. He's such a romantic."

Mac and I hadn't been able to leave Mac's son's place in Montana for a honeymoon as soon after our wedding as we'd planned. Mac had a bad head injury just before the wedding, and the doctor insisted he stick around until the danger of seizures was past. And now, of course, we were on this dinosaur detour. "You're sure we've never met? The Dallas area in Texas?"

"No. I haven't been to that part of Texas."

"Maybe it was an RV park somewhere."

"We've never had an RV."

"I was in Arkansas before Texas. My niece lives there. And then Oklahoma?"

She shook her head again and offered me a selection of teas. I chose orange spice. She poured water from the kettle over the tea bag in a cup and changed the subject. "Where are you going after you leave here?"

"Arizona. Maybe the Bullhead City area. Or Yuma. Perhaps we knew each other before I ever left home back in Missouri," I persisted. "Madison Street?"

"No, I've never been to Missouri."

I was still curious, of course, but I sensed a definite chilling in Kathy's friendly attitude and, a bit reluctantly, I dropped the inquiry. I broke off the dinosaur's head and tasted it. "This is really good."

"Thank you. I make everything from scratch, not a mix. I do dinosaur and goat cookies too, but they're all gone. I'll start baking them again when the park opens in the spring."

"Being Dolly Dinosaur sounds like fun. Where do you get a dinosaur costume?"

"I make my own. I'm working on a new one right now. But what I'd really like to have is a baby dinosaur puppet. Brian and I went to this exhibit that travels around the country and has

15

an *awesome* display of all kinds of dinosaurs. Unlike our dinosaurs, these *move*. Heads, tails, legs, everything! And they *roar.*"

"They didn't feel hostile to you?"

"Oh, no. Maybe I'll try to make a baby dinosaur myself."

I admired her talents, but I was more interested in Kathy herself. Not asking nosy questions is difficult for someone with what a law officer friend once rather grumpily called my mutant curiosity gene.

I was still sure I knew her from somewhere, and her stiff insistence we hadn't met simply agitated that gene. Why didn't she at least want to explore the possibility we may have known each other at some earlier time?

MAC

Brian Morrison led the way across the parking lot to the gate into the fenced area. A ticket booth with another Closed sign stood beside the gate. He pulled a key from his pocket and unlocked the padlock. The swing of the tall gate jiggled the overhanging foliage, which showered the back of my neck.

"The fence isn't to keep the dinosaurs in, of course. They're a rather docile herd. We haven't had any problems since I've been here, but Duke says in the past he had trouble with vandalism and graffiti. So he finally had the front and part of the sides of the park fenced in. The back part of it is so steep that a fence didn't seem necessary."

I picked out the name he'd mentioned before. "Duke?"

"Duke Lancaster. He owns the dinosaur park." Brian motioned to the travel trailer set back in the woods at the end of the parking lot. "He managed the park himself for years, after he inherited it from his uncle Hiram, but he doesn't get around too well now. Nice old guy, but, you know, set in his ways. Behind the times."

16

Ghost Goat Dinosaur Park didn't have a website, but I'd run across the Hiram Lancaster name when I researched the park earlier. Hiram had started the park years ago. I'd assumed Brian managed the park for current out-of-area owners, and the information that the owner lived right here was a pleasant surprise. "Can I meet Duke?"

"I'll have to check and see what kind of day he's having. He has to take pain pills and sometimes his mind gets a little—" Brian's wavy wiggle of fingers suggested Duke's mental processes might also have some squiggly areas. "Great guy, though. He's dedicated a lot of years to the park."

Brian held the gate open, and I stepped onto the walkway leading through the jungled growth.

"Be careful of the puddle," Brian warned.

Right. A muddy puddle nearly straddled the pathway. The winding path, outlined with a rather prim white picket fence that was at odds with the dinosaur statues and rough, tangled foliage, had an occasional narrow log bridge more in tune with the lush vegetation. The ground outside the path was rough and steep, cut with ravines and covered with fir and pines and brush. Big ferns lined the pathway, and exotic-looking, shoulder-high plants with oversized leaves filled the ravines. Water trickled under them. The air smelled of damp growth. Vines clambered over boulders and big trees fallen long ago. The skeleton of a dead tree loomed on the hillside. We paused on a log bridge with water visible below. Brian puffed from the climb.

"That's Hungry Man Creek." Brian smiled. "I'm not sure if the name came from hard times in the early history of the area or if old Hiram named it from his own experiences. As you may have guessed, the park isn't a big moneymaker."

The brontosaurus—a plaque identified it—stood close by, but all I could see of it through the overgrown foliage was its feet at the bottom and that towering neck above. "Are all the

17

plants here native to the area?"

"I don't think so. I think Hiram brought in some exotic plants to make the park look more dinosaur-era authentic."

He'd certainly succeeded in that. The area outside the park was thickly forested, with heavy undergrowth, but the park itself looked like something out of a *Jurassic Park* movie. Except for that incongruous picket fence. I asked about it, and Brian said all he knew was that old Hiram had built it that way and Duke hadn't changed it. I gave a prolific species of plant with enormous leaves along the creek a wary glance. "I hope none of this vegetation is of a man-eating variety."

Brian laughed. "Me too. Although we get an occasional park visitor that I'd be happy to toss to a hungry plant. Those big plants down by the creek may look as if they came from some exotic jungle, and I tell tourists it's *cabbai giganticus*. Actually, it's skunk cabbage, native to the area. Which isn't exactly exotic." He sounded pleased with how he hoodwinked park visitors.

We strolled along the path winding around the side of the hill. Brian puffed some more and stopped to catch his breath a couple times. I didn't say anything, but it certainly looked to me as if Brian was shirking his duty taking care of the park. A little ditching with a shovel would drain the puddles on the path, and some prudent pruning would offer a better view of the dinosaurs. All I could see of one creature identified by a plaque as an Archelon, a giant turtle of the late Cretaceous period, was part of a huge, curved shell and one baleful eye.

Perhaps Brian planned a big cleanup and repair job before reopening in the spring.

"Were the dinosaurs constructed here, or were they moved in?"

"Duke's uncle Hiram built them right here. By himself. Though no one seems sure how he did it alone, especially that one with the long neck. I've heard he liked to tell people he just found these big eggs and hatched them out." He laughed again. "Concrete eggs, I assume."

"That's what the statues are, concrete?"

"Duke says they're concrete and wire over a metal framework underneath. Other dinosaur parks show much more realistic ones now. Kathy and I went to an exhibit last fall with movable dinosaurs. Much more interesting and exciting. I suppose I could add realistic sounds like they had at the exhibit, but here, with the dinosaur statues just standing around, sounds would probably just make them seem more unmovable than they are."

"Are they scientifically accurate?"

"I think so. Full-size too. Although I'm not as knowledgeable as ol' Duke about dinosaurs."

I wasn't impressed with that area of his park management, either. Why didn't he educate himself about dinosaurs and their lives so he could talk knowledgably with park visitors?

"If the uncle wanted to attract tourists, he could have chosen a more accessible spot," I suggested, as Ivy had earlier.

"I'm not sure old Hiram cared much about tourist business. I think the dinosaurs were more a labor of love thing for him. A family trait, I guess, because Duke has them all named, as if they were pets."

I wasn't into naming inanimate objects, but the brontosaurus back there—definitely a Benny.

We followed the steep, winding trail through the park, past dinosaurs identified by a metal plaque for each. Many of the plaques were tilted or fallen. I set one upright that was lying face down on the ground.

"How big is the park?"

"Four or five acres, something like that."

"Duke lives here alone? Except for you and your wife, I mean?"

"Duke's wife took off for parts unknown not long after he inherited the place. I guess she didn't care for life among the dinosaurs and skunk cabbage. They didn't have children, but Duke has a couple of nephews who live back East somewhere."

"Do they come visit?"

"One was here a couple months ago. He said he might move out here after he retires. Duke also has a lady friend who visits and takes him for an occasional outing. She's quite a bit younger than he is, but I guess you'd call her a girlfriend."

I jotted bits of information in a notebook I always keep in my shirt pocket. I'd have to make another trip through the park to take photos. Maybe bring a pair of clippers to get a better view of the dinosaurs.

As we circled back to the starting point at the gate, Brian told me about a little girl who had found a big, slimy slug in the park. She thought it was a baby dinosaur and proudly handed it to her mother. Mom screeched and tossed it in the air. It landed in another woman's hair.

Brian smiled. "And let me tell you, you've never heard a shriek until you've heard one from a woman with a slug in her hair. Some visitors really enjoy the park, but others find it a waste of time. I heard one teenage girl say, 'You see one of these dumb dinosaurs and you've seen 'em all. Bor-ing.' In that tone only teenage girls can manage, of course."

He locked the gate again when we went out. "I'll take Duke's almond milk over to him and see how he feels about a visitor."

"Thanks." Out of curiosity, never having even tasted almond milk, I had to ask, "Does Duke need a special diet?"

"No. But Kathy says almond milk is better for him. She's into all that health and diet stuff. A while back it was coconut oil and chia seeds for both herself and Duke. Personally, I'd rather have a good steak."

"That's good of her to be concerned about his health."

"Yeah, well, sometimes I think he's in better shape than he

lets on. That maybe he just likes having both his girlfriend and Kathy fussing over him."

I wondered if Brian planned to remove the plastic bags stuck to the triceratops in the parking lot, but he still didn't seem to notice them. We were almost back to the Porsche by then. Apparently he saw me comparing the vehicle to the economics of the dinosaur park.

He brushed a hand across the back fender of the sleek Porsche. The car looked freshly washed and waxed, unlike the old Honda standing out in the weather. "We like it here, but I have business interests independent of the park."

"Business can be handled from almost anywhere these days, with computers and smart phones and all."

"Right. Say, maybe we can get together for dinner? I have brochures and copies of some old articles about the park that might interest you."

"Sounds good."

A light rain had started again by the time we reached the apartment door at the back of the gift shop. I figured Ivy and I would wait out in the motorhome while Brian went over to Duke's trailer, but she pulled me inside when Brian opened the door.

"Take a good look at Kathy," she whispered. "Does she look familiar to you?"

I glanced at the back of Kathy's generously sized figure as she reached into the refrigerator to retrieve the almond milk. "No, I don't think so. Why?"

"Because I'm sure I know her from somewhere."

"Did you ask her?"

"I did, but she insists we've never met. That she's never been in any of the places I mentioned. Never stayed in any RV parks."

"So?"

"So, I think it's odd, that's all. Strange that she's so *insistent* about it. She won't even try to figure out where we may have known each other. Look at her again. You're good at remembering people."

"Ivy, you've met all kinds of people I don't know." Before we were married, we both had motorhomes, but we didn't always travel in unison. "I don't recognize either of them, and their names don't sound familiar to me."

I'm good at getting information for magazine articles, but Ivy can know more personal details after talking to someone for a few minutes than I'd know in a couple hours. People like to confide in her. Her memory about people is also very good.

So it seems unlikely she'd be so certain she'd met Kathy Morrison before if they hadn't actually met, and it was also odd that Kathy didn't even want to explore where they might have known each other. I studied the woman more closely when she turned around.

Nope, no help from me. I'd never seen her before.

Chapter 3

MAC

Ivy and I walked back to the motorhome in what was now a drizzle. I toweled off from the drenching I'd taken in the park, changed from my wet shoes to rubber boots, and took BoBandy out for a walk around the puddled parking lot. He sniffed the toes of the triceratops, not intimidated by the size of the creature, but interested in visitors who had been there before him. Smell identification is a rather enviable talent, one I wouldn't mind having. Although I wouldn't want to stick my nose in places BoBandy does.

Brian hadn't seemed concerned about the plastic bags clinging to the triceratops, but they bothered me. I found a blown-down branch and managed to scrape off the bags and take them back to the trash sack in the motorhome. Brian knocked on the door a few minutes later.

"I'm sorry, but this isn't a good time for Duke. Kathy said you were on your way to Arizona, so if you have more questions, I'll be glad to answer them. I brought one of our brochures."

The touristy brochure looked too superficial to be of much use, but I thanked him and asked, "Maybe I could talk to Duke tomorrow? I need to take photos too."

"I can take you back in the park so you can get them now."

I held an open palm out the door. Heavier drizzle. "Maybe it won't be raining by morning. We aren't in any big rush to get to Arizona."

"I see." He sounded reluctant to leave it at that, but finally he said, "Before I forget, Kathy wanted me to tell Ivy—"

Brian peered around me, and Ivy stepped up to the door when he mentioned her name. "She said you'd been trying to remember where you'd met before and that you mentioned Arkansas as a possibility. I reminded her about when we rented a motorhome and drove around in Arkansas for a week. She'd forgotten that, but you must have met in some RV park there. You have an impressive memory." He nodded approvingly, as if memory was a remarkable accomplishment for someone our age, like one of the dinosaurs suddenly exhibiting mathematical skills. "Kathy was quite embarrassed that she'd forgotten."

"Umm . . . well, thank you," Ivy said.

"Is it okay if we park somewhere around here for the night?" I asked.

"There aren't any hookups for the motorhome."

"We can get along without them."

Brian looked as if he were trying to think of more reasons we shouldn't stay, but he finally turned to leave without suggesting any particular spot where we should park.

"We usually look for a local church wherever we happen to be on Sunday," Ivy added. "Perhaps you know one close by that we might visit tomorrow morning?"

"I've never noticed any."

"We'll see what we can find, then," she said, and Brian just kept walking.

I closed the motorhome door, and we both watched Brian stride across the parking lot without looking back.

"He doesn't want us hanging around," Ivy said. "He'd rather we'd just pick up and leave right now."

I agreed with Ivy's assessment. Brian certainly wasn't as friendly and sociable as he'd been when we went through the park. No mention of our getting together for dinner now. "I wonder why the sudden change."

"He talked to Kathy."

"What difference would that make? You have a knock-down, drag-out battle or something with her?"

Ivy wrinkled her nose at my facetious question. Ivy is not a

24

knock-down, drag-out sort of person, though she's a lot tougher than she looks. There's steel and rawhide and a bit of fire under that sweet exterior.

"Kathy and I got along fine until I persisted in asking about our having met somewhere before. Now she 'remembers' our probably meeting at some RV park in Arkansas. Except there's a problem with that."

"You stayed with your niece in Arkansas. You didn't even have a motorhome yet."

"Right. If Kathy and I have met before, and I think we have, it wasn't at any RV park in Arkansas."

"So why are they saying you did?"

"Because, for some reason, they don't want me to remember where I really know her from."

I might scoff at that as too much of a cloak-and-dagger explanation, but Ivy doesn't invent such situations. Although she does seem to attract them.

"What about Brian?" I asked. "Does he look familiar too?"

"No, but if he didn't have the beard and mustache . . ." Ivy tilted her head and squinted as if trying to bring up a hologram of a clean-shaven Brian. "Men have this do-it-yourself system of disguise. Grow a beard, and any man can look totally different. Especially if he colors it."

Dye your beard? I'd be as likely to paint my toenails as color my beard. But I suppose some people don't like the gray-beard look. Fortunately, Ivy isn't one of them. But maybe Brian and Kathy are. Brian's beard does look a little too black-bearish to be natural.

"Does their changed attitude make you want to pick up and leave?" I asked.

Ivy crossed her arms in a stubborn way that said Brian would have to hitch up a dinosaur and drag her off before she was going anywhere. "No way. It just makes me wonder *why*."

Exactly how I felt. I also felt we might just hunker down

and stay for a week. Or a month. That's what happens when you arouse the curiosity—and stubbornness—of the MacPhersons.

IVY

Mac didn't move the motorhome for the night. We stayed right there in the middle of the parking lot, sharing space under the lone parking lot light with the gloomy triceratops. While I fixed chiliburgers for dinner, Mac unhooked the old Toyota pickup we pulled behind the motorhome so we could look for a church in the morning. We'd left my car in a shed back at his son's place in Montana.

After dinner we tried to access the internet with the laptop, but Brian's Wi-Fi connection was apparently password protected, as most systems are these days, and we couldn't tap into it. Mac worked for a while on his magazine article about the park, and then we finished the evening with our usual Scripture study. We were in the book of Ruth now. I've always loved Ruth, but it's all new to Mac, who is a fairly new Christian. A CUC—Christian Under Construction—as he refers to himself. Biblical Ruth had known some upheaval and moving around in her life, as both Mac and I have. Unfortunately for Ruth, she lacked the comforts of a motorhome that we enjoy. Although she did have good-guy Boaz waiting at the end of her journey, and with him she even wound up in the genealogy of Jesus. God's mysterious plans at work.

***

I woke up early, before Mac and Koop, but not before BoBandy, who wiggled and danced with eagerness to go outside. This day was a different world than yesterday's gloomy rain. The coast temperature was chilly enough to warrant a jacket, but early-morning sunlight slanted through the tall trees

26

from a blue sky overhead. The fall air held a crisp scent of fresh-washed evergreens and unseen ocean.

I let BoBandy take his time leading me around the parking lot and gift shop. No sign of Kathy or Brian this morning, but I jumped when a voice called from the direction of the travel trailer back in the trees.

"Over here," the voice called again, and I spotted him. An elderly man sitting in a spot of sunshine in a . . . chair tree? Tree chair?

Because that's what it was. A tree with narrow branches trained to grow in the shape of a chair, then turning into leafy shade overhead. A striped pillow softened the branches under the skinny old guy sitting there. He had a white beard and mad-scientist hair, but his smile looked almost boyishly friendly. He had a cat in his lap and a walker stood beside him.

"Hi," I called as I walked down the overgrown driveway toward him. "You must be Duke Lancaster."

"That I am, young lady."

Usually I feel an urge to kick shins at "young lady" nonsense, but Duke said it with such gallantry that I accepted the term without grumbling.

"I'm Ivy Mal— Ivy MacPherson," I corrected. Sometimes I still stumble over the change from Malone to MacPherson. "My husband is here to write an article about the dinosaur park for a travel magazine. We were hoping to talk to you."

"Brian mentioned that yesterday, but I was kind of under the weather. Got a bum knee." He patted his left knee, then smiled and whacked the other knee as if it annoyed him. "Actually, got two of 'em. Sorry I couldn't talk to you yesterday. But Sheila brought me some pills, so I'm not hurting now."

I hadn't realized it until now, but a suspicion that Brian had made up some excuse so we couldn't talk to Duke had simmered in my subconscious. Apparently, a mistaken simmer,

27

because Duke was now saying he really hadn't been up to talking to visitors. The black-and-white cat in his lap stood up, spotted BoBandy, and hissed.

"Now, Scarlett, don't you go throwing a hissy fit," Duke admonished with a soothing swipe of hand along the cat's arched back.

BoBandy backed away, but his tail wagged. He and Koop get along fine and often curl up together. Scarlett didn't suddenly become friendly, but she didn't repeat the hiss. She turned her back on BoBandy with royal disdain and curled up in Duke's lap again.

"Scarlett seems an unusual name for a black-and-white cat," I said.

"I didn't name her for her color. It's for her feisty attitude, like that woman in *Gone with the Wind*. Scarlett, with two t's."

"You read a lot?"

"Oh yeah. What else is there for an old guy with bad knees to do? This thing"—he held up a cell phone I hadn't noticed— "is pickier about when it works than Scarlett is about where she sleeps. Right now I might as well be trying to make a call with a toadstool."

"Cell phones can be like that."

"I like reading that Grisham guy's books. Lee Child too, and that Rowling woman and those Mitford books. Not so fond of that weird stuff Stephen King puts out. Maybe I ought to get a computer. Brian's always on his. There are all kinds of games you can play on them."

"Is Duke a real name or a nickname?"

"It's real, all right. My mother had some fancy ideas. I had a brother named Prince and a sister named Duchess. Both gone now, sad to say."

Which made me think of the sister I'd lost, niece DeeAnn's mother, and my beloved husband Harley too. And the son who had been gone longer than either of them, without ever a

28

chance to say goodbye. But it was always a comfort to know I'd see them again someday beyond this life. I jumped to another subject. "Tell me about that chair you're sitting on."

"Kind of neat, isn't it?" He patted the branch trained to become an arm for the chair. "I've been working on it for, oh, twelve to fourteen years now."

When Mac and I finally settle down somewhere, maybe I'll try training tree branches into a chair too. A double chair, of course, so we could sit together. Although, given the unpredictable effect of my thumb on plants, I might wind up with a springboard into space instead of a chair.

"Would it be okay if I go get my husband so he can talk to you about information for his article?"

"I'd rather talk to a pretty young lady like you, but sure, you go get him. I'll go inside and fix coffee."

I went to the motorhome, and Mac accompanied me back to the trailer. We left BoBandy in the motorhome. I noticed, when we reached the trailer, that it had a ramp rather than steps, easier for Duke to navigate with his walker. Inside, the trailer was a bit cramped but warm and cozy, not immaculate but bachelor-level clean. A window looked out on the gravel road going toward the coast. Kathy had mentioned liking to look for shells and rocks, so there must be a nice beach out there. Shelves overflowed with books, and a bear-shaped honey container stood on the kitchen counter. Duke took three steaming cups out of a microwave and added instant coffee granules.

"Cream's in the fridge." Inside the trailer, Duke seemed fairly self-sufficient without the walker, but he motioned to the small refrigerator rather than going to it.

I opened the refrigerator and reached for the quart of half-and-half. I stopped with my hand on the container. Duke noticed my surprise.

"That's my Celebration Champagne," he said.

"You have a celebration coming up?" Mac asked.

"No, but if one comes, I figure on being ready," Duke said cheerfully. He added a dribble of honey to his coffee.

Mac and I exchanged smiles. When we were Duke's age—which, to be honest, wasn't all that far off—I hoped I could still expect an event worthy of a champagne celebration to be coming soon.

Although the next thing I noticed when we settled on the sofa with our coffee was the handgun casually hanging in a leather holster on a hook by the door. Duke saw me looking at it.

"Never know what kind of varmints might come sneakin' around." He smiled. "I figure on being ready for them too."

Another hook beside the holster held an oversized key ring with an unlikely number of keys for one older person in a small trailer.

A surprising man, Duke Lancaster. He made me think of that man in the TV ads, the one they call "the most interesting man in the world."

The first thing Mac asked Duke was about the unusual name of the park, Ghost Goat Dinosaur Park.

"It comes from the name of the mountain—well, it's really just a big hill, isn't it? But there was an old hermit with a bunch of goats lived here back in the 1930s.When he died, the goats went to living wild. Eventually they died out too, except over the years someone claims to see one or two of them now and then. Or maybe their ghosts." He went on to tell us how he'd once tried to build another dinosaur to add to the "herd."

"I thought it couldn't be all that complicated. After all, Uncle Hiram built them alone. But that one I tried to build just collapsed. Looked like an oversized turkey after a collision with an eighteen-wheeler." He scowled as if the memory still irked him. "Sometimes I wonder if the old coot maybe did find some old dinosaur eggs and hatch 'em."

"How many dinosaurs are there in the park?" I asked.

"Nineteen. The place would probably be closed by now if it weren't for Brian and Kathy. I don't know what I'd do without them. Brian built the ramp for my trailer, and Kathy is always sending over goodies from her kitchen and fussing about what I eat. They take care of everything about running the park and gift shop."

"You don't get out in the dinosaur area much now?" Mac asked. He'd mentioned earlier how run-down and overgrown it was out there, and he'd wondered if Duke knew Brian wasn't the greatest caretaker.

"Nah. These old knees, they're about done for. Though sometimes I manage to get over to say hello to ol' Tricky."

"Tricky?" Mac repeated.

"Tricky the Triceratops. There's Tex the Rex too. And Danny the Dimetrodon."

"Benny the Brontosaurus?" Mac asked.

Duke looked surprised. "Yeah. How'd you know?"

Mac smiled. "You know the old saying, 'great minds think alike.'"

"You probably didn't see Sammy the Saber-Toothed Tiger. I don't know why Uncle Hiram built him, because saber-toothed tigers aren't from the dinosaur era. I diverted the trail away from him, but I used to climb over the fence and visit him once in a while. He's not in good shape. One of his saber-teeth actually fell out. Sheila helped me glue it back in."

"How did you happen to get Brian and Kathy to run the park for you?" Mac asked.

"Fate or destiny, I guess. Whatever you want to call it. I was digging on the hillside back there beyond Sammy—"

"Digging?" Mac repeated.

"It's kind of embarrassing." Duke had removed Scarlett from the rocking chair and sat there himself, but she'd jumped right back in his lap. "There's this old story about a treasure chest of gold buried out there along with a couple of bodies. The story is vague on where the gold came from. Maybe a stagecoach robbery. Maybe pirates. Though I don't know that this coast ever had much pirate activity or why they'd bring their treasure this far inland and haul it up a hill. But maybe the coast line was different a couple hundred years ago."

"It changes," Mac agreed.

"Right. I'd never really believed either version of the buried treasure story, but I was up in there looking for something I saw moving, and then I spotted this strange circle of stones. They looked like they might be a marker of some kind. So I got a shovel and started digging and got down pretty deep. I leaned over to look down in the hole, and first thing I knew, I fell right into it. Almost as if it *pulled* me in. Like the dead bodies were guarding the treasure and weren't going to let anyone find it. If you want to believe in weird stuff like that. But I sure couldn't get out. The sides caved in around me, and I was stuck like a dinosaur in a tar pit."

"And so—?"

"I was afraid I could be dead there for a month before anyone found me. I started yelling my head off. And then, like angels dropping out of heaven, Brian and Kathy showed up. They'd just been passing through, stopped because the place looked interesting, and heard me yelling. They took me to a doc and then we got to talking, and they weren't headed anyplace special. So here we are. We kind of traded living quarters, so they live in the apartment in the back of the gift shop, and I moved into this trailer they'd been traveling in, and it's all worked out fine."

"That's great. For both you and them. But you never found any skeletons or treasure chest of gold, so maybe they're still buried back there somewhere," Mac suggested.

"Right. And if you believe that, there's a nice bridge down in San Francisco I'd like to sell you." Duke waggled his eyebrows and chuckled at his own humor.

I was a little uneasy hearing about the possibility of buried bodies because my first reaction to the park, that it looked like a good place for a dead body, was confirmed. But it was all long ago and only a tall tale at that.

"Sheila doesn't much like Brian and Kathy," Duke went on, "but I think that's just because she figures if they hadn't come along we'd of got married and closed down the park and be living happily ever after in her big double-wide. Or some fool idea like that."

"And Sheila is—?"

"Sheila Weekson. She calls herself my girlfriend." His cheerful smile shifted into a grimace, as if he didn't concur with that title. "But she's okay. She brings me books and magazines and stuff. She makes great spaghetti and meat loaf, and we play chess and cribbage or Monopoly. But she's a bulldozer in high heels about the marriage thing."

"She thinks you and she should get married?" Mac asked.

"Oh, yeah."

"What do Brian and Kathy think of her?" I asked.

"They're always telling me I ought to marry her and sell this place to them."

That surprised me. The dinosaur park didn't look like any great investment. But maybe the Morrisons just wanted to help Duke out, give him a little push into a better life. With Porsche-level money, they could probably afford to be generous.

Mac took notes while Duke talked more about the history of the park and some famous visitors who'd been here. Then, since it was time to get ready for church, I asked Duke if he knew of any nearby church we might attend.

"There's the one Sheila goes to once in a while. Just drive back out to the highway and go straight across it. The church is a half mile or so on the right. I don't recollect the name at the moment, but you can probably recognize a church when you see it."

"How will we recognize Sheila if she's there?" I asked.

"Fine lookin' woman. Hair as red as a flaming tomato, and a hat. Always wears a hat. She might come talk to you. She kind of likes to manage things. But some Sunday mornings she chases around to yard sales looking for stuff for her junk store or sometimes she rides her bicycle or runs out to the cove. Or she likes to go to some exercise place in town and lifts weights or something." He frowned. "Doesn't seem fittin' for a woman, getting big muscles. But she says she has to exercise to keep her backside from getting wide as a barn, but I don't think there's anything wrong with a generous backside."

I tried not to smile. If Sheila was smart and she wanted to ease him into marriage, she'd better not beat him at arm wrestling.

We went back to the motorhome, changed clothes, and took off in search of Sheila's church.

Chapter 4

IVY

We found the North Coast Community Church without any problem, an old-fashioned little white church with a big bell in the belfry. We took seats in a middle pew.

I immediately spotted Sheila standing in the aisle several pews ahead of us. As Brian had said, quite a bit younger than Duke. Flaming red hair, a purple beret jauntily dipped to one stylish eyebrow, and a purple-and-yellow plaid cape swirling as if she might levitate with it at any moment. On me this would have been an ELOL look. Eccentric Little Old Lady. But on her it was artfully sassy, a bold statement of personal style. I was fascinated by her large, dramatic gestures as she talked to another woman sitting in the pew. What was she describing? An oversized watermelon? A whale with wings?

The service began with a combination of old hymns and newer praise songs. The young pastor played guitar, along with an older woman on keyboard and a young woman on drums. The pastor's interesting message was about the different responses of the two criminals who were crucified with Jesus and how this relates to people's reactions to Jesus today. I was glad we'd come. After the final prayer, several people greeted us, and Duke was right. Sheila rushed over to introduce herself and pepper us with nosy questions. I told her we'd met Duke.

Sheila flung up her cape-clad arms in a theatrical gesture of despair, a Batwoman in plaid. "Duke is a wonderful man, but I've been trying to get him here to church for *years*."

An admirable project, but if she went about it in the same way she apparently tried to bulldoze him into marriage, I had to think the effort might be doomed to failure. Although she had strong shoulders under the cape and looked capable of dragging him to church or altar, or anything else she had a mind to do.

"I'm taking minestrone soup and lasagna over to Duke's for dinner this evening," she added. "Would you come join us?"

Inviting us to dinner at Duke's place without checking with him first struck me as a bit forward, but to my surprise, Mac jumped on the invitation. "Sounds great! How about if we bring salad?"

"That would be wonderful! Kathy and I are always trying to get Duke to eat more vegetables. And having visitors will be good for him."

We settled on six-thirty for dinner. She gave us each a big hug, and I found myself liking her more than I expected. She might be a bit pushy, but she really did seem to have Duke's welfare at heart.

We'd barely gotten back to the motorhome when Brian knocked on the door and said he could take Mac through the park now to take photos. Mac hastily changed to jeans and rubber boots, grabbed his camera, and they took off. I had texts from teenage grandniece Sandy in Arkansas and Mac's ten-year-old granddaughter Elle in Montana. I answered both, and then the cell phone tinkled with an incoming message. I was delighted to see who was calling.

"Magnolia!"

Magnolia and Geoff are old friends and neighbors from back in Missouri. They'd come up to Montana for our wedding and then taken off in their motorhome on another of Magnolia's genealogy expeditions. Most people investigate genealogy by internet these days, and Geoff helps Magnolia do some of that, but she likes to accompany that cyberspace research with in-person pursuit. Often with rewarding results, although a few people have been less than welcoming about the arrival of a large woman enthusiastically claiming a family relationship of some distant degree.

36

"Are you in Arizona yet?" Magnolia asked. "We thought we'd come down to wherever you are for a while too."

Magnolia and Geoff and I had often arranged meetings in various places around the country when I was on the road alone. Although back then I was also hiding from the murderous Braxtons, who were intent on making roadkill out of me. Thankfully that's all over now, various Braxtons awaiting trial or incarceration back in Missouri. I explained that we'd taken this detour to the Northern California coast and I wasn't sure how soon we'd get to Arizona.

"Where are you?" I asked.

"Somewhere in Oregon. Where are we, dear?" Magnolia said in an aside to her husband, Geoff, who did all the driving. A brief conversation between them ensued. "We'll be there tomorrow! Oh, this is wonderful, especially after the experience we just had."

I gave directions on how to find us. "Just watch for the triceratops out front. You can't miss it."

I expected her to respond with a puzzled silence, or at least a question about what *is* a triceratops, but Magnolia rose to the occasion, as she often does.

"Oh yes, that's the three-horned one, isn't it? With the big ruff on its neck. See you soon."

I had to shake my head. How did she know that? Even after all these years of friendship, Magnolia can still surprise me.

Looking out the window, I saw Mac and Brian returning from their photo excursion. When they reached the motorhome, I opened the door and invited Brian in for coffee.

"Thanks, but I'd better get back and see how Kathy is doing. She's headed into one of her killer migraines, so I'll say goodbye for her. We've enjoyed meeting you. And you folks have a good trip on down to Arizona." He backed off with a smile and a wave as if we were already on our way.

"We aren't leaving yet," Mac said. "We're having dinner

with Duke and Sheila this evening."

"And Magnolia and Geoff are arriving tomorrow. She just called," I added by way of explanation to Mac.

"Hey, great!"

Brian's response was less enthusiastic. His heavy eyebrows drew together, and the smile flattened to a stiff line. "We've been glad to have you folks with us, but we can't have a whole contingent of RVs staying here. There are regulations even out here in the country, you know." He sounded very righteous. The property owner defending his territory from marauding RVs. "We'll have to ask you to move along."

"We can be gone by tomorrow, but I really need more information from Duke first."

"No longer than tomorrow," he ordered.

After he stalked off, I said, "I wonder if Kathy really is having a migraine or if that's an excuse to keep us from seeing her again. I don't think she wants any more discussion with me about our having met before."

Mac nodded. "I'm interested in finding out what Sheila knows about the Morrisons when we have dinner with her and Duke this evening."

Which, I realized now, was why he'd responded so quickly to Sheila's invitation.

"Brian was very adroit at keeping himself out of the photos I took," Mac added. "He laughed it off, saying it was because he always comes out looking like something the dinosaurs dragged in, but he was quite determined about it."

"So you didn't get any photos of him?"

Mac winked at me. "I wouldn't say that."

***

We ate a late lunch, and then Mac suggested we take the rough gravel road that went on past the dinosaur park and see if it went to the beach. It did, and Mac parked the pickup under a wind-twisted coastal pine near a cove with a sandy beach.

38

Beyond the cove, wild waves surged around offshore rocks, spray shooting skyward in geyser bursts. Within the protected area of the cove, however, the waves lapped almost gently. An old wooden dock stuck out into the cove, a handful of seagulls and even a couple of seals in residence.

Looking back, we could see the western side of the hill on which the dinosaur park was located. This side broke off in a steep cliff with a jumble of broken rocks below it. More forested land separated the cliff from the ocean.

"I wonder what that used to be?" I asked as we also surveyed the burned skeletons and foundations of what had once been several buildings near the cove. It didn't look like a recent burn, but it wasn't old enough for brush and trees to obliterate the site. Tall weeds and blackberries were making a strong attack on it, however, growing around crumbling foundations and surging up through the old asphalt of a parking area.

We took off our shoes to stroll along the sandy beach and afterward put them back on to wander around the burned buildings. The whole area had the lonely feel of a vanished civilization, but it was still a lovely setting with a magnificent view. The wind came up and skittered balls of sea-foam across the shoreline.

It was almost dark by the time we got back to the motorhome. I'd just started a salad when someone knocked on the door. Mac was in the bedroom changing his jeans to go over to Duke's for dinner. I opened the outside door warily. I expected to see Brian again, perhaps returning to wave a shotgun and a list of unfriendly county regulations about RV parking at us. Instead, Sheila stood there in the early darkness of coming winter. She was still wearing the plaid cape and purple beret, but she'd changed to snug black pants and high-heeled boots.

"Hi. I came over to bring you some lasagna and soup and

tell you we won't be able to have dinner with Duke this evening." She handed me two plastic containers. "I'm really sorry, but his knees are bothering him again, and the pain pills make him kind of woozy."

"I'm sorry to hear that. We were looking forward to an evening with both of you. But thanks so much for the soup and lasagna." I sniffed the warm, spicy scent drifting from the containers. "Smells wonderful! Come on in for a few minutes, won't you? We didn't have much chance to get acquainted at church this morning."

Sheila managed the step up to the motorhome gracefully. In her spike heels I'd probably have somersaulted through the door. Which makes me sigh. I used to love wearing high heels. I still do, but it takes a very special occasion, and a certain reckless disregard for consequences, to wear them now.

We sat down and talked about the weather and Duke's bad knees for a few minutes. I thought about the pickup parked out by the trailer and asked if Duke still drove.

"He hasn't driven for quite a while. I always take my SUV when we go anywhere. I suppose he *could* still drive, though I'm not sure he *should* drive. But you know men and their vehicles." Roll of eyes. "Take away their ride and you'd think you'd cut off some vital part of their anatomy."

Mac came out of the bedroom, and I explained about the change in dinner plans. He expressed regret and then sat down with us and asked about the burned ruins we'd seen over near the beach.

"Oh, isn't that a terrible eyesore?" Dramatic fling of hands from Sheila. "The county has been trying to get it cleaned up ever since the fire a few years ago, but the owner died and the heirs have been squabbling, and it still looks like a disaster area. Some big resort outfit wanted to buy and build there, but nothing ever came of it."

"What was it before it burned?" I asked.

"Kate's Kabins. One larger building with rental rooms and a small restaurant, plus a half dozen or so rustic cabins. All outdated, but some families stayed for a week or two and came back year after year. They gave the dinosaur park some business. Kate's dead now, of course."

Mac headed the conversation in a different direction. "We got the impression from Duke that you might have a few reservations about the Morrisons."

Sheila's dramatically lined eyes looked mildly alarmed at our knowing that. "I'm not fond of Brian," she admitted. "Kathy is okay. But she hates it here."

"Hates it? She told me she loved it here."

"She tries to convince herself of that, but I know she hates the dinosaurs."

"She did mention she felt as if they were 'hostile' to her."

"She hardly ever goes out in the park. I think she's afraid a goat is going to sneak up and butt her in the behind. Of course, she does make kind of an obvious target." Sheila slapped herself on the cheek. "Oh, I shouldn't say that. It sounds catty, and she's really a sweet person."

"I wonder why they stay here, then."

"Because Brian wants to, of course. Kathy is such a *wimp* where he's concerned."

"Wimp?"

"Oh, you know. Whatever Brian wants, Brian gets. I think she's a little older, so maybe that has something to do with it. Afraid she'll lose him to a younger woman if she makes any waves. He doesn't appreciate her enough, and she's so good with the kids in her Dolly Dinosaur costume. She tries to look after Duke too. But Brian . . ." She paused and then, as if she found it necessary to find some good point about Brian, added in a virtuous tone, "Of course Brian did build that ramp for Duke's trailer."

"But?" I finally said, because there was an obvious *but*

41

lurking in there.

"I just don't feel, well, *comfortable* with how Brian manages the park. I mean, he's just let everything *go*."

"Does Duke know the foliage in the park is so overgrown you can barely see the dinosaurs?" Mac asked.

"Really? I didn't know that. Of course, I haven't actually been out in the park for years. I don't go along with Kathy's silly idea about dinosaur *hostility*, but I don't care for the smell out there."

"I didn't smell anything," Mac said.

"Well, that *is* skunk cabbage down by the creek, and *I* can smell it. But I have a more sensitive sense of smell than most people." She sniffed as if to give a demonstration of that superior talent. BoBandy sniffed back, taking a good whiff of her feet. "But I was mostly thinking about how the parking lot is all run down and poor old Tricky has lost part of a horn." She gave Mac a sideways glance, and I had the unexpected feeling she wanted to say something else but not in Mac's presence.

He saw it too. With admirable insight, he jumped up. "If you ladies will excuse me, I think it's time to take BoBandy out for a walk." He put on a jacket and briskly snapped a leash on BoBandy's collar.

Sheila did not instantly provide more derogatory information about Brian after Mac was gone. She talked about her daughter Vivian living down in Las Vegas, Duke's knee problems, and how the church was having trouble getting accustomed to a pastor's wife who played drums. I tried to ease her back to the subject of the Morrisons.

"I keep feeling I know Kathy from somewhere, but she doesn't seem to recognize me. Or doesn't want to recognize me," I added with careful casualness. "Duke told us about how he fell in a hole he'd dug out in the park, and they rescued him. Do you know much about them?"

"Not really. I'm not even sure where they came from." Sheila's forehead creased in a frown. "Kathy has mentioned that Brian is into investments. He spends a lot of time on his laptop, and he tells her he's looking at investment properties when he jaunts off to Eureka so often. Poor Kathy. She's so . . . gullible."

"Brian said she sometimes has migraines."

"Yes, terrible migraines. Although it's a wonder she doesn't have them full-time, being married to that man. If I were Kathy, I'd pick up that laptop and whack him over the head with it."

I didn't ask her to elaborate on that. In fact, I was now inclined to back away from this discussion entirely. The conversation felt as if it might be sliding into busybody gossip. We'd been mistaken about Brian coming up with excuses for us not to talk to Duke, and apparently I was just as mistaken in suspecting he'd invented migraines as a way to keep Kathy from having to talk to me again. He didn't strike me as particularly likeable, but I didn't want to jump to some other unfair conclusion about him.

"I had one of Kathy's very good dinosaur cupcakes earlier," I said. "I think I'll ask her for the recipe."

Now that Sheila was started on this subject, whatever the subject was, she was not going to be distracted. She lowered her voice. "This hasn't anything to do with Mac's article for the magazine. It isn't for print."

I was curious, of course. Being wary of gossip doesn't, unfortunately, cancel curiosity. But I managed not to ask questions. "Perhaps Duke will feel well enough in the morning to talk to Mac again."

"I've been thinking I should get Duke a better cell phone," Sheila said. "That ancient old thing he has now is always dropping calls, and he complains that it doesn't ring loud enough. He needs something better in case of an emergency."

I wasn't sure what she was getting at. With Duke's age and health problems, I agreed he needed a reliable form of communication. He might fall out there in the trailer, and the gun hanging by the door wouldn't do him much good in that kind of emergency. But Sheila almost sounded as if she had some darker emergency or danger in mind. Before I could agree on the need for a better phone, however, Sheila jumped to a different subject. Or perhaps it was the subject she had been headed for all along.

"The thing is, I'm almost certain Brian has a girlfriend. Well, nothing *almost* about it. Brian *has* a girlfriend. She's a real estate agent in Eureka, Renée Echol. Divorced. Attractive, but pants so tight they look painted on. Necklines so low it's a wonder she doesn't trip over them in those stiletto heels she wears."

I managed not to make a giveaway glance at the heels on Sheila's own boots.

"I've been undecided about whether or not to tell Kathy about her. I think she has a *right* to know, but I don't want to be a tattletale . . ." Her shoulders lifted in a gesture of vexed dilemma.

"Kathy said Brian was interested in possible real estate investments in the area."

"Yeah, right." Sheila's tone made a snide comment on that possibility. "I saw Brian and Renée having lunch together in a back booth at the Red Dragon and they didn't look as if they were discussing real estate. Not unless she had a property map printed on her neck."

I had to admit that neck exploration didn't sound like a standard way to discuss a real estate investment, but I'm reluctant to think the worst of people. Especially since I'd already been wrong about Brian a couple of times.

"After lunch I followed them, discreetly, of course, back to her house on the south side of town. Brian was in there over an hour. I don't think they were discussing real estate."

44

When I didn't make a comment, Sheila threw her hands in the air, apparently exasperated with my denseness. "Ivy, the man is a *sleaze*. He's cheating on his wife, and who knows what kind of con game he's playing with Duke? I think he wants the dinosaur park, though I don't know why. And Renée Echol is a sleaze too. They were together in The Fisherman's Retreat one evening. That's a *bar* in Arcata, not some therapy organization where fishermen gather to discuss the psychological problems of men at sea," she added with sarcastic emphasis.

I have to admit I immediately wondered what Sheila was also doing at a bar in Arcata, but maybe they had exceptionally good french fries or fried fish, so all I said was, "You didn't want Mac to know about this?"

She gave an exaggerated shrug. "You know how men tend to stick together. I figured he'd say it was none of my business. Although I had a run-in with Renée myself a while back."

"About her relationship with Brian?"

"No, it was before I knew about that. Actually, at one time, Renée and I were fairly good friends. We met at a health club where we both worked out. Sometimes we went out for lunch after a workout session, or maybe a drink in the evening. But then another friend wanted to sell her house in Eureka, and I recommended Renée as a real estate agent. The house didn't sell, and when a very lowball offer from some out-of-town buyer came in, Renée advised her to take it."

I raised my eyebrows, waiting for the connection.

"Lexie took the offer and moved down to Modesto. Purely by accident, I found out *Renée* wound up owning the house. She'd just used someone as a front to get the place for herself at a bargain price. She's using it as a rental now."

"That sounds rather unethical. Maybe even illegal."

"Right. And I was appalled that she'd done something like that to my *friend*. I called Lexie and told her she should sue the socks off Renée. She said she wasn't up to getting involved in some big lawsuit and wouldn't do it. But I was so upset with Renée that I stormed into her real estate office and gave her a piece of my mind."

I made some noncommittal murmur.

"A few other people happened to be there, and Renée started screaming about suing me for defamation of character or libel or mental anguish, some ridiculous thing like that." Sheila shook her head. "I told her to go ahead, sue me. And then I said, who knows what all might come out if all this got into a courtroom?"

"You mean about her relationship with Brian?"

"No. I didn't know about her and Brian yet. It was just a shot in the dark. I figured someone who's unethical on one business deal is probably unethical on others. And then she *threatened* me."

"Threatened you?"

"On weekends I open up my garage and sell a few antiques and whatnots. You know, just a yard sale kind of thing. Renée started yelling about how it was a lot more than a yard sale, that it was an actual *business,* and I wasn't complying with zoning and business permit regulations."

"A threat, then, that she might turn you in."

"I'm sure what I do is perfectly legal, but she could still make trouble for me."

Sheila's mention of the threat from Renée reminded me of Brian's grumpy push to get us out of the dinosaur park parking lot. "Brian says we have to be out of the parking lot by tomorrow. County regulations about RV parking."

Sheila made an unladylike p-f-f-s-t sound. "You could park here for a month and nobody'd say anything. In fact, you can come park at my place for a month. Or more. Some friends from Texas did it for six weeks last summer. I have five acres, so there's plenty of room."

"Thanks. I appreciate that. But some friends are arriving in their motorhome tomorrow."

"Bring them along." She jumped up abruptly, again managing the spike heels nicely. "I'm half inclined to go over there and tell Kathy about Renée right now," she declared.

"Duke said the Morrisons think he should sell the park to them—"

"Right. At some bargain-basement price, of course."

"And then he should marry you."

"Oh." Sheila was obviously a bit taken aback at how she'd been bad-mouthing the Morrisons only to have me tell her they were promoting exactly what she wanted.

"You don't know anything more about Brian and Kathy?" Quickly, before she thought I wanted more details about Brian's possible involvement with a girlfriend, I added, "I mean, how they happened to be going through here or what Brian did before coming here?"

"Not really. He might have had a business of some kind." Sheila made a vague gesture, well below her usual dramatic level of expression, and sat down again. More of a *plop* this time, as if my information about the Morrisons had deflated her.

"He must be successful," I suggested. "If his ride is any indication." I don't feel quite comfortable with that expression, *ride*, but grandniece Sandy tells me it's the word that's used now.

"The Porsche?" Sheila said. "Yes, I guess so. Although Kathy has gone into Eureka with me a few times, and she's always very careful about the price of anything she buys. But maybe Brian limits her to some skimpy household budget. That would be just like him, spend big bucks on that Porsche for himself but make her search for the cheapest paper towels in the store."

"Maybe she's just the thrifty type." I'm careful about money

47

and probably would look for the best buy on paper towels even if we owned a Porsche. Which I can't imagine us ever owning. But that's fine. We have enough. The Lord may not provide all the luxuries magazine and TV ads tell us we should want, but he supplies our needs. "I keep feeling I've met Kathy somewhere before. But I can't remember where, and she says no." Except for a meeting that never happened at some RV park in Arkansas.

Sheila unexpectedly went philosophical. "Well, who knows? Maybe they have some big secret in their past. Maybe they're in that witness protection program or something."

Maybe. Or maybe time travelers headed for the dinosaur era but missing their mark and winding up in a deteriorating dinosaur park in the twenty-first century instead.

"Thanks for the lasagna," I said when she stood up again.

"That's a real invitation to come park your motorhome at my place. It's not far, just before you get to the church on the other side of the highway." She noticed the laptop still sitting on the dinette table and added, "You can use my Wi-Fi there too." She scribbled an address on a piece of paper from a scratch pad in her purse. "Your friends too."

"I'll see what Mac says."

***

Mac, obviously just waiting for Sheila to leave, came inside only a minute after she headed back over to Duke's trailer. I relayed what she had said about not knowing much more about Kathy and Brian than we did. After hesitating, I also passed along the gossipy information about Brian and a girlfriend. Sheila had said it wasn't for print, but she hadn't put any don't-tell-anybody restrictions on it.

"Are you thinking we should do something about it?" Mac asked.

"Not necessarily. But we could check it out, I suppose."

Yes, we could do that, I agreed with myself. We could go

48

into town and inquire about available real estate from Renée Echol. We might also ask about food at the Red Dragon and an office in her home. And how would she react to the fact that we were staying at the dinosaur park?

Then I stiffened my shoulders. No. I may have snooped into a murder or two, but I was not snooping into gossip no matter how tempting it was.

We ate the salad I'd started, plus Sheila's soup and lasagna, which was very tasty. Afterward, with the moon shining, Mac suggested we drive down to the cove again.

I started to ask why, but then I gave myself a mental whack. Walking hand in hand beside a moonlit sea. A sweet, newlywed kind of thing to do, right? And romantic of Mac to suggest it.

So we drove over to the cove and parked under the same wind-twisted tree. Even though the evening was chilly, we took off our shoes, held hands, and walked along the curve of the cove. Stars sprinkled the sky, and the moon cast a magic glow over sand and waves and turned a twisted piece of driftwood into a silvered work of art.

Gazing up at a starlit sky always brings out my thoughts about God along with awe at the immensity of his creation. *Is there anyone else out there, Lord? Someone on a planet maybe like ours?* The Bible makes no mention of anyone, but the Lord hasn't necessarily told us everything, has he? He leaves things for us to discover. Quantum physics and the string theory, creatures under the sea and why a hard-boiled egg sometimes just won't peel. A psalm came to mind.

What are human beings that you care for them, mere mortals that you think of them? Them meaning *us,* of course. *Me.* This peek into the universe of stars in a night sky always does this to me. Why should the Lord care about me in the immensity of all this? But he does. *Thank you, Lord!* Then Mac interrupted my thoughts.

"I've been thinking about having this tattoo on my arm removed."

49

Chapter 5

IVY

"Remove the tattoo?" I've had this ongoing curiosity about the tattoo ever since I first saw it. Why a blue motorcycle? Mac has never shown any particular interest in motorcycles, and he's always been uncommunicative about the tattoo. Which has just made me more curious, of course. Mystery of the Tattoo. "Why remove it?"

"I've been thinking about doing it for a long time."

Not exactly an answer to my question, so I asked it again. "Why?"

He pushed his sleeve back and held his arm up to the moonlight. As always, there it was. A rather classy looking motorcycle, actually, with lots of fine-line detail, especially in the wheels.

"They can remove tattoos with a laser now. It may take eight or nine treatments, with seven or eight weeks in between treatments, but it can be done."

"You've checked into this, then."

"Yes. Yes, I have." He nodded. "I checked into it a long time ago, actually, but back then all they could do was try to sand it off or remove the skin surgically. Or you could tattoo over it."

Since the tattoo still decorated his arm, that was apparently what he'd done. "The tattoo was something else before it was a motorcycle?"

"Yes."

"Were you a spy with an important message hidden in code in the tattoo? Or maybe a secret messenger for Interpol or the CIA?"

"No." He smiled at what he apparently considered my

50

facetious speculations. Although I didn't necessarily consider them facetious. Mac had lived most of his life before I came along. He knows about dinosaurs, and I never knew that about him. Who knows what intrigues and adventures he may have been involved in that I don't know about? "I'm afraid the secret of the tattoo is much more mundane than that. As you may have noticed, the wheels are a little close together for a regular motorcycle."

Never having paid much attention to spacing of motorcycle wheels, no, I hadn't noticed. "What was it before?"

He rubbed the arm as if he'd like to erase the tattoo rather than talk about it. "That's the embarrassing part. The reason I always avoid talking about it."

Okay, as much as I wanted to know, I wasn't going to push Mac into some awkward admission that made him more uncomfortable than he already was. Though I have to admit, I was instantly curious about *why* he was so uncomfortable.

"I was only nineteen when I first got the tattoo. It was just before I went in the navy. A friend—long dead now—and I were enlisting together." He paused. "Two nineteen-year-old guys who are excited about what they're about to do, but also a little scared, do not necessarily have the best judgment in the world."

"Bad judgment about enlisting in the navy?"

"Bad judgment about getting tattoos before we became sailors."

I surreptitiously tried to see a battleship hidden within the lines of the motorcycle, but I couldn't. What else would an almost-sailor tattoo on his arm? An anchor? A sea monster? But no reason to be embarrassed by either of those. An old girlfriend's name? Possibly embarrassing, but I couldn't see any hint of that in the tattoo, either.

"My friend Eddie got the back side of the bottom half of a rather curvy woman on his leg." He swallowed. "A naked back

51

side."

I digested that for a moment. I looked at the tattoo again, still not seeing anything. But if friend Eddie had gotten the naked *bottom* half . . .

Mac saw my realization dawning. He nodded. "Yes, I also got part of the . . . anatomy of a curvy woman. Front side, top half. See these wheels?" He outlined them with a finger.

It took me another minute to get the full extent of what he meant. Then I saw it. The full, round shape of the wheels. The less-than-normal distance between them. My swallow was more like a startled gulp. "A very . . . well-endowed top half of the anatomy." Without any complication of head or arms.

"Yes. It was that way all the time I was in the navy. After the first few weeks, I was appalled at what I'd done, but about all I could do was cover it with long sleeves whenever I could. Then I got out of the navy and met Marguerite."

Marguerite was Mac's first wife, whom he'd lost several years before I met him.

"I wore the long sleeves for the first three months I knew her, even in hot weather. But finally I figured she had a right to know about my . . . youthful foolishness."

"You also realized you weren't going to be able to keep the tattoo hidden indefinitely."

"That too," he admitted ruefully. "So I showed it to her." He groaned. "In all its buxom glory. I'm sure tattoos can't *grow,* but somehow this one looked as if it were expanding second by second while she looked at it."

"So what happened?"

"Marguerite was a sweet and generous woman. She didn't berate me or laugh at my foolishness, at least not out loud. Instead, she politely asked if the tattoo represented any particular female anatomy, and I said no. It wasn't anyone I knew. Just a tattoo the artist had in his repertoire."

Some repertoire. Where were the battleships and sea

monsters? But I didn't comment.

"So then, also very politely, she asked if it was a permanent fixture there on my arm. I said not necessarily, and that was when I looked into how it could be removed. I was willing to go the surgical route, including the skin graft that would be necessary because a fairly large piece of skin would have to be removed."

That was Mac. If he was in the wrong, he was willing to do whatever needed doing to make the wrong right. Including surgery and skin graft.

"It was Marguerite herself who suggested the alternative of turning it into something other than the . . . gross exaggeration of female anatomy that it was. She even suggested the motorcycle."

A gracious way to handle the situation. With something of a sense of humor too. I think, if I'd known her, I'd have liked Marguerite.

He pulled the sleeve down. "So now you know the story of why a man of elder years has a blue motorcycle tattooed on his arm."

I just stood there with my toes in the sand and looked at the rueful, chagrined expression on Mac's face. A breeze off the sea ruffled his silvery hair and stirred his beard. I halfway wanted to laugh, halfway wanted to swat him for pulling such a macho-kid stunt, even if it was so many years ago.

But I've made a foolish mistake or two in my life too. Back in my teenage days I'd once stuffed a too-large swim suit with cotton balls to fill it out, with the ensuing embarrassment of that strangely soaking-wet portion of my anatomy when the rest of the suit had dried. I put my arms around him. "I love you, Mac MacPherson. With or without a tattoo."

"Thank you, Mrs. MacPherson. I love you too."

So he kissed me there in the moonlight, and we strolled hand in hand around the cove. And I had this wonderful all's-right-with-the-world feeling of happiness and satisfaction.

Honeymoon is, after all, a state of mind.

***

In the morning, Mac spent time on the laptop working on his magazine article, and then we went over to Duke's trailer so Mac could check some remaining details. Duke looked at the digital photos Mac had taken and said the plaques on two of the dinosaurs had been switched, and what was identified as a psittacosaurus was really an ankylosaurus, and vice versa. Mac said he'd see about getting the plaques put back in their right places and take new photos.

When we walked back to the motorhome, Brian was just crossing the parking lot in his Porsche. On his way to see his girlfriend in Eureka? I felt like giving him a meaningful thumbs down when he went by, but I managed a polite wave instead. Brian gave us a stiff nod. Then Mac changed his wave to an upraised hand to stop the Porsche. Brian rolled down the window as we approached.

"I was just talking to Duke," Mac said. "He noticed in the photos I showed him that a couple of the plaques in the park have been mistakenly switched. Okay if I go in and change them?"

"I'm just leaving, but you can get Kathy to unlock the gate for you. Though you might want to be careful. I spotted a cougar in there a few mornings ago when I was doing my usual walk-through." He smiled maliciously and took off in a blast of muddy puddle water. I suspected he hoped the cougar would consider us a tasty snack.

We'd just gotten back to the motorhome when Geoff and Magnolia's big motorhome pulled up beside us. She stepped out first, and we hugged as if we hadn't seen each other in months instead of a few weeks.

"It's so good to see you!" she said.

Magnolia isn't overweight or fat, but she's a large woman,

and when Magnolia hugs you, you know you've been hugged. Her hair had been a delicate orchid when she walked me down the aisle at the wedding; now it was majestic purple. We stepped back, hands held, and studied each other affectionately.

If I tried purple hair, it would definitely be an Eccentric LOL look, but Magnolia was quite regal in purple hair, as if she surely had queenly robes and a crown tucked away somewhere.

"You're looking *marvelous,*" Magnolia said. "Marriage agrees with you. But I always knew you and Mac were meant for each other." She nodded wisely. "I felt the vibes from the very first minute I introduced you."

Magnolia places great stock in her "vibes." She has them, vibes good and bad, about everything from matchmaking to political choices to hair color. Strong vibes encouraged her to vote for a mayor who later embezzled a million or so in city funds to finance a South American gold mine. But I have to admit the vibes had been right about Mac and me.

I squeezed her hands. "I'm so glad you're here."

"What a beautiful place!" Magnolia looked off toward the jungled park. "So lush and green. But it's closed now? We won't be able to see the dinosaurs?"

I was surprised that she sounded so disappointed. "Did you really want to see them?"

"Yes, indeed. Several years ago I took a class about prehistoric eras, remember? I found the dinosaurs fascinating. Some of them were quite small, not all huge and vicious like that triceratops over there. We might even be keeping them as pets today, if that asteroid hadn't wiped them all out."

I couldn't quite imagine a dinosaur, no matter how small and even-tempered, as a pet for myself. But Magnolia? Yes, I could see her with a pint-sized dinosaur on a leash. I couldn't recall her taking the class about prehistoric times, but Magnolia is a determined believer in self-improvement, and I knew she'd studied everything from Butterfly Identification to Appreciation of Street Art. Taking a class was actually how her passion for genealogy began.

"The manager isn't here at the moment, but his wife can let us in," Mac said. "I need to go in and change a couple of identification plaques anyway. We can do it right now, unless you're too tired from being on the road?"

Magnolia and Geoff assured him they weren't too tired. I thought I knew Mac's real reason for wanting to get into the park immediately. Brian didn't yet know there were now *two* motorhomes in the parking lot, and when he came back and surely did notice, he might do more than wave regulations at us.

Mac headed for the Morrison's door to get a key. I went back in the motorhome to get Mac's camera, then followed Magnolia and Geoff to the park gate. A minute later Kathy stepped outside, key thrust ahead of her like a weapon. She headed for the gate, determinedly avoiding eye contact with me. But she didn't get to the padlock on the gate before a call from Magnolia stopped her. And startled me into a stumble as well.

"Genevieve! Ivy didn't tell me you were here. What a lovely surprise!"

Chapter 6

IVY

Kathy stopped so short she stumbled over her feet. Yet even with shocked recognition written all over her face, she managed to say, "I'm afraid you've mistaken me for someone else. I don't know you. My name is Kathy."

I hadn't yet had a chance to tell Magnolia about Kathy, so Magnolia had no idea Kathy had also pulled this we've-never-met act on me. I hadn't been able to refute it, but Magnolia was having none of it.

"Of course you know me," she scoffed. "My hair color may be different, of course, but so is yours."

Kathy touched her hair but didn't retreat from her stubborn stance. "No, I-I really don't know you."

"You'd just moved into that little house over on Jefferson Street, remember? Two blocks over from our home on Madison. And you came to my St. Patrick's Day potluck. I had corned beef and cabbage for everyone. A lovely man came to play the bagpipes. You admired my magnolia trees."

Hey, I remembered that St. Patrick's Day potluck. I also remembered that the lovely man may have imbibed a bit too much Irish whiskey before he arrived, and his bagpipe playing occasionally sounded more like the bellow of a lovelorn goose. But something else about that day was even more memorable. Magnolia likes to get into the spirit of the day at her get-togethers, with appropriate outfits to match.

"Oh, it's you! I guess I—" Kathy might not want to admit she knew Magnolia, but her finger moved to point as if pulled by a magnet. Maybe a green magnet, because Magnolia as a large green elf is not a sight to be forgotten. Green from peak of her pointy hat to the curled toes on her pointy shoes. And hair delicately green as well.

I couldn't remember Kathy at that crowded potluck, but now I knew why she looked so familiar. And Magnolia was right. Kathy's hair was different now. It was mousy brown back then. "I remember now! I occasionally walked over on Jefferson, and sometimes you were out working in your flowers. Once, when you were transplanting geraniums to hanging baskets on the front porch, you even gave me a little pot with a beautiful red geranium in it."

Kathy still didn't admit knowing either of us, but she did make a generic statement. "I've always loved having flowers in hanging baskets. Especially geraniums."

"And then your husband became ill—" Magnolia broke off and reached out to touch Kathy's hand. "Oh, my dear, I'm so sorry. We're bringing up painful times and upsetting you, aren't we?"

Kathy blinked and twisted the key in her hands. Her mouth opened as if she still wanted to deny what Magnolia and I were saying about knowing her, but finally her shoulders slumped. "Your St. Patrick's Day potluck was the only neighborhood event he was ever able to attend. I don't think he went out of the house except to go to the doctor after that."

"And then he passed away." Magnolia's voice was gentle and regretful. Magnolia can be blunt, but she's never unkind. "A sudden heart attack."

Kathy tucked her hands around her waist as if trying to comfort herself. "It wasn't really *sudden*. He had heart trouble, and I knew it could happen. But still, it was a terrible shock."

Magnolia turned to me. "It was after you'd left Madison Street, so you wouldn't remember."

Mac and Geoff had remained silent. Mac had never met either Kathy or her now-dead husband back in Missouri, and Geoff, though he sometimes takes charge, usually lets Magnolia do the talking.

"I used my first name back then, of course. Genevieve. Genevieve Higman. But when I had to start a new life without Andy, I decided to use my middle name, Katherine. Kathy. It was kind of a . . . you know, closure thing."

Magnolia gave her a big hug. "I'm glad you were able to make a new life for yourself."

Kathy looked up and blinked. "Yes. Brian and I are very happy together. I hope Andy would have wanted it that way."

"I'm sure he would," Magnolia said.

I hadn't said anything all this time, but now Kathy gave me a wary sideways glance. "I know you mentioned Missouri and I said I hadn't been there, but it was the saddest and most heartbreaking and stressful period of my life, and I avoid talking or even thinking about it as much as I can."

A tacit admission that she remembered me from Madison Street from the first time I mentioned how familiar she looked. Although it wouldn't have been surprising if she hadn't remembered me. I've never been the kind of woman who's a magnet for every eye the moment she enters a room, and it was back then I first realized I seemed to have aged into this state of invisibility. A good many people, both then and now, just don't *see* me. An invisible LOL. I guess it happens to a lot of older women. It can certainly be a frustrating non-reaction from people but can also be a handy asset for someone who has a peculiar tendency to stumble into murders.

Kathy gave herself a little shake, as if to dismiss the sad past and orient herself to a *now* state of mind. "Well, let's see. I'm here to open the gate, aren't I?"

She did that, and we all trooped inside. Except for Kathy; she didn't stay to accompany us to the mislabeled dinosaurs. "Click the padlock when you come out," she said as she headed back to the house, and I was undecided whether this meant she just didn't want further communication with us and our reminder of her sad past or if she was feeling hostile

59

emanations from the dinosaurs. Maybe she and Magnolia should get together and compare vibes.

Mac and Magnolia had a learned discussion about the various dinosaurs as we walked the winding path. She didn't mention anything about dinosaur vibes, but she did mention how difficult it was to see the dinosaur figures properly through such overgrown foliage. Although it seemed to me the dinosaurs were perhaps just a bit shy and hiding behind the foliage, that with a little coaxing they might come out.

Then I gave myself a mental slap. *They're just concrete statues, ma'am.* Not shy or hostile. No more feelings than a fireplug and just as immovable.

Mac found the switched identification plaques, corrected them, and took new photos. I took a few photos of Magnolia and Geoff with my cell phone camera too. They turned out quite nicely, much better than the one I'd accidentally taken of myself when I first got the cell phone. I'd never before realized it was possible to get such an oversized and detailed look up your own nose.

Afterward, I fixed lunch, and we discussed whether we should move the motorhomes over to Sheila's five acres or just head on down to Arizona. Magnolia and I decided to take a walk while Mac and Geoff drove over to look at Sheila's place. They took BoBandy with them, and I left Koop sleeping on the bed in the motorhome. I'd once thought I'd teach him to walk on a cat leash, but usually calm Koop turned into King Kong Cat and climbed the leash as if it were the Empire State Building. Now, he often does accompany us on walks but only on his no-leash terms.

Magnolia changed into her safari pants with all the pockets and brought along a carved walking stick acquired from a found relative who said he'd carved it himself for hiking in the Himalayas. Maybe true, although I suspected it more likely once had a "Made in China" sticker attached and hadn't been any closer to the Himalayas than I have. I also thought that Kathy, now that our prior acquaintance had been established, might come out to join us for a walk, but then I saw that both vehicles were gone.

Magnolia talked about their search for the relatives in Idaho as we walked, but I have to admit I wasn't really listening. Instead my mind wandered around in these newly revealed facts about Kathy.

She'd told me that she and Brian had been married a "few years," but, if her husband's death had come after I first left my home on Madison Street to escape the murderous Braxtons, there couldn't have been much time between his death and when she married Brian.

Was that really why she hadn't wanted to acknowledge she knew me when I first said I was sure I recognized her from somewhere? Because if she did admit she'd lived near Madison Street back in Missouri, she knew I'd realize she'd remarried within a very short time, maybe within days, of her husband's death?

Another thought ballooned through that one. Had Kathy been in a relationship with Brian even before the ill husband died?

That got into the slimy ooze of gossip, but then an even more ominous thought balloon exploded through the others. What if the husband's death hadn't been a natural heart attack? What if Kathy had somehow brought it on so she and Brian could be together? Was there a way to do that? Withhold his heart medication? Give him a triple dose of it? Was grandmotherly-looking, dinosaur-cookie-baking Kathy really a husband killer?

Back off, Ivy, I chastised myself the instant those thought-balloons threatened to expand to spaceship size. Because, just like my wondering about a dead body in the house when Kathy hadn't immediately opened the door, this rocketed into sleazy tabloid territory with alien-baby stories and bloody novels with toothy vampires on the covers. In real life, ill spouses die; living spouses get on with their lives and remarry. Perhaps sooner than old-fashioned rules might consider proper, but nothing sinister about it.

My mind resisted that logical thinking and instantly hoisted another red flag: maybe it was Brian who got impatient and somehow hurried the first husband's death along.

I hastily shut off this line of thinking, and all its subversive tentacles too, and turned to Magnolia. "You said you'd had some kind of 'experience' with the last relatives you were looking for?"

"Ivy, I've just been *telling* you."

"I'm sorry." Not wanting to admit I'd been rambling around in murder plots again, I determinedly moved on. "You did find the relatives you were looking for, then?"

"After chasing all over Idaho. A bill collector said they'd written enough bad checks to paper a jail cell. A landlord claimed they'd made meth in the kitchen of his rental house. A neighbor said he'd loaned them a pickup for an emergency, and they just disappeared with it."

"But you kept searching for them anyway?"

"Well, that information *concerned* me, of course, but mistakes and misunderstandings happen." Magnolia looked uncomfortable, but she's always reluctant to admit her gene pool may have some swampy areas. "But when we finally caught up with them at a place out in the mountains, they stuck a shotgun out the window."

What could I say? *Good thing they didn't grab the semiautomatic rifle and just start blasting?*

"And then, when we finally convinced them we weren't bill collectors, drug agents, or vengeful neighbors, that we were relatives with a mutual ancestry, they hit us up for money. Can you imagine that?" She gave an innocent rock an un-Magnolia-like whack with her walking stick. "I think I may give up on searching for people in my family tree."

Magnolia had made similar statements before, so I suspected this was only a temporary withdrawal. I waited what seemed a respectable length of time to change the subject and then asked if she remembered anything more about Kathy back in Missouri.

"I didn't really see much of her because her husband was so ill, and she didn't stay there long after he passed away. It was an abrupt departure, as I recall. No services for the husband, no goodbyes."

"Where did she go?"

"I have no idea. I don't think she kept in touch with anyone."

No, she probably wouldn't have, if she'd instantly rushed into marriage with Brian Morrison.

We didn't walk all the way to the cove, but we got far enough to see the cliff on the far side of Ghost Goat Mountain and the ocean in the distance, a rippling jewel on this sunny day, a ship far out on the horizon. When we got back to the motorhomes, Magnolia decided to take a nap until the husbands got home.

I had too much on my mind to nap. Kathy Morrison had been Genevieve Higman back in Missouri. With a husband named Andy. Which was probably Andrew. I tried exploring for information with my cell phone but got frustrated with that and dashed off a text to my grandniece, Sandy, in Arkansas. Sandy isn't a hacker, but, like so many of her generation, she was apparently born with a new gene that enables her to zip through cyberspace at cyberspeed. I asked if she'd see what she could find out about Genevieve and Andrew Higman, especially details of his death back in Missouri, and also information on Katherine and Brian Morrison.

She texted back and said she'd see what she could find. She

also said she had a little gift to send me. I said thanks and told her to send it to General Delivery in the closest town, Trinidad, California. I have to admit I felt a slight trepidation. Sandy is sweet and generous, and I always appreciate her gifts. Though I must admit they're sometimes a bit . . . unusual for an LOL. Thong panties. Toe rings. A blue garter for our wedding. What would it be this time?

Then I used my own snail-with-rheumatism pace on my cell phone to look for more recent information about Brian's girlfriend in this area. I found Renée Echol on the website of a real estate agency in Eureka. Information was minimal, but there was a professional photo. She looked thirty-five-ish, with dark hair in a perky pixie cut and an equally perky smile. A cheerleader type aging nicely. She was quoted as saying she enjoyed her own home in Eureka so much that she had made it her goal to help others find homes that made them as happy as she was with hers. Very admirable. Maybe she'd been a beauty pageant contestant too, with world peace as her goal.

Okay, I had something of a built-in snarky attitude toward Renée. Not fair, I reminded myself. I didn't even know the woman, and Sheila could be totally mistaken about a backstreet relationship between Renée and Brian.

The statement about having a home that made her so happy suddenly wakened a new thought. Was the real reason we were on this detour not just because an editor needed something to fill a space in his magazine but for some other reason entirely? Had the Lord led us on this detour for a different purpose?

Chapter 7

MAC

Sheila was headed out for a bicycle ride, but she took time to show us the space where her friends had parked last summer. The grassy area sheltered by several trees was out behind her double-wide manufactured home, certainly enough space to accommodate both the motorhomes. Water and one electric hookup were accessible, but there were no sewer hookups. Sheila said her friends had visited a dump station at an RV park in Trinidad to empty their tanks every few days. Not ideal, but workable.

RV living gives a wonderful freedom in life, and I've loved it, but it isn't—as it's sometimes optimistically pictured in magazine ads—all carefree fun. There's all this grubbing around with hookups and wastewater tanks. Some people have maps showing interesting places all over the country; my old maps are marked with an X for "good dump station."

When we got back to the motorhomes, Magnolia got up from a nap and we all sat around their dinette and discussed plans. Magnolia and Geoff decided they'd stay a couple of nights at Sheila's and then head on down to warmer temperatures in Arizona. I thought that would work for Ivy and me too, but she said there was something she'd like to check into before we left.

I was curious, of course. Maybe even a little uneasy. I dearly love my wife, even if she does have this tendency to get involved in dead-body and murder situations. I sometimes think, if there is a murder anywhere within gunshot distance, Ivy will gravitate to it. Or maybe they gravitate to her.

Right now, what she wanted to do was go over and say goodbye to Kathy. I was surprised. Kathy had finally acknowledged Ivy's and Magnolia's past acquaintance with her, but she wasn't exactly enthusiastic about the reunion. But maybe women feel some need to try to repair old acquaintances, because Magnolia wanted to do it too. So, while Geoff and I moved the motorhomes to Sheila's pasture, Ivy kept the pickup so she and Magnolia could drive over after they did the goodbye thing with Kathy. We planned to thank Duke and tell him goodbye later, before we actually left the area.

At Sheila's, Geoff and I maneuvered the motorhomes into place, got the water and electricity connected, and the jacks lowered to level and stabilize both motorhomes. I checked the gauge showing contents of both our gray and black water tanks. We were good for several more days. Geoff and I got out canvas chairs, and BoBandy explored the pasture.

Even though this was not a convenient detour, not the honeymoon Ivy and I had anticipated, Sheila's big field was a nice place, peaceful and quiet, with a pleasing scent of damp earth and grass. Ivy talks to the Lord all the time. I don't feel quite that familiar with him yet, but I could comfortably say, *Thanks, Lord,* and fall asleep right there in the chair.

IVY

Brian's Porsche still wasn't in the carport, but Kathy's Honda was now parked near the door of their living quarters. Kathy answered my knock quickly enough, but she didn't open the door more than enough to peer out with one eye.

"We just stopped by to say goodbye," I said. "We'll be parking over at Sheila's for a couple of days, but we may not see you again before we leave."

"Oh. Well, that's nice of you. Goodbye, then."

I don't know what I expected. Not a tearful farewell, of course, but something more than this. Didn't Kathy want to know about any of the neighbors on Madison and Jefferson Streets? What the area was like now? What we'd been doing since she lived there?

Apparently not. Was she afraid a chat might get into messy details of her first husband's death and the timing of her marriage to Brian? Her hand clutched the door so hard her knuckles looked like white knobs. She was definitely stressed about something.

Finally I said brightly, "We appreciate you and Brian letting us stay here in the parking lot. It's been good seeing you again."

She did not prolong the conversation. "You, too." She didn't slam the door, but I heard the quick click of the dead bolt on the door.

Magnolia and I looked at each other as we walked toward the pickup Mac had left for us. "Was there anything unusual about Kathy's husband's heart attack? Any investigation?" I asked.

"No, I don't think so." She stopped short. "Why? What are you thinking?"

"Just curious."

Magnolia frowned, perhaps remembering other instances of my curiosity, but she started walking again. "It happened in the middle of the afternoon. Franny and I . . . you remember Franny Lisbon? No, I guess you wouldn't. She bought the Lithgow place after you left and got in a big to-do with the city about those two potbelly pigs she kept in her backyard. Anyway, Franny and I were sitting out on our patio drinking tea, and we heard a nearby siren. That's all there was to it. I didn't even know what had happened until that evening."

"It was on the news?"

"Oh, no. Franny came back over and told me. Franny always knows what's going on in the neighborhood."

A polite way of saying Franny Lisbon was gossip central on Madison Street and surrounding area. "Does she still live there?"

"Yes, I believe so. Why?"

Yes, why had I asked? Madison Street was old news. I'd sold my house there before Mac and I married. Most of the old-timers are already gone from the neighborhood now, and I don't keep in touch with anyone but Magnolia. Magnolia and Geoff had sold their place once, gotten it back when the buyers ran into financial difficulty, and were now thinking about selling it again. I wasn't suspicious enough of Kathy to consider contacting this Franny who always knew what was going on . . . was I?

I decided I'd remember the name, just in case I ever needed it.

Well, maybe I wouldn't remember it. My mind occasionally slips into some sticky pit, more euphemistically known as a senior moment. I wrote the name on a scratch pad in my purse as soon as we reached the pickup. Just in case. I also remembered, with regret, that I hadn't asked Kathy for her dinosaur cupcake recipe.

MAC

Geoff and I were still sitting outside when Ivy and Magnolia arrived in the pickup. It was such a nice evening, with a spectacular sunset, that I got out the barbecue, and when Sheila got back from her bicycle ride, we invited her over for steaks. It wasn't until later, when Ivy and I were getting ready for bed, that Ivy brought up the subject she'd been waiting to talk to me about.

"I've been thinking about that property by the cove where the old cabins burned down."

I was surprised. I'd assumed she wanted to talk about something to do with Kathy and Brian and the dead husband. "Thinking about it in what way?"

"Thinking it might be a great place for a home."

"Really?" I cycled that around in my brain. A beautiful spot,

68

yes, if you ignored remnants of the old fire. But— "It doesn't exactly fit our requirements as a place to settle down permanently."

"No, it doesn't," Ivy agreed. "But the view of the cove and ocean is spectacular, and we both like walking on the beach."

The burned-out ruins as a site for a home hadn't occurred to me before, but now that Ivy mentioned the idea, I could see possibilities. Yes, great possibilities! A garden. A place for BoBandy and Koop to prowl and run. Privacy. Fishing in the cove or surf. Walking the beach together. "It would take a lot of cleanup work. With a bulldozer, not a broom."

"We could live right there in the motorhome until we could have a house built."

"It wouldn't be like trying to find a house that suits us," I mused. "We could build exactly what we want." I nodded. The site had growing appeal. "Are you serious about this?"

"Yes. Quite serious. And the place does fulfill one of our most important requirements." Ivy smiled. "No murders. No dead bodies."

"We'll check it out."

IVY

Mac finished his article about the dinosaur park and, using the Wi-Fi connection through Sheila's internet service, sent everything to the editor the next morning. Magnolia and Geoff stayed two days, and we spent the time doing touristy things. "Goofing off" would describe it. Sheila went along a couple times to show us places to go and things to do. We had to take Magnolia and Geoff's Subaru, of course, and once Sheila took us in her SUV. Our pickup wasn't big enough for all of us.

The giant redwood trees in the Lady Bird Johnson Grove we visited deserved the term "awesome." We strolled through the Old Town part of Eureka, drove around to look at the much-photographed Carson Mansion and other Victorian houses in Eureka, and ate at a restaurant right beside the picturesque bay at Trinidad. I was surprised, when we passed the dinosaur park on our way out to show Magnolia and Geoff the cove late one afternoon, to see an empty spot in front of Duke's trailer where the old blue pickup usually stood. Had he actually driven it somewhere? Or maybe he'd decided he'd never use it again and gotten rid of it?

I was a little sad when we watched the familiar magnolia mural on the back end of Magnolia and Geoff's motorhome go down the road on Thursday morning, but we'd keep in touch and probably meet later in Arizona. Unless buying the cove property and staying right here worked out. Did I want that to happen? Maybe!

Even with the earlier interest Mac had expressed, I was surprised when, as soon as Magnolia and Geoff were gone, he immediately suggested we drive into Eureka and see what we could find out about the property. I wasn't eager to work with Renée Echol, so we picked a real estate agency just by spotting a sign on a small white office on the edge of town. An older man with a weathered complexion stood up behind a desk to greet us. We exchanged names—his was Delmer Johnson—and Mac told him about the property that interested us.

"Sure, I know the place. It was listed at one time, but I think it's been off the market for a while. Let me check." He sat down and clicked keys on the computer, talking even as his fingers sprinted over the keyboard. "I haven't been out there for a long time. Has the mess from the fire been cleaned up?"

"No, it still looks pretty bad," Mac said.

"What caused the fire?" I asked.

My mind tends to ramble around in crime possibilities, so I was thinking *arson*, but Delmer said, "A malfunction in the old electrical system, as I recall. Everything out there was old as the hills, of course. I guess you know it used to be a little resort with some rustic cabins?"

"Kate's Kabins," Mac said.

"Right. Did you folks have in mind something like that? Maybe a bed-and-breakfast?"

"We're thinking it might be a nice place to build a house just for us," Mac said. "But it may be a larger and more expensive piece of land than we'd want to buy."

"I don't remember the price, but I'm sure it was hefty. Even with that burned mess on it, any property with ocean frontage like that is pricey. But it isn't all that large a property." He glanced up at us, and I suspected he was trying to decide if we were richer than we looked. "Size of the property was a problem when some big resort outfit looked into buying it a while back. Regulations now require a much more extensive and expensive sewage system than what that old resort had, and there just wasn't enough space there. Especially since so much of the property is swampy. That may be a problem for any kind of commercial enterprise there."

"Would it be a problem for a homesite?"

"Probably not. A septic system for a private home doesn't have to be anywhere near that large. The company tried to buy the old dinosaur park for more space." He laughed. "Shrewd old guy out there let them wine and dine him. People said he always ordered lobster or prime rib when they took him out. But he wasn't really interested in selling all or even part of it, and they finally figured that out. Although, if you ask me, he'd have been smart to grab the money and run. Take life easy in his old age instead of coping with deteriorating dinosaurs and aggravating tourists."

"He still lives there, but he has someone running the place for him."

"Oh? I didn't know that."

"His property is quite some distance from the old cabins," I said. "I can't imagine how buying it would help a resort company."

"Actually, his property adjoins the resort property. It's kind of complicated, as I recall. The road to Kate's Kabins goes through that old guy's property, and I don't think there ever was a legal easement for it. Probably just one of those old-time handshake deals from way back when. He must have forty or fifty acres. The dinosaur park takes up only a small part of his property."

We certainly hadn't known that. From what Brian had said, we'd assumed the four or five acres in the park was all Duke owned.

I admired Delmer Johnson's multitasking abilities as he worked the computer and talked to us at the same time. I really have to concentrate when I do anything on the computer or I find myself stumbling around in anything from a medical site about obscure but horrendous diseases—and checking to see how many symptoms I have—to a site offering to tell my future if I'll just provide my date and place of birth and favorite color. And my credit card number, of course. But Delmer Johnson zipped smoothly from screen to screen as he tapped keys and at the same time talked about the old resort and a cousin's wedding he'd gone to there long ago.

"You've never really seen a wedding until you've been to one with seagulls," he added, laughing, but before I had time to picture the calamities possible in a seagull-attended wedding, he announced that yes, the listing on the property had run out some time ago.

"So it was never sold?" I asked.

"The last I heard, the heirs were still squabbling." A few more clicks, and then the agent peered more closely at the computer, obviously surprised about something. "It hasn't actually sold yet, but there's an option to buy on it. A local real estate agent, Renée Echol, has it. It was written up just a few days ago."

I couldn't tell if it was the sale that surprised Delmer Johnson or if the surprise was the identity of the buyer, but he was definitely surprised.

Mac and I looked at each other. Brian's girlfriend had an option on the property? What did that mean?

It didn't necessarily mean anything, of course. Renée was probably a smart investor who knew local real estate and was quietly snapping up the property as an investment for the future. Or maybe she already had another buyer lined up. I wasn't convinced of Brian's romantic relationship with her, no matter what Sheila said. Sheila's pejorative view of Renée may have been colored by her previous run-in with the woman.

"I wonder what she intends to do with it," Mac said.

"Good question. She owns a few rental properties around town." But this was obviously no rental property. What he quickly said, however, was, "We have other listings near the ocean that might interest you."

"No. Thanks anyway. Say, could you give us the name of a good restaurant here in town? Some place kind of special." Mac looked at me and winked. "We have a little something to celebrate."

Hey, we did. How could I forget? Today was our one-month anniversary! The man gave us a name, the Hideout, and directions. At the door, Mac turned back to ask a question.

"Renée Echol works for an agency called LeHigh Realty, doesn't she? Could you tell us where it's located?"

We knew the name of the agency because of my earlier nosiness checking out the website, but I hadn't noted the address then.

With hand motions to demonstrate the instructions, Delmer Johnson told us how to find LeHigh Realty. Then he surprised me by adding, after a pause, "Actually, until a few months ago, Renée worked here with our agency."

My first thought, of course, especially because that little

pause seemed somehow meaningful, was to wonder if Renée's departure had anything to do with Sheila's noisy accusations about Renée's handling of her friend's property. However, whether from business ethics or maybe just because he was a gentleman, Delmer Johnson didn't add further information. "Renée's a real go-getter," was all he said.

Which could mean anything, of course, from a compliment about her talents as a real-estate saleslady to a comment on her *go-getter* abilities involving someone else's husband.

***

We found the Hideaway, a rustic log building with wagon wheel chandeliers and log booths, and I forgot about Renée Echol and the cove property as we ate Caesar salad and oh-so-good crab cakes. The friendly, middle-aged waitress, when she learned we were celebrating our one-month anniversary, even brought us a miniature chocolate cake adorned with a single candle. Mac does have his romantic moments, and we made a sweet celebration of sharing a kiss and dipping our forks into the cake together, complete with a selfie using Mac's phone.

It wasn't the greatest picture. How do people get those flattering selfies I'm always seeing on the internet? We looked oddly egg-headed in ours. But it memorialized the occasion. We looked like happy eggheads.

Afterward Mac suggested that we contact Renée Echol and see if she intended to resell the cove property. I hesitated. I still felt squeamish about getting involved with her in any way. But seeing her about buying a specific property wasn't the same as inventing an interest in properties just to snoop on her relationship with Brian Morrison.

At LeHigh Realty, a middle-aged woman came out of a back office to greet us. She had an impressive upswept blond hairdo and equally impressive blue fingernails decorated with sparkly silver stars. Mac told her we'd like to see Renée Echol.

"She hasn't been in for a couple of days, but her SUV is out in the parking lot. Maybe she went to breakfast or lunch with a friend." Without actually saying so, the woman managed to make not being in the office sound like a flaw in Renée's work ethics. I also detected a hint of disapproval in her emphasis on *friend.* Maybe she knew about Brian? "But I'll be glad to help you with whatever you're looking for. I'm Donna Feldman." She held out her hand, apparently eager to snatch business out from under Renée if she could.

We both shook hands with her, but Mac said, "Thanks, but we need to talk to Renée herself." He paused, and I wondered if he was going to say anything about the property at the cove, but this was Renée's private option deal, not an agency listing, and he didn't mention it. "Will she be in later?"

"She *should* be in now, so I really can't say. I can give you her card with her cell phone number if you'd like." Said with all the enthusiasm of introducing a boyfriend to the hottest girl in town.

"Thanks," Mac said. "We'd appreciate that."

She disappeared into the back hallway and returned with a card in hand. I thanked her, took the card, and saw the same perky face I'd seen on the website. In the pickup, I read the number off to Mac and he tried calling her but only got voice mail. He left a message with his name and number and asked her to call.

We drove back up the coast to the motorhome. It was a windy afternoon, not really conducive to outside activity, and I caught up on housekeeping. Sheila offered her laundry room so I could do a couple of loads of washing. Mac tried calling Renée late that afternoon and again that evening. By the third call he didn't bother leaving another message. Apparently, she didn't want to talk to us. Had Brian warned her to stay away from these people?

In the morning, with windblown rain pounding the windows, I tried the number once more. Still the same voice mail recording. We discussed just heading off for Arizona immediately. Mac's work was done here, so there was no real reason to hang around. The weather was not an encouragement to stay. We could be on the road in twenty minutes.

I had to wonder, if we actually settled down somewhere, would I miss that freedom to just pick up and go?

But before Mac got the pickup hooked onto the motorhome, I suggested we drive out and look at the property once more, this time paying special attention to it as a possible homesite. Even if Renée did want to sell, the property was probably far out of our price range, but we'd never have another chance to look at it if we didn't do it now. If it looked like a real possibility for a home, we'd wait to talk to Renée Echol; if not, we'd head down the road. We left BoBandy and Koop curled up together in his doggie bed.

When we drove by the dinosaur park, I noted that the blue pickup was back at Duke's trailer. I wondered what had prompted him to drive somewhere himself, since he apparently hadn't done so for a considerable time. Looking for a new girlfriend? More likely he and Sheila had gone off together to do something, and he'd just asserted his manly driving rights.

At the cove, we parked under the same windblown tree as we had before. It wasn't raining hard now, but drizzle and fog blotted out everything beyond the ridge of sea-foam edging the sandy beach of the cove, the end of the dock lost in mist. Unseen surf roared beyond the cove. Even the scent was wild and raw, like something God had left unfinished.

Not an ideal day for inspecting property to buy. And the place felt somehow different today, as if something had changed. Definitely higher on the creep scale.

"So, what do you think? The place doesn't look very appealing at the moment, but if we don't look at it now, we'll never have another chance," Mac said, echoing my earlier

76

thought.

I had to agree with the "non-appealing" statement. At the moment, the place looked almost sinister.

But he was right. This would be our only chance.

I pulled the hood of my jacket up over my head, and we wandered through the remains of what had been the main building. In spite of the blackened skeletons of old timbers, the fire had been too long ago for any odor of burn to remain. Now the scent was just soggy earth and wet vegetation, as if anything built here might mold before the last nail was driven.

The eight cottages had been irregularly spaced, giving each one some privacy, although close enough together that fire had jumped from one to another. From the layout of the foundations, they appeared to alternate between one- and two-bedroom cabins, each with a small kitchen/living room area. Soggy old mounds of half-burned mattresses and sofas remained, and in one cabin the smashed and half-burned remnants of a crib lay in one corner.

Now I felt a real dismay about the site. No one had mentioned deaths, but had there been victims here, mothers and fathers and even children who'd lost their lives in the fire?

I suddenly felt uneasy prowling here, even a little squeamish. A blackberry vine snagged my pants leg, and I stepped on an old can that clamped around my foot like some hungry metal predator. On a practical note, although no Keep Out signs were posted, and cans and broken bottles and old fast-food burger wrappers suggested many people had wandered here before us, this was private property. Property on which Renée Echol had an option to buy.

By the time we got to the last cabin, I had almost decided the drawbacks of the site outweighed the good points. Because, in addition to all the bulldozer work needed to clean up the place, there was something unsettling here that went beyond remnants of the old fire, wet weeds, and thorny vines, something I could neither see nor smell nor hear.

But something that sent a spidery shiver up my back and wakened an unpleasant prickle in my nerves. Something that made me peer into the oversized ferns behind the cabins and hunch my shoulders against something unseen. Something that made my ears strain to catch some sound just beyond my hearing. I tried to scoff at the uncomfortable feeling, but it clung like cat hair to black pants.

At what remained of the last cabin, Mac said he was going a little farther to see if an old shed vaguely visible in the drizzle and fog was the pump house for a well. He plunged into the brush, and I stepped into the shelter of a still-standing corner of the burned cabin. A layer of matted leaves covered the uneven floor, areas where fire had burned through the flooring now sunken booby traps, the scent musty in spite of the fresh rain. A pile of old beer cans filled one corner. Momentarily, the impression of a vanished civilization, the where-have-all-the-people-gone feeling that I'd had when we came here before, surrounded me.

And then I heard a sound that was very much current civilization.

Music. *Music?* Yes, something a little rowdy but not unpleasant. Upbeat. Kind of a *Let's dance!* sound, totally at odds with the gloomy day.

But how—? Who—?

Then I recognized what it was. The ringtone of a cell phone.

Not mine. All mine had was a phone-sounding tinkle.

My cell phone was also, I realized as I felt in my pockets, back in the pickup. I'm not as welded to the phone as a lot of people are, and it often gets left behind.

I threw back the hood on my jacket and peered around cautiously, eyes trying to dart in all directions at once. Was someone in the wreckage of the burned-out cabin with me? Someone furtively hiding from my view?

78

Someone hiding with nefarious intentions directed at me? I cautiously turned a full circle without moving in any direction, feet shuffling in the matted leaves, skin prickling.

A movement there by a burned cabinet? Malevolent eyes peering in from outside?

No. No movement, no watching eyes. Just that incongruous upbeat tune on a phone.

I cautiously crunched over broken glass to circle a sodden, burned lump that had once been a sofa. Nothing there. The phone still played its dancy beat, something vaguely otherworldly about it. I turned and edged toward an oblong of burned two-by-fours that had once framed a doorway to a bedroom.

She lay sprawled faceup on the far side of a sodden mound of old mattress, her body sunk into the soggy remains. A petite woman, small boned. Slim and dark haired. I recognized her from the perky photo on the business card and website. The phone went silent.

She didn't look perky now, not with rain pounding her half-open eyes and slack mouth, plastering her hair to her head and puddling in her upturned palms.

She just looked dead.

Chapter 8

IVY

She wore skinny-legged jeans, gold hoop earrings, and a black leather jacket open to reveal a red turtleneck.

And a dark hole in her chest.

An irrelevant but stomach-twisting thought hit me. The music from the phone had stopped, but those calls we'd made to Renée—the cheerful *Let's dance!* music—had danced against a dead woman's body. While we grumbled about her not answering.

I screamed. Well, I thought I screamed, but only a squeak came out. I swallowed and backed away. There was no need to check for a heartbeat. Renée was so not living. I made it to the warped bedroom doorway I'd come through.

"Mac?" My voice had gone hoarse as well as squeaky. I tried again, hoarse-squeaking louder. "Mac?"

No answer. All I could hear was the lonely shriek of an unseen gull and the roar of surf. I stumbled to the outside doorway and held onto the burned framework for support. All I could see beyond a few feet of ragged ferns and blackberry bushes was a world of mist and drizzle. Everything familiar was gone. Mac was gone.

I took a deep breath and called again, this time a full-fledged blast the dinosaurs back at the park could have heard. "Mac!"

He crashed out of the brush. "What? What's wrong?"

Husband from the Black Lagoon. Mud from hair to toes. Mud on shoes and legs, mud on hands and arms and chest, mud in beard and ears and eyebrows.

"What *happened* to you?"

"I fell in some kind of swamp or marsh back there. It's covered with reeds or something, and everything was so foggy

I didn't even realize they were growing in water until I was all tangled up in them. They tried to eat me alive! The mud must be ten feet deep!"

No doubt a bit of exaggeration there, although he did look as if he may have been floundering in ten feet of mud. Broken reeds clung to his hair, strands of swamp scum draped his arms, and blackberry thorns stuck to his shirt and legs of his pants. Rain hit his muddy hair and dripped off his muddy beard. Why hadn't he been wearing his hooded jacket, or at least a cap?

"Are you okay?" I tried to pick a strand of slimy stuff off his arm.

"Do I *look* okay?"

Well, no, he didn't look okay. He didn't smell okay either. The scum left a green streak when I wiped my hand on my pants leg.

"I don't think this is a good place for a home." Mac, master of the understatement. He scraped mud off his face and flung it aside. "No telling what other booby traps or ambushes are hidden out there."

He didn't yet know the biggest reason this was not a good spot for a home, a reason that turned my nerves to icicles and removed this place from any list of places we might ever settle down and live.

"Let's go back to the motorhome so I can get this stuff washed off." Mac stomped his feet and flapped his elbows.

I ducked to avoid flying mud. "We have to do something first. Do you have your phone?"

"If I do, it's probably full of mud," he growled. Then he planted his muddy hands on his muddy hips and gave me an exasperated look. "You want to make a phone call *now?*"

"We have to call nine-one-one. There's a dead body in there." I motioned toward the skeleton of burned cabin.

"A dead body?" His mouth gaped open. I think he intended

81

to say something about this being no time to kid around, but he closed it without saying anything. Maybe because he realized I wouldn't joke about a dead body. Maybe because rain and mud tend to dribble into a mouth gaping open.

I grabbed his muddy hand, and we stumbled through the burned framework where the door had once been. I led him past the soggy sofa to the bedroom doorway. If I'd hoped I was somehow mistaken about a dead body, I was wrong. She still lay there, body still sunk into the sodden mattress, still dead.

"I-I think that's a bullet hole in her chest."

Mac shook his head as if he couldn't believe what he was seeing. I think he mumbled something about *not again*, or maybe that's what I was thinking.

"You recognize her, don't you?" I reached in the back pocket of my jeans and pulled out the card I'd stuck there after trying to call Renée that morning. I handed it to him. I saw now that one of her shoes had fallen to the leaf-matted floor. Not a stiletto, but the black leather with a chunky heel and lots of silver studs still looked a little upscale for tromping around in a place such as this. When I leaned forward I could see the name printed on the inner sole, and I was startled. Jimmy Choo. Could Renée afford shoes in that price range? Well, she had an option to buy this property, so maybe she could.

Mac looked back and forth between the card and the face on the body sprawled on the misshapen mattress, then searched his clothing for a phone. Unfortunately, all he found was mud-filled pockets. Or maybe fortunately, because mud probably means quick death to a cell phone. His phone must be at the pickup, same as mine.

I hesitated a moment before starting back to the pickup. I didn't like leaving her like this, soggy mattress beneath her, a crumpled beer can beside her foot, rainwater drizzling on her pale skin and half-open eyes through the nonexistent roof. She was dead, but she still looked so . . . vulnerable and lonely and abandoned.

But there was nothing we could do for her, nothing to cover her with, and we surely shouldn't touch anything anyway, so we just slogged back to the pickup. Once there, I dug my phone out of my purse. I had some concerns about the value of a 911 call since we'd never been in this area before. Maybe it would go to some 911 location back in Montana. Or Missouri. Or outer space. But the call went exactly where it should, the local 911 site. Something about 911 calls and nearby cell phone towers, Mac said.

I told the woman who responded who and where we were and what we'd found. The woman was efficient but not impersonal. I told her I didn't think we were in any danger, but she said we should stay in our vehicle until help arrived. "Be careful, okay?" So, after I found an old T-shirt of Mac's behind the pickup seat and wiped mud off his hair and face, we climbed in our vehicle and waited.

We spoke a few words, but we didn't have a real conversation as we sat there. We were both a little dazed as well as cold and wet. One of us was also sitting in mud. It oozed around him and dripped to the floorboard. He started the engine to run the heater, though that didn't seem to help much.

"I wonder if she was killed here or killed somewhere else and brought here." I kept myself from saying *dumped here.* "She didn't drive here in her SUV because it was in the real estate agency's parking lot."

A few minutes later Mac said, "I wonder how long she's been dead."

Rain now battered the top of the pickup with a clackety-clack that sounded as if we were stranded in a tin can under attack by a dozen nail guns. The mud smelled even worse in this enclosed space—definitely Black Lagoon-ish—although I didn't mention that to Mac. He shivered, and I rummaged under the seat and found an old burlap bag he used to spread on the ground when he needed to crawl under the pickup. The bag was oily and dirty, with a surprise touch of dried mustard, but he mumbled grateful thanks when I wrapped it around his shoulders.

Me, more minutes later and somewhat warmed by the heater: "I wonder who was trying to call her when I found her."

"Maybe the phone will tell the police something important."

Me again, after more minutes: "I wonder what happened to the gun."

Finally, Mac asked the questions that really mattered. "Who killed her? And why? And why way out here?"

I thought of possible answers.

She may have been here looking at what might soon be her new property, and someone saw her vehicle and wanted it. A vehicle theft that escalated into murder. Nothing personal. Maybe she'd encountered the thief while he was in the act of stealing the vehicle and he shot her and carried her to the far cabin.

The facts punched an instant hole in that scenario. Renée's SUV wasn't stolen; it was in the parking lot in town, according to the upswept-hair lady.

Of course, she may have owned some other vehicle in addition to the SUV and had come here in it. Maybe something sleek and pricey, like Brian's Porsche?

Awful as it was, I wanted to believe the car-theft version of her death. It was an impersonal kill-the-owner-of-the-car thing, not a personal *kill-Renée* murder. Not that it mattered, I reminded myself. Dead was dead.

Renée had been playing a dangerous game involved with another woman's husband. Especially if that other woman, sweet and gentle as she might look in a Dolly Dinosaur costume, had already killed once and probably wasn't about to let Renée snatch the husband she'd killed to acquire. This put a new spin on Kathy's nervousness that last time Magnolia and I saw her when we went to say goodbye. She very likely would be nervous if she'd recently put a bullet in Renée's chest. Did she know anything about guns and shooting? Did she or Brian own a gun?

Or maybe Brian never intended to leave his wife. Renée was just a fling, and he got rid of her, maybe in the heat of an argument when she forced a showdown. *Kathy or me, Brian. Make a decision.* And his answer was a bullet in her chest.

Though the isolated, burned cabin seemed an odd place for a showdown. Had Brian killed her somewhere else and brought her to the cove?

I felt as if I were floundering in sleaze as deep as the mud Mac had fallen into. Affairs. Infidelity. Murder. I took a mental sidestep and pointed out to myself that it could be some business thing, something totally unrelated to Renée's messy personal life. Hadn't I recently read about some real estate woman being murdered when she was holding an open house? Although the burned-out cabin was hardly open-house territory.

Not my job to figure it out. We'd called 911. Help was coming.

Sooner than I expected, a siren wailed in the distance, and then a white police car with Sheriff and an official emblem emblazoned on the side skidded up behind us. We both opened our doors and got out, although from the way the officer warily put his hand on his gun maybe we should have stayed in the pickup and let him come to us.

"You called nine-one-one? About a dead woman?" He looked around warily, reminding me that 911 calls have been used to ensnare law enforcement officers in deadly ambush.

"She's back there." Mac pointed to the line of burned

cabins only partly visible through the fog and encroaching brush and vines.

"How'd you find her?"

"We were looking at the property, thinking about buying it, and I heard a phone ringing," I said.

I thought the officer might insist on more information, especially since he eyed muddy Mac warily, but apparently he figured the first priority was to make sure the woman was actually dead, not in need of emergency medical care. Non-law-enforcement people like us probably aren't noted for their expertise in such matters. I didn't see any need to tell the officer this wasn't our first dead-body encounter. Not that such earlier encounters made us experts.

He took a minute to take our names and check driver's licenses for identity. He called them in on his car radio and then we headed across the old parking lot. The asphalt was buckled and rough, weeds rampant in the cracks, but it was easier walking there than struggling through the brush and ferns and vines growing around the burned cabins. Even with the old burlap bag draped around him, Mac looked shivery and miserable. At the cabin, the officer stuck out a hand to stop us.

"Stay back," he ordered, his other hand on his gun as he stepped through the doorway.

I hadn't seen a shoulder mic, but the officer must have been wearing one under the heavy jacket, or maybe he carried some handheld radio, because, although I couldn't make out the words, I could hear him talking. I wished Mac had the officer's wide-brimmed hat for protection from the rain. I guiltily corrected my wishing. I wished Mac had a hat *like* the officer's; even in a wish I shouldn't be depriving the deputy of his hat.

After several minutes, the officer came back to the doorway. "Did you see anyone else? Any vehicles?"

"No," Mac said.

"Did you touch anything in here?"

"No," I said.

"Did you see a weapon?"

Mac's turn to answer. "No. But we didn't look for one."

"You know who she is?"

I had the feeling he recognized Renée and was just checking to see if we did. I got out the card and handed it to him. It bore muddy fingerprints from when Mac had handled it with Black Lagoon hands.

"You were meeting her here?"

"Oh, no. We'd been trying to get hold of her, but she didn't answer her cell phone, so we decided to come out and look at the property by ourselves. Her cell phone is how we found her body. I heard it ringing. Look, can we go back to the pickup? Or maybe on back to our motorhome? Mac is freezing."

"Let me get some information first. It'll only take a minute." He dug out the little notebook law enforcement people always seem to carry even in these times of high-tech equipment. He sheltered it under his jacket while we gave him phone numbers and where we were staying in the motorhome. He'd already written down the license number of the pickup, but now he also wanted the motorhome license number. Can anyone remember their license numbers right off the bat like that?

We couldn't, and I had the uncomfortable feeling that not remembering was somehow a black mark against us. He closed the notebook. "Just don't pick up and leave. I'll come to your motorhome to talk to you later."

"Okay."

He gave Mac a final wary glance. Rain had washed off some of the mud, but he still looked like a mud zombie from a horror movie. "What happened to you?"

Mac apparently didn't want to admit what he considered a dumb move in falling into the swamp, so all he did was mutter, "Little accident."

"Do you need medical attention?" the officer asked.

"I need a shower."

The officer nodded without comment, but he asked, "The property is for sale? I didn't see a sign."

"That's why we were trying to get hold of Renée," I explained. "We learned she had an option to buy it, and we wondered if she planned to sell. We're in the area because Mac was doing an article about the Ghost Goat Dinosaur Park for a travel magazine, but we're also looking for a place to settle down and live."

I had the uneasy feeling that was TMI. Too much information. Like a thief offering too much information about why he has a ham and two packages of steak under his coat.

"We're going to leave now," Mac said. He held his arms away from his body as if the mud in his armpits might be hardening into solid lumps. "We'll be at the motorhome."

We went back to the pickup, and Mac drove carefully to Sheila's. I tried not to breathe too deeply of the swamp-mud scent that hung like a miasma around us. We met two more cars with sheriff department insignias on the sides, plus one from the California Highway Patrol.

MAC

Back at the motorhome, Ivy wanted to rush me into the shower, but even though rain had washed away some of my mud covering, this was still too big a project for the motorhome's little shower system. Like trying to clean up a wallowing pig with a Waterpik. I got another hose out of a storage compartment under the motorhome, hooked it up to a faucet, and stood in the grass while Ivy hosed me off. I shivered. Even so, I was tempted to strip down to an elemental skinny-dipping state right there outside the motorhome. Inside the clothes, I could still feel mud in my belly button and between my toes and every other available spot.

Ivy hustled me inside the motorhome before I got beyond loosening my belt. She tossed my wet clothes back outside, and I took a hot shower. She brought me slippers and clean, dry clothes from the skin out. By the time I'd dried off and dressed, she had the motorhome warmed up, her own clothes changed, and coffee made.

Thank you, Lord, for Ivy. Hey, I'm getting better at this everyday talking-to-you stuff, aren't I?

And every day I'm more and more grateful he blessed me with Ivy.

We sat at the dinette drinking coffee, and Ivy checked her phone.

"There's a text from Sandy. I'd asked her to see what she could find out on the internet about Kathy and her first husband back in Missouri, when she was Genevieve Higman. And also about Kathy and Brian."

"Why?"

"Oh, you know, just curious."

I didn't question the *why* of her curiosity. Ivy is curious about everything, from shooting stars to shooting guns. Her mutant curiosity gene, as a friend of hers once put it, hard at work. "So what does she say?"

"It's pretty long." She scrolled down the text. "And full of those abbreviations texting people use."

I knew some of those from deciphering messages from my grandkids. U for *you*. Ur for *your*. I even liked some of them. B3 for *blah, blah, blah* makes a useful comment in any number of situations. I've been tempted to use it in some live, person-to-person conversations too. But I'm still clueless about HAK and SLAP.

"Do you want to read it?" Ivy asked.

"Give me the highlights."

"Okay. Starting with Genevieve Higman and the dead husband Andrew. Sandy located several Andrew Higman death

89

certificates, one of which she thinks might be him because of the city where he died. He died of acute myocardial infarction."

"More commonly known as a heart attack."

"Right." Exactly as Kathy had said. "Sandy couldn't come up with birth or marriage certificates for Genevieve and Andrew, but she found several interesting articles. One from an Alabama newspaper was about an Andrew Higman who was involved in the development of a new soft drink that was going great until various medical reports about severe intestinal complications surfaced, and it was pulled off the market. There was quite a stink about it." She paused. "No pun intended."

"None taken."

She still paused, frowning, and I knew what she was thinking. This generation is changing the whole concept of spelling. Ivy, as a long-time librarian, probably didn't approve. But maybe some spelling needs changing. Even after writing a couple hundred articles for travel magazines, I still have trouble with the spelling of "traveling." Or is it "travelling"?

"Then Sandy says she found an earlier newspaper article with the Andrew Higman name in it as part of an investment group building a shopping mall in Illinois that went bankrupt. And then there's an Andrew Higman who showed up in a couple of criminal activities in Alabama. One for fraud in a car sales scheme, one for some kind of investment fraud scheme with stock in a mining company in Utah. He went to prison for that one."

"Do you think any of those could have been the first husband of our Dolly Dinosaur?"

"If they were, wifehood may have been a roller-coaster existence for her." And Brian and a quiet dinosaur park may be just what she needed.

It occurred to me that Kathy and Brian probably didn't expect to run into anyone they knew here at an obscure dinosaur park and, even if they did, a dinosaur costume probably made an effective disguise for Kathy in the gift shop. Was that the reason they were here? But why would she not want to be recognized? What difference did it make?

"Did Sandy find out anything about Brian and Kathy as man and wife?" I asked.

"Very little, actually. She found birth records on several Brian Morrisons, but it isn't really an unusual name and none of them were the right age. No marriage records. Most states have tightened up access to driver's license records, and she didn't get anything that way on any of them. Neither Brian nor Kathy seem to have made their way into any news articles."

Just a nice, quiet, well-behaved couple. Although the thought occurred to me that their quiet life at a deteriorating dinosaur park might also be described as *lying low*. Even *hiding out*.

"The last thing she says is that she's mailing the surprise she has for me."

"You asked Sandy to find out about Kathy and her husbands even before we knew Renée was dead," I pointed out.

"I've thought about Kathy's first husband's death and how soon afterward she married Brian," she admitted.

I leaped over several tall buildings and landed in the middle of Ivy's sometimes outside-the-LOL-box thought processes. "You're suspicious about the first husband's death."

"Not exactly *suspicious*, but . . . interested."

I tried to follow her trail of thinking. Actually, this pathway wasn't as convoluted as some. Or maybe my mind is starting to work like Ivy's. "You wondered if Kathy may have had a relationship with Brian before her husband's death. You wondered if she may have hurried that death along."

Ivy nodded. "I've also wondered if Brian could have done the hurrying."

"And now you're wondering, since Brian was involved in

91

an affair with Renée, if he killed her. Or wondering if Kathy did it."

She nodded. "Those possibilities have occurred to me."

Either Kathy or Brian sounded like obvious possibilities to me too, and in real life, obvious possibilities often turn out to be the right ones. The killer is someone the victim knew. The husband or wife, girlfriend or boyfriend. But there is danger in making easy assumptions and jumping to wrong conclusions.

"Maybe someone else is involved," I suggested. "Unknown Man. Renée was an attractive woman. Maybe she had some other man in her life. A man who becomes enraged when he finds out she also has a relationship with Brian. He pulls a gun and *bang*. Or it could be that Brian objected to Renée's involvement with this other man. You think we should mention any of this to the officer when he comes to interview us?"

"I think what I'd really like to do is head on down to Arizona and get on with our honeymoon and not get any more involved in this," Ivy declared. "If there was another man in Renée's life, the official investigation will surely uncover it."

I agreed. Non-involvement was an excellent plan. "As soon as we've talked to the officer, we'll take off."

"You mean leave yet today after he comes?" She peered out a window. BoBandy got up to look with her. "It's almost dark."

"So? As soon as the officer leaves we'll go over and tell Duke goodbye, and then we'll just keep going." I was suddenly impatient to be on the move, away from here, and there was nothing holding us here now. "You start putting stuff away. I'll wash the mud out of the pickup and get it hooked up."

Ivy immediately started tucking the toaster and various other loose items into cabinets where they wouldn't fly around when we were on the move.

It occurred to me that this ability to just pick up and *go*, to stop in a rest area for the night or drive all night if we wanted to, was really a wonderfully free way of life. Free as a bird. Did we really want to give up our bird freedom and settle down in one place?

Ivy's cell phone rang before I got out the door.

Chapter 9

IVY

"Mrs. MacPherson?"

"Yes."

"This is Deputy Hardishan. I told you I'd be there to interview you today, but I'm still here at the crime scene and won't be able to get away for a while yet."

My head was full of questions. Had the medical examiner arrived? Had Renée's body been removed? Had they found the gun or any other evidence? Had anyone else fallen in the swamp? But I knew how far asking questions would get me. I've struck out in this ball game before. Besides, we'd already decided on Non-involvement. I didn't need to know anything. One thing I should tell him, however.

"In case you don't already know, Renée's SUV is in the parking lot at that real estate agency in Eureka where she worked. LeHigh Realty."

"You saw it there?"

His question gave me the impression he already knew about Renée's SUV and our inquiries about Renée inside the LeHigh office. I was uneasily reminded that someone who finds a body often heads up the suspect list. Often with good reason. Then I had to explain our visits to the two real estate offices, which somehow made us sound more *involved* with Renée than we really were. "So you'll be here when?" I interrupted myself. "Tomorrow?"

"Yes, but I'm not sure what time. I'll call you."

This changed our plans about scooting on out of here tonight, but I supposed one more day wouldn't matter. As I kept reminding myself, honeymoon is a state of mind. Although a dead body, an oversupply of mud, and an upcoming questioning by a deputy did not add to the already shaky honeymoon ambiance.

I thought that took care of everything, but then Deputy Hardishan added, "You understand that you can't leave, of course."

"You mean we have to sit right here all day waiting for you?"

"No, I mean you can't pick up and leave the area."

That sounded as if he suspected we might take off to avoid talking to him. I didn't like his imperious-sounding order that we couldn't leave the area.

Because we *could* pick up and leave. No matter how many times in books and movies, and maybe in real life, people are told they can't leave, it isn't so. Info courtesy of a police officer friend back in Missouri, now with the FBI. Law enforcement might not like it if you left. Your leaving might frustrate and anger them. They might make it sound as if you couldn't leave, as Deputy Hardishan was doing. But they can't keep you from leaving unless you're actually under arrest. Which Deputy Hardishan surely knew.

Then he added, "Whether you realize it or not, you may have vital information. Your cooperation is important to us, and we appreciate any help you can give us."

Okay, I'd consider this a request rather than a high-handed order to keep us from disappearing. "We want to cooperate and help any way we can. We were planning to leave this evening, but we'll stay to talk to you tomorrow. Thanks for calling."

We discussed whether we should go over and tell Sheila about Renée's murder but hadn't yet decided if we should do so when someone knocked on the door.

"Everything okay out here?" Sheila asked.

It was almost dark by now, but the oblong of light from the open door illuminated Sheila's hooded plastic rain jacket over

95

flowered leggings and knee-high rubber boots, also flowered. She looked as if she'd just sprouted from the ground in full bloom. I didn't intend to invite her in. I liked Sheila fine, but I felt as if I'd run a marathon and then been pulled through a knothole, and I knew Mac felt the same or worse. Finding a dead body will do that to you, and he'd had the additional ignominy of a fall in the swamp. But before I could think of some polite excuse to keep her out, she'd scooted inside with the expertise of a shyster salesman. Mac, who apparently felt even less like chatting with Sheila than I did, instantly disappeared into the bedroom.

"I saw you out there hosing Mac down."

Her playful smile startled me. She'd been *watching*? Now I was extra glad I'd yanked Mac inside before he went into skinny-dipping mode.

A little coyly she added, "Fun and games among the newlyweds? I saw that pile of wet clothes outside, his *and* yours. I remember once when Stan and I were first married—"

I didn't want to picture whatever Sheila might be remembering. Or what she was imagining now. "Mac fell in a swamp out at the old Kate's Kabins place," I said hastily. "He was covered with mud."

"What were you doing out there?"

"Just looking around."

"Mac falling in the swamp was what brought all the police cars? I saw them heading out that way with sirens screaming when I came home from town. I've been thinking I should run over and check on Duke. I worry about him. Sometimes he seems so . . . naïve and defenseless."

Although he seemed capable enough at avoiding marriage.

"The police came because we called nine-one-one. Not about Mac falling in the swamp. We found Renée Echol's body in one of the old burned-out cabins."

"You found Renée's *body*?" Sheila gasped. Her hand

touched her throat. "You mean she's *dead*?"

"I'm afraid so."

"What did you see? I mean, did she just *look* dead? Or did you feel for a pulse or do that breathing test like I've seen on TV? You know, where you hold a mirror under the person's nose to see if it fogs up? I wonder, does that really work?"

The rush of questions sounded almost voyeuristic, like the gawking people who gather at the scene of an accident, so I may have been a little sharp with my response. "She had what looked like a gunshot hole in her chest."

"How *ghastly*." Sheila patted her own chest and breathed deeply, as if to see if she still could. "Are you saying she took her own life?"

I was startled. That thought hadn't even occurred to me. For one thing, the gun would have been right there if she'd killed herself, wouldn't it? Although it could have been there and we just hadn't noticed it. But shooting yourself in the *chest* . . .

"The police will figure it out," I said. "We'll be leaving as soon as an officer comes to interview us tomorrow."

She ignored my statement about leaving and dropped to the sofa. "Oh, this is so . . . so *sad*, isn't it? I didn't like her. You know that. What she did to my friend Lexie ended our friendship. We had words. She was not an ethical person either in business or personal life. But to *kill* herself, and in such a lonely, forsaken place . . ."

"You think she had some reason to kill herself?"

"Well, no, not necessarily." Sheila's slump on the sofa straightened. "It was just my first thought, considering the awful situation she was in with Brian. Maybe he broke up with her, and she'd decided she couldn't go on living without him. Although that seems a little melodramatic, doesn't it?"

"She'd just gotten an option to buy that old Kate's Kabins property. You wouldn't think she'd do that if she was in a

97

mood to kill herself."

"Maybe it wasn't really planned. Maybe she was giving Brian the drama-queen treatment, *threatening* to do it. You know, waving a gun around and then making a mistake and accidentally *doing* it."

"At a burned-out old cabin?"

Then, as if my statement about Renée buying the property just got through to her, her hand dropped from her throat and her tone went inquisitive. "Renée was *buying* that old place? What in the world for? How did you find out about that?"

"We stopped to inquire about the property at a real estate agency."

Sheila didn't ask why we'd made the inquiry. Something else apparently interested her more. "I wonder where she was getting the money."

I also hadn't thought about that, but it was an interesting question. From what the real estate man had said, the ocean-front property, in spite of its condition, was worth a bundle.

"I got the impression she was fairly well off. I noticed she was wearing Jimmy Choo shoes."

"Oh, *that.*" Sheila waved a dismissive hand. "She bought name-brand stuff at some cheapie site for secondhand clothes and shoes on the internet. Though I doubt if some of the big-name items she bought were even *genuine.* That's where she got that Coach bag she carried."

I hadn't seen any bag with her body. "How do you know that?"

"Like I told you before, we were friends way back when." This time it was a shrug that dismissed that old-friends era. She squinted into space. "Maybe she was buying the property for someone who didn't want his name known."

"Why would she do that?"

"I know it's not polite to speak ill of the dead, but Renée was sneaky. A real hustler. A wheeler and dealer, not necessarily on the up-and-up. Maybe she'd gotten some investor to put up the money and they had some scheme going. Or maybe she was trying to put something over on an investor."

Considering her hidden affair with Brian, Renée apparently did have a sneaky and/or scheming side. Could an investor be the Unknown Man Mac and I had contemplated? Or could it be Brian himself? He apparently had some money.

In what sounded like something of an afterthought she added, "Is there anything I can do?"

"I don't think so. Going over to see Duke might be a good idea. All the police cars going by might upset him. His pickup was gone when we drove by there a couple of days ago, but I think it's back now."

Sheila looked surprised and a bit annoyed. "I didn't know he'd gone anywhere by himself. I wonder where he went?"

Obviously not somewhere with her. Maybe he did have another girlfriend or had gone looking for a new one? I didn't mention that possibility and just repeated what I'd said, that checking on him would be a good idea.

"I'll do that right now. I wonder if Brian and Kathy know about Renée." She shuffled her flower-booted feet and gave me a sideways look. "Of course, if Renée *didn't* kill herself . . ."

Her voice trailed off, but that sly look suggested she was thinking what had already thundered into my mind like a drum roll. If Renée hadn't killed herself, Brian or Kathy, or the two of them together, might already know she was dead because one of them had pulled the trigger. I thought again about how edgy Kathy had been when Magnolia and I went over to say goodbye.

None of your business, Mrs. MacPherson, I reminded myself firmly. *Non-involvement, remember?*

Maybe I'd better jot that on the palm of my hand.

Sheila's SUV pulled out of the driveway a few minutes later. Ivy stood at the window and watched her go. BoBandy jumped up to watch with her. He's always interested in whatever Ivy is doing.

"What are you thinking?" I asked.

"I guess I'm thinking about Sheila's 'run-in' with Renée about her friend's property. She'd said that Renée threatened to retaliate by getting her in trouble with county authorities about her garage sales. That it was really a business and needed a business license or permits or something."

"You're thinking Sheila could have had something to do with Renée's demise, then?"

"Renée's threats surely weren't enough to make Sheila resort to *murder*. I was just, you know, *musing*. Sheila may have drama-queen tendencies, and she seems like something of a pushy busybody, but she hardly seems like a *murdering*-type person."

She hesitated momentarily after saying that. We both knew she'd run into other killers who hadn't seemed like "murdering-type" people.

"She seemed quite surprised when I told her about finding Renée's body." Ivy tapped the arm of the sofa. "But was she *really* surprised?"

Interesting point. But not something that involved us.

"I'm sure the investigation into Renée's death will turn up Sheila's clash with her," I said. "Apparently several people witnessed the altercation."

"So we'll be on our way as soon as we talk to the deputy tomorrow."

Right. Non-involvement.

***

The next day—in that abrupt way the coast does weather changes—turned bright and sunny. I hoped the deputy wouldn't be long in coming. The open road called, and I itched to answer. Ivy spent the morning in Sheila's laundry room washing and drying clothes that were still wet from yesterday. I helped her fold and carry the dry load back to the motorhome. She said Sheila had told her Duke was fine when she went over to see him but shocked about a death out at the cove, of course.

"Did he know Renée?" I asked.

"Sheila said Renée had represented the company that tried to buy the dinosaur park a couple years ago so they could put together a larger property for a resort. According to Sheila, Renée really tried to bulldoze Duke into the deal. Renée hinted to him that the state might be unhappy about some safety aspects of the dinosaur park unless some expensive improvements were made."

"A threat that if he didn't sell, she'd tell the authorities about safety problems, which might force a shutdown of the park. Rather like that I'm-gonna-tell-on-you threat she made to Sheila about her yard sales," I said.

"Right. So Duke's feelings toward Renée probably weren't of the warm, fuzzy variety."

"Did Duke tell her where he'd been, off driving by himself?" I asked.

"She said he told her he'd had a 'hankering' for pancakes at McDonald's, so he went off to get them." Ivy paused. "I had the impression she didn't necessarily believe him. But they do serve breakfast all day now, you know."

No, I didn't know. Sometimes we like pancakes for supper. Actually, pancakes at McDonald's sounded like a good idea. Maybe we should stop when we went through town on our way south and get some.

101

I went outside and checked the engine oil and radiators on both the motorhome and pickup so we'd be ready to go and took BoBandy for a walk. Koop came along. By noon the deputy still hadn't arrived.

Sheila had the garage open for her yard sale, and various customers came and went. I saw one carrying out a lamp and a waffle iron, and Sheila herself carried a bulky old TV out to a pickup for an older woman. All her bicycling and jogging apparently kept her in strong shape. After lunch we went over and looked around. She had the garage efficiently set up with shelves and counters and an old-fashioned cash register. It did look like an ongoing business, not a few-times-a-year, yard-sale thing. Ivy bought a pocketknife, and I bought a cap with a whale embroidered over the visor. I seemed to have misplaced the cap I usually wore.

I've never been a fan of incense, but the garage had a pleasantly spicy scent that came from a stick Sheila was burning on a little stand. She had an oversized cup filled with sticks of incense of various scents. Twenty-five cents each.

It wasn't all customers buying stuff. Some guy came in with some lures, and Sheila bought a whole tackle box full of fishing gear from him. He asked about renting the little apartment over her garage, but she said the refrigerator wasn't working and she'd have to get a new one before she rented it again. I hadn't realized there were living quarters above the garage, but I saw now that there was a stairway inside the garage.

Afterward Ivy texted Sandy thanks for all the information she'd sent us. I got a text from the magazine editor approving the article and photos, no revisions needed. Great. We were good to go. I kept looking at my watch.

About 5:00, without calling ahead, the deputy finally showed up. He pulled around Sheila's double-wide and parked beside the pickup. I saw him take time to jot down the motorhome license plate number we couldn't remember yesterday.

"Sorry to be so late," he said when I opened the door before he knocked. He looked a little rumpled, and some blobs of mud clung to his uniform. A strong aroma, a smell I remembered from up-close experience with the swamp, also came with him.

By now clouds and a gusty wind scented by the sea had moved in. When he came inside, he looked around in a way that, if he weren't a law officer, might make me think he was, in old detective-novel terms, "casing the joint." A moment later I realized he had something else in mind.

"I need to interview you separately," he said. *Separate* isn't all that easy in a motorhome, as he was obviously noticing. He made a quick decision. "One of you can come out to the car with me." He didn't ask who wanted to go first. He pointed at Ivy. "You."

IVY

We went to the car. There was wire mesh between the front and back seats. When Deputy Hardishan opened the passenger's side door for me, I stopped short, hit with a rank aroma of swamp plus something else.

"The vehicle used by our K-9 unit broke down this morning," the deputy said. "We had to use this one instead."

Ah, that was it. The memorable scent of wet dog. "You had a dog working the crime scene?"

I thought for a moment he was actually going to explain, but all he finally did was give one of those generic non-explanations that can be used to answer anything from why a mechanic is pulling the innards out of your car to why the bank is charging you some exorbitant new fee. "Standard procedure."

"Did the K-9 find anything useful?"

103

I didn't get an answer, of course. Deputy Hardishan closed the door, circled the vehicle, and slid in on the driver's side.

The interview started with routine questions. Full name, age, residence, occupation. I gave Mac's son's address in Montana as a mailing address. He'd noted that our pickup and motorhome weren't licensed in the same state. I explained our having purchased the motorhome only recently, which then led to the one-month state of our marriage.

That didn't bring congratulations, but it seemed to interest him. He had questions about how long I'd known Mac and what we'd both done earlier in our lives.

"I was a librarian for many years before my retirement. You can ask Mac what he did in his younger years."

"I'd like to know what *you* know about Mr. MacPherson's past. What he's told you."

I peered at the deputy in the relatively dim light of the police car. Was he trying to catch us giving different versions of our lives? Why would that matter? The worst I could say about Mac was that he had a motorcycle tattoo with a shady past, and I saw no point in mentioning that. If they were so interested, I figured they could do background checks on us. If they hadn't already done so.

Finally he got around to questions about our finding the body. Why were we looking around in the burned cabins? Had we been there before? What time did we get there? Had we known Renée Echol before finding her body? How did we know she was buying the property? Had we talked to her on the phone? I tried to sneak in a couple of questions of my own as I answered his: Was Renée killed in the cabin or her body brought there from somewhere else? How long had she been dead? Did they know who'd been trying to call her on the cell phone at the time I found the body?

I might as well have been asking questions of the mud blobs on his shirt, for all the response I got. His questions kept going.

Did we own a gun?

"No. I sometimes think we should carry one when we're on the road, but so far we haven't done it."

Where had we been during the three days preceding finding the body?

Three days? Did that mean Renée's body had already been autopsied and a tentative time of death established? Or was he just covering a general time period around a possible time of death?

"We had friends visiting and we spent most of two days looking around with them."

"Did you or Mr. MacPherson go anywhere by yourself during the time your friends were here or after they left?"

"Mac went to the convenience store over on the highway to pick up a newspaper and toilet tissue. We have to buy a special kind. Regular tissue can clog up motorhome tanks."

The deputy gave an impatient sigh, no doubt figuring he had better things to do than discuss the merits of toilet tissues. "He didn't go anywhere else without you?"

The persistent questions about Mac made me feel a bit snappish. "Not that I recall. But I don't have a sign-out sheet for his comings and goings."

He ignored my snarky comment. "Did you go anywhere without him?"

"No."

There were more questions about our activities in the three days, more questions about our relationship with Renée Echol. I kept telling him there was *no* relationship, but he continued digging, attacking the same subject from different angles. Did we know anyone who'd had business or personal dealings with Renée? Did we know any of her friends? Had our visiting friends met her? He wanted a phone number for Magnolia and Geoff. He also wanted to know about our relationship with Sheila, how long we'd known her, how we happened to be

105

parking our motorhome here, what we'd noticed about her activities since we'd been here.

Finally he let me go and took Mac out to the car. By then I felt drained, as if he'd squeezed my brain dry as an old tea bag. I also felt a definite aroma of wet dog clinging to me. He kept Mac just as long as he had me, and he came inside with Mac when the interview was over. Mac, too, now had a distinctive aroma.

"We appreciate your time and information," Deputy Hardishan said politely. "You've both been very helpful."

"Glad we could do it," Mac said. "We hope your investigation turns up the killer quickly."

"Is there any possibility she killed herself?" I asked.

I think my question caught him by surprise, because he actually answered. "No, that isn't—" Then he caught himself and switched to generic cop-speak. "Our investigation will consider all possibilities, of course."

I nodded. "Of course."

He wasn't about to tell me that suicide hadn't so far even been a consideration, but it did apparently catch his interest now. "Did she have some reason to kill herself?"

Maybe. The affair with Brian. The possibility of losing her real estate license because of unethical dealings on Sheila's friend's property and/or other property dealings. Maybe getting in over her head financially with purchase of the property.

But surely a woman with Jimmy Choo taste in shoes wouldn't kill herself in an ugly, burned-out cabin by a swamp. Much too tacky. This had to be murder. When I didn't say anything, the deputy gave me a speculative look that made me uncomfortable. Was he thinking I knew more than I was saying? That we'd met Renée, maybe even had dealings with her, but weren't admitting it? Or that I'd made the suggestion about suicide as a red-herring move to divert their attention

106

from murder?

"I realize it may be an inconvenience, but you will have to remain in the area as our investigation continues," he said.

The statement was phrased politely, but I immediately bristled. I pulled myself up to my full height. Which admittedly isn't all that impressive.

"Unless someone is under arrest, I don't believe you—" Mac's surreptitious but powerful elbow jab in the ribs stopped me. I blinked in surprise. Mac is not generally an elbow-jabber. Then I caught the urgent message.

Shut up!

Mac's message was clear. Make Deputy Hardishan suspicious enough and we might find ourselves actually under arrest. I shut up, linked my arm with Mac's, and gave Deputy Hardishan my best LOL smile.

Chapter 10

IVY

"They're suspicious of us," Mac said as soon as the door closed behind Deputy Hardishan. "They think *we* may have killed Renée."

Yes. Incredible as it seemed—one LOL and one silver-fox senior as killers?—I knew Mac was right. The deputy's questions were much more comprehensive and penetrating than he would have asked if we were just witnesses. We were *suspects.* "Why us?"

"It's probably just that at the start of an investigation, everyone's a suspect."

A hopeful thought. Was our finding the body enough to do it? The possibility had occurred to me earlier, but surely reporting a dead body is just an act of good citizenship. Doesn't everybody do it?

Although, take a man-on-the-street poll, and you probably wouldn't find all that many people who've been involved with as many dead bodies as I have.

"What kind of questions did he ask you?" I asked.

Mac slid into the bench seat of the dinette and rested his elbows on the table. "He wanted a detailed account of every minute of our last three days. Where we'd gone and what we'd done. If either you or I had gone off alone during that time. All I could think of was when you and Magnolia went into Trinidad so she could get her hair done."

Uh-oh. "I'd forgotten that. I told him I hadn't gone anywhere without you."

So now Deputy Hardishan no doubt figured he'd caught me in an outright lie. Would he also find out I hadn't been with Magnolia the entire time she was in the hair salon? I'd wandered through a couple of antique shops and a drugstore, but I hadn't bought anything, and then I'd found a bench to sit on overlooking the harbor. Would anyone remember me? Unlikely. At one antique store, a young woman ran her hand over my jacket, apparently not even noticing I was a live person and not one of the mannequins displaying vintage clothing. Invisibility at work.

"Did you remember to tell him about when you went to get toilet tissue?" I asked.

Mac shook his head. "I didn't think about that."

Caught in another "lie." I could see a lurid spread in some tabloid. *Elderly Couple Charged with Murder! Not the first time wife has been involved in death!* They'd no doubt dig up photos that made us look like zombie-weirdos capable of anything from decapitation to cannibalism. And a photo of the motorhome too. The Deathmobile in which we transported victims and dumped them in inconspicuous spots around the country.

Mac jumped up and paced back and forth the short length of the living room. I put the kettle on the stove and got tea bags out of the cupboard.

"He wanted to know about my past, before you and I were married," Mac said as he paced. "He asked about my familiarity with guns, if I owned one now or if I'd ever owned one in the past. He wanted to know all kinds of things about *you.* Including if you had experience with guns."

The deputy had imagination. Ivy the LOL gun moll. With a Glock tucked in her bra?

I was sitting on the bench seat of the dinette now, drinking my tea. Koop managed to squeeze under the table and into my lap. "He asked me the same things about you."

Mac sat down across from me. "This changes things, doesn't it?"

"In what way?"

"About leaving."

"If we're not actually under arrest, we can still—"

"But we're suspects now. How will it look if we just take off and disappear?"

Guilty, that's how we'd look. Yes, we could go, just drive off into the sunset. Or rainstorm. Whatever. But leaving—running off—would probably only make them more suspicious of us. It also might concentrate the investigation on us instead of on the real killer.

"But staying doesn't mean we need to go chasing around on some killer-hunting expedition," Mac said almost hastily, as if he figured that was what I was thinking. Was I? "We'll just be here, *available*, letting the authorities do their thing. We don't have to go looking for the killer for them."

When I didn't say anything, Mac's eyebrows lifted. "Right?"

Right. Non-involvement. "Who else do you suppose is on their suspect list?"

A minute later we had at least one answer. A frantic pounding on the door made me jump to my feet and started BoBandy yipping. I hesitated a moment. With a murderer on the loose, answering an unknown knock in the dark could be opening the door to a killer with a shotgun or machete or ten sticks of dynamite. I looked around for a possible weapon to counteract such an attack. Neither the toothpicks in the plastic dolphin holder on the dinette nor the cup of hot tea in Mac's hand looked as if they'd be particularly effective against machete or shotgun.

A moment later, Sheila's frantic voice joined the frantic pounding. Mac opened the door.

"That deputy stopped to talk to me after he left you!" Sheila was too upset even to barge inside. She just stood there with wind and rain tossing her red hair into a tomato froth, arms— no machete or dynamite visible—flapping like a demented windmill. "They think *I* may have killed her!"

"He said that?" Mac asked.

"He didn't have to *say* it. He knew about my argument with Renée and asked all kinds of questions about it." She paused, eyebrows moving in a wet frown. "I may have made some threats while we were arguing. I don't remember that, but apparently some other people do."

"Would you like to come in?" I said.

I barely had the words out before she was inside and dropping to the sofa as if her flowered legs had suddenly wilted. She'd come without rain jacket or hood, and wet red hair now plastered her face.

The sheriff's department was doing well with their investigation. After one day, they now had three of us as suspects. I tried to take comfort in that old adage about safety in numbers. There should be even more. Had they ferreted out Brian's relationship with Renée yet? That would give them both Brian and Kathy as suspects. Even Duke might be a suspect, given that he'd had hostile dealings with Renée in the past. He also kept a gun in a holster by his door and he'd been away from home for some length of time on an unusual solitary expedition. Would a clerk at McDonald's verify that he'd been in there for pancakes? If that was really where he'd gone.

Sheila jumped up. "Then he wanted to know where I'd been every minute of the last three days. I was with you two and your friends some of the time, but not all of the time, and yesterday I wasn't with *anyone*. I have no *alibi!*" she wailed. In spite of her distress, she paused long enough to wrinkle her nose. "It smells strange in here."

Neither of us offered an explanation. "I don't believe they're saying anything yet about actual time of death for which you or anyone needs an alibi," Mac said.

I was fairly certain they couldn't pin Renée's death down to the hour. Early on, there are details about lividity and rigidity and body or liver temperature that can come close. But, as the hours go by, time of death becomes ever more difficult to determine closely. I'd learned that from a few other instances of death in which I'd been involved. There was the bug and maggot thing for longer times between death and body discovery, but I guessed that with Renée they had chosen that three-day time period because they had information that three days ago was the last time anyone had seen her alive. And who, I wondered, was that last person?

"Did that officer ask you any questions about me?" Sheila peered at us suspiciously as she sat down again. "Did you tell him about my altercation with Renée?"

"We didn't tell him anything about you and Renée. Although he did ask about you," I admitted.

Mac turned the discussion in the opposite direction. "We also seem to be suspects, so I'm sure the deputy asked you questions about us. What did you tell him?"

"Well, uh, nothing really." Sheila's gaze zigzagged from floor to ceiling and back again. "Certainly nothing incriminating."

I couldn't tell if she was uneasy because she perhaps had told Deputy Hardishan something incriminating about us, or if she suddenly realized she might be sitting here cozied up to a couple of gray-haired killers. Which I found reassuring about *her* innocence, because she wouldn't be wary of us if she had killed Renée herself, would she?

Unless she was afraid we knew enough to incriminate *her* . .
.

Did we? No, all we knew was what Sheila herself had told us, that she'd had a "run-in" with Renée some time back. Although we also knew she'd had plenty of time to rush out to the cove and put a bullet in her former friend. Probably even enough time to kill her elsewhere and move the body to the burned cabin. She wouldn't even have needed a car to go to the cove if she'd killed Renée right there. Duke had said she sometimes went out there on her bicycle or even a run.

112

So she was right. She had no alibi. Maybe *we* were the ones who should be nervous. Maybe we were sitting here in the presence of a flower-booted killer furtively hiding her own guilt under a pretended wariness of us.

"Was the deputy going to talk to Duke?" I asked.

"I talked to Duke on the phone while the deputy was out here with you," Sheila said. "He said someone had already been there. They asked about what vehicles he'd seen in the area in the last few days. His trailer window looks out on the road to the Kabins, you know."

"Had he seen anything?"

"Oh, yes. He always keeps an eye on the road, and he knows cars. But he didn't have license numbers. His eyes aren't good enough for that, and he didn't know about Renée being dead then anyway. He also heard a couple of vehicles and a motorcycle go by during the night when he couldn't actually see them."

A motorcycle. Interesting. Maybe Renée had ridden out there on a motorcycle with someone? Someone who could have killed her and just ridden away.

"But Duke said he hadn't thought much about any of the vehicles at the time. Kids go out there to party. I've told him he ought to put a gate across that road. It crosses his property."

"I wonder why he hasn't done it," Mac said.

"He says he doesn't want to keep people from going out to enjoy the beach." She wrinkled her nose, apparently not in agreement with that generous attitude.

"Is he a suspect in the murder?"

She blinked. "I don't know. I didn't ask him that. But he couldn't be a suspect!" She jumped up again, fully alarmed. "Not *Duke*. That's ridiculous. Although Brian and Kathy are surely suspects. Especially Brian."

"But Duke could be a suspect too. You said he was unhappy that Renée had tried so hard to push him into selling out earlier," I pointed out. "Do the law enforcement people know about that? Maybe, since Renée was now buying the Kate's Kabins property herself, she'd approached him again about selling."

"He didn't mention her doing that." Sheila frowned. "But he doesn't tell me everything."

"Would it upset Duke if Renée again started trying to get him to sell?" Mac asked.

"It might. He finally told her the other time that if she came back again, he'd run her off with a shotgun. But that was just Duke playing tough guy," she scoffed. "He doesn't even own a shotgun."

Would she know if he did? But then, it didn't matter. I don't know much about guns, but I know enough to tell it wasn't a shotgun blast that put that neat hole in Renée's chest.

I didn't want to be suspicious of Duke. I like ol' Duke and his patient, tree-training abilities and his rescued Scarlett and his upbeat attitude about a champagne-worthy celebration coming soon.

But Duke had a handgun, and even guys who seem calm and peaceful have been known to take a wacko turn into violence. Isn't a description of Duke exactly how people usually describe the neighbor who suddenly turns killer? *He was always so quiet. Kept to himself. Never bothered anyone.*

"I'll talk to him again," Sheila said. "I'll tell him to be careful what he says to those law enforcement people. You're always hearing about some guy who goes to prison for *years* before DNA tests or something prove he was innocent all along."

"Before you go," Mac said, because she was edging toward the door now, perhaps anxious to get away from us, "do you know about any other personal relationships Renée may have had? Male relationships, someone other than Brian?"

Sheila stopped with a hand on the door. "I hadn't thought about that, but it's certainly a possibility. She might have had something going with an investor on buying the property."

I thought about the black leather jacket and studded shoes in which Renée had died. Not totally a biker-chick outfit, but maybe leaning in that direction. And Duke had heard a motorcycle.

"Maybe a motorcycle-ish investor?" I suggested.

Mac and Sheila both looked at me. "Motorcycle-ish?" Mac repeated doubtfully.

I scowled back. *Motorcycle-ish* is a perfectly good word. Quite descriptive, actually. Sheila didn't question it.

"I've heard biker gangs sometimes channel drug money into legitimate investments such as real estate. I doubt Renée would have had any scruples about dealing with dirty money."

"A lot of ordinary people like motorcycles. Not all motorcycle-ish guys are into gangs and crime. And there are some great Christian motorcycle groups," Mac said, and I appreciated his standing up for both my vocabulary and a Christian motorcycle group we'd met down in Texas.

"Now that I think about it, I remember hearing Renée's ex-husband is in the area, and he's been in prison. Maybe being involved with gangs and drugs was how he got there. They were divorced before she came here, but, who knows? Maybe they hooked up again."

Mac and I exchanged glances. Could an ex-husband be our Unknown Man? Either the killer himself or a motive for Brian killing Renée?

"Did she have children?"

"A son, I think. He got in trouble and lives with her parents back in the Midwest somewhere now."

Sheila scooted out without saying anything about church, and the next morning we saw her SUV pull out of the driveway before we were ready to leave. Attendance at church was a bit skimpy that morning. I inquired about her of a woman I remembered her talking to last week, but the woman didn't

115

know anything about Sheila's absence. Apparently, her not being there wasn't unusual. Actually, Duke had said as much when he mentioned she sometimes used Sunday mornings for garage sales or exercise.

After another good message, this time about the woman Jesus encountered at the well, Mac and I went back to the motorhome. I was just getting out of the pickup when my phone tinkled.

Magnolia's voice immediately boomed out of the phone. "Ivy, what is going *on*? We had this call from some deputy up there. He asked *all kinds* of questions about both of you, and what we did while we were there."

I explained about finding Renée Echol's body and that we seemed to be suspects in the murder.

"*Suspects?*" Magnolia gave an unladylike snort of indignation. "How did they come up with *that* preposterous idea? We're in Arizona, Bullhead City, but we'll come back there right away. We can tell them you were with us all the time and you've never done anything illegal or been involved with the law—" She broke off as if remembering that wasn't entirely accurate. There are those troublesome dead bodies I've had the misfortune to encounter on various occasions, and the law was involved.

"Well, you know what I mean," she muttered. "You haven't *broken* the law."

Much as I appreciated the loyalty and the offer and thanked her for it, I doubted Magnolia's and Geoff's character reference or even a claim of their being with us every minute would take us off the list of suspects. "We'd love to have you here again, but there's no need for you to drive all the way back up here. There are other suspects. Including us is probably just some standard procedure. We'll be out of here and down there with you in no time."

"You're not going to do anything about finding out who did

it, are you?" Magnolia's question sounded both concerned and suspicious. The woman does know me too well.

"Finding the killer is law enforcement's responsibility," I assured her primly.

I assured myself of that too. Non-involvement. Stick that overactive mutant curiosity gene in a mental closet. Lock a mental door on it. No searching for clues. No digging into suspects. We'd just sit around and take it easy until law enforcement rounded up the killer. Or killers. Because Brian and Kathy could be in it together. I was more suspicious of Brian than Kathy, but I could definitely see her helping him.

Then I repeated the important word here. Non-involvement. Which included Non-speculation about possible killers.

With rain pouring down, we just hung around the motorhome for the rest of the day. The editor of *Fun on the Road* called and suggested the old tale of buried treasure and dead bodies in the dinosaur park, which Mac had mentioned in his article, might make a good lighthearted piece for the magazine. Mac held the cell phone to his chest and told me about the editor's suggestion.

"It would give us something to do while we're stuck here," he said.

Right. Unspoken were other words Mac was undoubtedly thinking. It would give us something to do other than get involved in Renée's murder and the killer or killers who had committed the crime. I nodded, and Mac told the editor he'd look into the buried treasure thing. He didn't mention the real-life murder we'd encountered here.

Mac spent time on the computer trying to dig up old references to the treasure story. I read a freebie mystery on my e-book reader. Non-involvement, I kept reminding myself. No matter how energetically that mutant curiosity gene kept trying to crawl out of its closet, Non-involvement was the plan. I determinedly tried to wash the curiosity away with a hot shower. I did get rid of the still-lingering wet dog scent, but the stubborn gene still raised antennas quivering with curiosity.

And that evening Mac went to the little convenience store at the gas station out on the highway to get half-and-half for our breakfast cereal and came back with a local newspaper.

Chapter 11

IVY

Mac spread the newspaper on the dinette table. The article and photos about Renée's murder covered much of the front page. Most of the article repeated what we already knew, including that we'd found the body. A sidebar went into some history about both Kate and her Kabins. She'd been a well-liked character in the area, usually showing up in Trinidad or Eureka in a battered old Ford pickup with her shaggy mutt in the seat beside her. The only information new to us about the murder was that an employee at the Hideaway had seen Renée at lunch there with a heavyset, bearded man on Wednesday, apparently the last time she'd been seen.

Authorities were asking for information to help identify the man with her at the restaurant and also asking anyone who may have seen her since that time to contact them.

"Sound like anyone we know?" Mac said.

Heavyset and bearded? Oh, yes.

A photo of Renée showed the same perky face that was on her business cards. Other photos showed the entire layout of Kate's Kabins taken from the air both before and after the fire. Seen from above, the reed-covered swamp that Mac had fallen into was quite obvious and took up a big area. All the pictures, except the one of Renée's vehicle being hauled away for processing, had a file-photo look, nothing recent.

The newspaper article didn't name us, or anyone else, as murder suspects, but, in addition to being finders of the body, we were also identified as the persons who'd told the authorities where to find the SUV.

"They point a finger at us without saying a word," I grumbled. "As if we know too much to be merely innocent bystanders. How come they didn't identify by name the person at the Hideaway who saw Renée and this man, the same as they identified us?"

Mac's momentary silence suggested he agreed with me, but all he said was, "They're surely suspicious of this bearded man who was with her at the restaurant."

"He makes a better suspect than we do," I declared.

Mac finally put our personal suspicion into words. "So, you think the description sounds like Brian?"

"Of course. But we can't rush in and positively identify him just from that bit of description. There are probably any number of bearded, heavyset guys around."

I had an idea. I gave Mac a cautious sideways look. This idea sprinted around Non-involvement. Or maybe collided with it head-on. "Perhaps we could have lunch at the Hideaway again. We could talk to the employee and get a more detailed description of the man with Renée." A description that would stick to Brian like mud in the swamp clung to Mac.

I expected Mac to counter with Non-involvement, and I was prepared to fortify my suggestion with noble reminders about personal responsibility, civic duty, good citizenship, etc. Instead he said, "Or I could print out that photo I got of Brian when I was taking dinosaur photos for the article. We could take it along and see if the employee recognizes him as the man who had lunch there with Renée." He paused and added reluctantly, "As suspects, we seem to be involved in this murder even if we don't want to be."

Monday morning would have been a pleasant day, blue sky and no rain, but a strong wind rattled the air-conditioning unit attached to the top of the motorhome and swirled leaves from the maples in Sheila's yard into miniature tornados. At the door, when I opened it to let BoBandy out, I spotted Sheila headed out for a run, apparently undeterred by wind. Today she wore ordinary gray sweats and a baseball cap with her red hair swinging from a hole on the back side. A very wholesome look. I waved, but she must not have seen me. Or didn't want to see me? Maybe she was regretting allowing us to park the motorhome here.

Mac printed the lone photo he'd managed to get of Brian. In it, Brian was leaning over, hands in his pockets, studying something alongside the trail in the park, obviously unaware of Mac taking the photo. The photo definitely showed that he was heavy-set and bearded, but he didn't look murderous. It's hard to look murderous when you have the tail of a dinosaur growing out of your left ear.

We decided we'd drive over to Duke's trailer and talk to him about the old buried-treasure story before driving in to town for lunch at the Hideaway. I thought we might see Sheila on the way. Duke had said she often took the road to the cove on her longer runs. "Probably to keep an eye on me," he'd grumbled. But apparently she was running some other route this morning. Duke's pickup was in its usual spot by the trailer. Kathy's Honda stood outside the apartment, but the carport was empty.

Duke was inside on this windy day, but his wispy white hair still looked as if he'd combed it with a leaf blower. "Meet my new roommate!" he said. "This is Bovary. She showed up sitting on my tree chair a couple days ago."

Bovary. From the famous literary character, Madame Bovary, no doubt. Bovary was a somewhat nondescript looking, mottled-gray kitty now curled up at one end of the small sofa, Scarlett at the other end. Bovary looked up with surprisingly gorgeous golden eyes, and Duke introduced us.

"Bovary, these are my friends, Mac and Ivy."

We both acknowledged the introduction. Bovary yawned. "Are the two of them getting along okay?"

"Scarlett was a bit standoffish at first, but she's coming around." Then he instantly jumped to the subject of murder.

121

"But I can't believe it. A woman *murdered*, right out there at Kate's Kabins. Killer must have gone right by here." He peered out the window facing the road. "I might have seen his car or pickup go by."

"Or motorcycle," Mac murmured.

Duke snapped around with surprising vigor. "That's right. I did hear a motorcycle. But I understand it was you folks who found her body. That so?"

"We just happened to be wandering around out there," I said. "You knew the woman who was murdered?"

"Just as a business acquaintance from some time back." Duke dismissed the association with a bony shrug, not forthcoming about the hostilities stirred up when Renée had tried to pressure him into selling the dinosaur park property.

I turned and took a quick peek at the nail by the door. No holster. No gun.

Observant Duke saw the peek. "Got me kind of nervous, somebody getting killed so close to home. I got the Glock down to clean and make sure it was loaded."

Not an old-fashioned, six-shooter type weapon as I'd assumed. Glocks are high-powered, modern weapons, the kind professionals use. Professionals on both sides of the law. It occurred to me that cleaning a gun would probably remove from the barrel any indication that it had recently been fired. Where was the gun now?

Then I gave myself a mental thunk. Duke as a killer? He'd managed to drive somewhere alone in the pickup, but he needed both hands on his walker just to get around on foot. And besides, this was *Duke,* rescuer of stray cats and cheerful keeper of champagne for some yet-to-be-determined celebration.

Mac told Duke about the editor's interest in that old tale of buried treasure. We all sat down and Duke offered a couple of different versions of the story, one about pirates, the other

122

about a long-ago stagecoach robbery in the area. The stagecoach version had the victims of the robbery simply buried beside the treasure, but the darker pirate tale had bodies buried with it as some sort of macabre ghost-guardians. The wind made an appropriately eerie howl around the trailer.

"Could you show me where you found the circle of stones that prompted you to start digging?" Mac asked.

The wrinkles on Duke's old face gathered into a frown. "You planning to write about how I was dumb enough to fall into the hole I'd dug myself?"

"I can skip that detail."

I didn't mention it, but the thought occurred to me that this was a little like Mac's preference not to explain to the deputy about his awkward blunder into the swamp. Men and their egos.

"I'd like to help you, but I don't think these old knees could get me up there. Some of the hole filled in when it collapsed on me, but unless Brian filled it all in, it's probably still there. It was a humongous hole to begin with. I couldn't dig one like that now. Brian can show you."

I was doubtful about Brian's willingness to show us anything, but Mac nodded. "We'll talk to him about it."

It was getting close to lunch time when we finally stood up to leave. Then Duke opened a magazine to show us something.

"It's called a champagne saber." He pointed his finger at the photo of a silver sword with an elegantly curved blade and handle grip. "What you do, see, is slide the side of the blade up the bottle with enough force that it hits the lip and breaks it off. It's called sabrage, and you catch the champagne that gushes out in fancy flutes. They do it at elegant hotels."

"Are you going to buy one?" I asked.

"Not right now."

"Expensive?" Mac guessed.

"In the twenty-five-thousand-dollar range." Duke grinned.

"But, who knows? Maybe I'll be celebrating a million-dollar surprise, and twenty-five thousand will be peanuts to me."

Twenty-five thousand sounded considerably overpriced to me, even if the saber was silver and came in a satin-lined box. I figured, at that price, at least a few nights at one of those elegant hotels should be included. But if Duke could believe in the coming of a champagne-worthy event, he may as well believe in a twenty-five-thousand-dollar silver saber too. Good for him, I decided. Somewhere I remember reading that optimistic people live longer.

When we left, he insisted we take a couple of fig-filled cookies from a batch Kathy had brought over.

***

At the Hideaway we sat in the same booth as before, and the waitress recognized us. "Hey, the happy newlyweds! Good to see you again."

Being recognized and remembered is nice, but it also makes me uneasy. I've gotten to where I rather like my invisibility. I mean, who knows? Maybe sometime I'll have an irresistible urge to hop on a table and do a whirling flamenco, and it would probably be better if I were invisible at that point. Of course, I'd first have to learn to do the flamenco. And then manage to get this aging body up on a tabletop. Okay, cancel that little fantasy. But I still like my invisibility. Now I noticed from the tag on our waitress's peasant-style red blouse like all the women employees wore that her name was NancyLou.

We ordered a shrimp salad to share, and when NancyLou brought it, Mac had the newspaper spread on the table. He didn't have to bring up the subject of the murder. She jumped on it as soon as she saw the newspaper.

"Isn't that the most horrifying thing? I knew old Kate. She was a real character. Always telling jokes, usually a little on the risqué side. Then there was the fire. It just about broke poor old Kate's heart. And now *this*. *Murder*, right there in one of her old cabins."

"Was it you who saw Renée and the heavy-set guy having lunch in here together?" Mac asked.

"No, that was one of the waiters. Ron." NancyLou sounded regretful that she hadn't been the one to see them. "But I knew Renée too. She came in every now and then. She also handled the deal when I sold my house a couple years ago. A deputy talked to me for quite a while." She sounded gratified by that.

"Did Renée always come in with that same guy?" I asked.

"I don't remember her ever coming in with a guy who looked like the one Ron described. Sometimes she was with clients. Or if she was alone, she was usually busy on the phone."

"Business calls?"

"Well, I didn't listen in, but she was, you know, probably the sharpest real estate agent in town. My daughter said I'd never sell that old place of mine, but Renée had it off the market in a month. And at almost full price. Though I remember once her taking a call on her cell phone and afterward she laughed and said, 'Ex-husbands! Can't live with 'em, can't live without 'em.' So I guess it was her ex on the phone that time." NancyLou rolled her eyes. "Although I can definitely live without *my* ex."

Mac and I exchanged a quick glance. The ex-husband again.

"How long ago was that?" I asked.

"I'm not sure. Maybe a month or two."

"I wonder if he called from somewhere else or if he was right here in town," I said.

"That's a good question." NancyLou's expression brightened. "Maybe I should contact the deputy and mention the ex-husband to him. I didn't think about him when I talked to the deputy before."

"Do you suppose we could talk to this Ron who saw them?" Mac asked.

125

"You could, except he isn't working here anymore."

"Fired?"

"No, he quit. He was a good waiter, and he'd been here six months or so, but he just came in and quit a couple days ago."

"Right after he talked to a deputy about Renée and the bearded man being in here?" I suggested.

"Well, I hadn't thought about it that way, but I guess that's so." Her brow wrinkled as if that possibility troubled her.

"How did someone from the sheriff's office happen to talk to him?" Mac asked.

"He must have contacted them when he heard Renée was dead. They didn't come in *looking* for him. Actually, I didn't know anything about him talking to them until I saw it in the newspaper." She sounded somewhat aggrieved about that. "Then I called them too, of course. Because, like I said, I knew her."

"Could you describe him?" Mac asked.

"Ron? Just a kid, really. Early twenties. Five-nine or so. Slim build. Dark hair. Good looking in that kind of bad boy way girls always go for." She smiled in a reminiscent way, as if she understood the appeal, then hastily added, "Although he really is a *great* guy. He has a tattoo of a mermaid on his arm. I don't think he has a car. He always came to work on a motorcycle."

Mac and I exchanged another glance. A motorcycle-ish guy.

"Did he know Renée outside of working here?" Mac asked.

"I don't know—" Then NancyLou broke off with a startled look, as if a different meaning to Mac's question had just gotten through to her. "You mean know her in a romantic way? Renée and *Ron?* Oh, I don't think so. I mean, he's so *young.*"

I didn't know Renée except by reputation, but somehow I doubted a few years difference in age would be an obstacle for her. It might even be an attraction. So, was Ron our Unknown Man? Although he didn't sound like the kind of guy who'd be a big investor in some high-priced real estate scheme.

Somehow the ex-husband worked better in that role for me. He could have come out of prison and retrieved some big stash of illicit money he'd tucked away somewhere. And which he now needed to launder through a legitimate real estate deal.

"Do you have any idea where we might find Ron?" I asked.

"Why?" NancyLou's tone suddenly had a wary edge and her eyes narrowed. Protective, I decided. She didn't want us making trouble for him.

Mac pointed to our names in the article. "Because we found Renée's body."

"Oh!" She backed off and touched a fingertip to her lips as she gave us a startled inspection. Two nice but insignificant older folks who'd suddenly taken on an aura of celebrity. "I didn't realize that was *you.*"

I thought about adding that we seemed to be under suspicion ourselves, but then I decided that might just make her suspicious of us too, so I stuffed a crouton from the salad in my mouth instead. Excellent croutons, nicely crisp and garlicky.

"We think we may know the man who was in here with Renée," Mac added. "But we need to talk to Ron before we mention this man's name to the authorities. It wouldn't be fair, you know, to involve the man if we're mistaken and he really wasn't involved at all. We have a photo we'd like to show Ron."

"Okay, well, *sure.* That's very conscientious of you. Let me think." NancyLou's narrowed gaze turned into a squint and she tapped a finger on her cheek before giving Mac a sideways glance. "Maybe I'd recognize him if I saw the photo."

I wasn't sure if she really thought she could be helpful or if this was just an excuse to get a peek at the photo. Mac hesitated, but finally he nodded, and I pulled the manila envelope out of my purse. I like to carry a big purse. I mean, who knows when you may need a screwdriver or a bag of Hershey's Kisses? The 8x10 print of the photo fit in it nicely.

NancyLou opened the envelope and studied the photo for a long minute. Finally, she shook her head regretfully. "He may have been in, of course." She smiled a little ruefully. "But unless he was a regular customer or a really big tipper—or a really *lousy* tipper—I might not remember him."

She handed back the photo, and I stuck it in the big envelope and in my purse again, pushing it down between a calendar for next year and the new pocketknife I'd bought from Sheila.

"Do you know Ron's last name or where he lives?" Mac asked. "If he hasn't left town, of course."

"His last name is Sweeney, but I don't know where he lives. But I see a bunch of biker guys hanging out at a motorcycle shop near the highway out south of town. Maybe someone there would know him."

"What kind of bike did he have?" Mac asked.

NancyLou touched her chin thoughtfully, and I thought she was going to come up with a brand name or something technical. But finally, she gave the kind of answer I might have given. "A big red one. Cranberry red. With big thingies on the side."

"Saddle bags?" Mac suggested.

"Yeah, I think that's what they're called. Saddle bags."

We finished our salad and Mac left a generous tip for NancyLou. We waved to her on our way out.

***

The motorcycle shop was easy enough to find. Several motorcycles with high handlebars were parked around it, and a green pickup with rusty fenders and an orange tailgate stood off to one side. Fancy script painted across the rear window of the pickup identified it as a *Redneck Cadillac*. A handful of guys clustered around a dismantled bike spread on the ground, like 3-D pieces of a jigsaw puzzle. I know it's a mistake to stereotype anyone, but several of these guys did have a stereotyped big-belly, leather-jacket, bandanna-tied-around-the-head, tough-biker look. We got out of the pickup and strolled over.

"We're trying to locate a young man named Ron Sweeney." Mac spoke to the cluster in general, his voice louder than normal because no one seemed to notice us. Was my invisibility expanding to cover Mac too? "He worked at the Hideaway restaurant for a while. A friend said someone here might know him."

The biggest-bellied guy with a stubby gray pigtail sticking out from under a blue bandanna tied around his head turned and eyed Mac. "What you want him for?" The question wasn't threatening, but his tone and the frosty look in his blue eyes sent a message. *Do we look like guys who'd give information to someone who looks like you?*

Several of the other standing-around guys, apparently interested in what might be shaping up as a confrontation, drifted over to cluster around us. I warily wondered if they came as observers or if they were participants in something we didn't yet know about but involved us.

"We just need to talk to him," Mac said. He didn't sound or look intimidated by the cluster, but I felt like an undersized mouse surrounded by a herd of feral cats. Hungry feral cats.

"About what?"

"We need to discuss that with Ron."

"You don't look like nosy cops, but you sound like nosy cops." Biggest-Bellied Biker eyed me over his bulbous nose and big mustache as if trying to decide if I could be undercover in disguise. I found that somewhat flattering, although I really prefer invisibility. "We don't much like *nosy*."

"Ron said someone might come around looking for him," one of the feral cats offered.

"That couldn't be us. We've never even met him." That statement didn't seem to endear me to anyone, and I felt an interior panic button beginning to self-activate. "All we know is, he rides a red motorcycle. Cranberry red. With—" I broke off, at the moment unable to remember the word I wanted. "Big thingies on the side," I added lamely.

One guy snickered and said his bike was police-uniform blue and it had big thingies on the side too. "And what's yours, Bo? Lilac? Or maybe it's mauve?" They laughed as they drifted back to huddle around the bike bits, which were apparently more interesting than we were.

Biggest-Bellied Biker laughed too. "I'm afraid your description may have been too technical for the guys." It was obviously a facetious comment, but he said it with a straight face. He unexpectedly gave me a rather kindly look, and I guessed I may have sounded like his mother or grandmother.

"Ron wasn't a regular here, but he did mention someone might come looking for him," he said. "But I kind of figured it'd be someone a little more . . . ."

"Intimidating?" I supplied.

Biggest-Bellied Biker laughed again. "Yeah, something like that. You family or something?"

I wouldn't have claimed a family relationship that didn't exist, but I might not have denied it, either. Mac surprised me by laying out more of the truth. "Actually, we need Ron's help. We seem to be under suspicion in the murder of a woman Ron may have known."

I guess that old adage about honesty being the best policy was right in this situation because Biggest-Bellied Biker cocked his head. "I can't believe anyone'd be suspicious of you two," he scoffed.

"Well, you know. Everyone's a suspect to law enforcement," Mac said.

Biggest-Bellied Biker nodded, as if Mac had hit on some universal bit of wisdom. "Ain't that the truth."

"We heard Ron may have left town," Mac added.

"Might be a smart thing for him to do."

"Why is that?" Mac asked.

"He knew that chick that got herself killed a few days ago. She rode around with him sometimes. I figured she was just slummin' and Ron would figure that out too, sooner or later."

"You mean Ron might have killed her?" I gasped.

Biggest-Bellied Biker squinted at me, as if I'd made some baffling, little-old-lady leap in logic. Maybe I had.

"Nah. He was all shook up about her getting offed. What I mean is, I think someone didn't like him associating with her. Dude told him he'd better find himself another chick. With kind of an 'or else' on the end of it."

"But he didn't say who this person was?" Mac said.

"No. He just said if someone came looking, don't tell 'em anything. And I wouldn't. Ron was an okay guy. Trying to save up enough money to get back in college at San Diego State. But, since I don't know anything anyway, I don't have to worry about making trouble for him by saying something."

"That's too bad. We could really use his help."

"We found her body," I added impulsively. "I guess that's why the police are suspicious of us. Ron was apparently the last person to see her alive, and a man was with her then, and we just thought Ron might help us figure out who the man was. It might help us out of a bad spot."

Biggest-Bellied Biker shuffled his boots with what I thought was uncharacteristic uneasiness. "You look like good people and I wouldn't want to see you get hurt or dragged into something." Good people? Or harmless ones? Another foot shuffle. "Actually, Ron may still be around. Maybe holed up with a friend up around Orick." He paused. "Maybe not."

Mac nodded and thanked him, and we returned to the pickup. Mac sat there twiddling the key but not turning it in the ignition. "He thinks someone might take a dim view of our snooping around in this."

131

"Deputy Hardishan wouldn't like it."

"Right. But I think our biker friend out there is thinking more of someone not on the side of the law."

We considered unpleasant consequences for a few minutes. A guy came out of the motorcycle shop and got in the Redneck Cadillac. The vehicle looked as if it might not make it out of the parking lot, but it gave an impressive roar of hidden power when the man pulled onto the street.

"I'd guess it almost had to be the ex-husband or Brian who threatened Ron. Someone who didn't like Renée chasing around with some other guy," Mac said.

"If someone actually threatened him," I suggested reluctantly.

I didn't like to think that. Ron Sweeney had voluntarily come forward with the information about seeing Renée and a man at the Hideaway. A decent kind of guy, probably scared, but trying to do what was right.

But there was a different, less admirable possibility. Maybe Ron killed her, and the threatening caller and/or the bearded man in the Hideaway were inventions to try to turn suspicion away from himself. I could picture a midnight ride out to Kate's Kabins, two people on a red motorcycle, laughing, enjoying the night and the speed and the adventure, the metal studs on Renée's black shoes flashing in the moonlight. And then, only one person riding away from the burned-out cabins . . .

But why? What reason would motorcycle-ish guy Ron have to kill her? Maybe because she was in the relationship just for a lark and he had a meltdown when she made that clear?

I didn't like any of these thoughts. Okay, I'd rather the killer was wife-cheater Brian, or if not him, the felonious ex-husband.

But truth is what it is, not what we'd prefer it to be.

"Now what do we do with the photo?" I asked.

"I suppose we could go up to Orick and see if we can locate Ron. Or we could take the photo directly to the sheriff's department and suggest this might be the man who was with Renée at the Hideaway."

"We could just send them the photo with an identifying name and let them take it from there," I said. "You know. An anonymous tip. Non-involvement."

"Yeah, I guess we could." Mac still fiddled with the key in the ignition without turning it on. "Law enforcement gets lots of anonymous tips whenever there's a sensational murder."

"I think they investigate all but the freakiest of them." I sighed. This was an irrelevant conversation. We are not anonymous-tip type people.

We asked at a nearby service station and got directions to the sheriff's office, which was in a wing of the county courthouse. I was expecting something grim and old-timey, but the courthouse turned out to be a modern building of several stories. We got out of the pickup and started toward the door to the wing on one side.

And met someone just coming out of the building.

Chapter 12

IVY

"Well, if it isn't our famous writer and spouse." Brian looked from Mac to me with a smirk that I interpreted as both condescending and smug. "What brings you two to our local bastion of justice?"

"We found Renée Echol's body out at those old burned cabins," Mac said. "Maybe you heard."

"Yes, I did. I also saw in the newspaper that the last time she was seen alive was with a bearded man at a local restaurant, so I came in to let the authorities know I was that person."

"You did?" I said. Dumb thing to say, of course. He'd just told us what he'd done. But sometimes dumb, meaningless things come out of your mouth when you're flabbergasted. It certainly had never occurred to us that Brian might come in and volunteer this information.

"Kathy and I have been thinking about investing in local real estate, and Ms. Echol had been looking into some properties for us. That's why I met with her at the Hideaway that day, to discuss several places she thought might be good investments for us. So it was a real shock to learn that I was apparently the last person to see her alive. At least the last one admitting it. There's a killer running loose out there somewhere."

Brian peered around as if expecting to spot a hooded killer scurrying among the parked cars, but I figured what he should do was look in a mirror.

Anyway, there was no point in our providing the sheriff's office with that photo now. And perhaps Brian's relationship with Renée *was* simply a business matter. Maybe Sheila had been mistaken about a personal relationship between them, and I was being unfair in my suspicions of his guilt.

Mac surprised me by saying, "I'm glad we happened to run into you. The editor of the travel magazine publishing my article about the dinosaur park is also interested in that old tale about a treasure and bodies buried in the park. He'd like me to do something lighthearted about it for the magazine. If you don't object, of course."

Brian hesitated, as if he were weighing something in his mind. I figured he was framing a nasty comeback, but finally he said, "No, I don't object."

"Duke said you could show me where he dug a hole looking for the treasure up on the hill somewhere."

Brian's answer wasn't enthusiastic, but it was compliant. "It's kind of a wild-goose chase. You're as apt to find buried treasure in your left shoe as anywhere out there. But sure, I can do that."

"Tomorrow morning? Maybe ten o'clock?"

Brian nodded.

So we left the sheriff's office without ever entering it. We sat there in the pickup and ate the fig-filled cookies Duke had given us, and I tried to applaud Brian for both his responsible-citizen move in voluntarily identifying himself as the man with Renée at the Hideaway and his unexpectedly cooperative attitude about the buried-treasure article. But it was the old one-hand-clapping thing, a little short of audible. Or authentic.

"I suppose Brian wouldn't identify himself if he had anything to hide." Although, even as I said it aloud, I wasn't convinced.

Apparently Mac wasn't convinced either, because he said, "Maybe that's exactly why he did it. Because he has a lot to hide. An affair. Murder. He figured the sheriff would find out about his relationship with Renée sooner or later, so he made a preemptive move to explain it."

Preemptive. Exactly. "Trying to pull off a good-citizen act.

135

Helpful. Responsible. Also, he's now established a business reason for anytime someone else may have seen them together."

"Right."

"I guess there's no point in locating Ron Sweeney now that Brian has identified himself to the sheriff," I said.

"I suppose not." Mac tapped the steering wheel reflectively. "Although it would be interesting to know who scared Ron enough that he quit his job and tried to make it look as if he'd left town. I'm under the impression he didn't share that information with the sheriff's office."

"Are we going up to Orick?"

"Does Koop like tuna in a can?" Mac asked by way of an answer. Yes, of course we were going to Orick.

We drove back up the highway to the small town. Orick was north of the dinosaur park and we'd passed through it when we came down the coast to get to the park, but I didn't remember it. Maybe because, although it looked like a pleasant little place when we got there, it wasn't particularly memorable. Several motels, an RV park, a market, gas station, post office, tavern, restaurant, and some modest houses. Small town, USA.

We described Ron to a couple of guys at the gas station, but neither remembered him or his motorcycle. Same results at the restaurant and two motels. It seemed the flashy bike, if not Ron himself, should have been noticed by someone, but apparently not. At least not by anyone who felt inclined to pass the information along to us.

By the time we got another negative response at the tavern flashing a neon beer sign, this definitely felt like a wasted trip. I reminded myself that a non-response said something too, in this case probably telling us that Ron had roared off to Sacramento or other destination unknown and had never even come up here to Orick.

We drove around on some side streets with the thought that

we might spot the bike parked at a house somewhere. No bike, but we unexpectedly came on a surprise sight, a herd of elk grazing in a green meadow. All were fat and sleek, and some had horns like intricate sculptures that looked almost too big and heavy for a head to hold up. Magnificent animals! Like something out of a medieval painting, the kind of creatures that remind me of what a creative Lord we have. I tried to count them, but it was difficult the way they kept moving around. Mac offered helpful advice.

"Just count the legs and divide by four."

He grinned when I swatted him on the shoulder.

We watched and took photos for a good twenty minutes, and I decided that getting to see that herd of elk turned this trip from wasted time into something special.

We were just about to leave Orick when Mac decided to drive through the RV park. And there it was, a flash of red tucked behind a travel trailer. Mac braked and backed up a few feet for a better look. Yes, a cranberry-red motorcycle with saddlebags. Which looked as if someone was trying to keep it as far out of sight as possible. A welcome mat lay below the step up to the trailer, but a printed sign with shooting stars and lightning bolts in the trailer window said *The Zombie Apocalypse Starts Here.*

Not today, I hoped.

We debated for a moment and then approached the door. I figured together we were a harmless looking older couple, although I rather doubted anyone would answer Mac's knock anyway. I most of all didn't expect that someone to be Ron, but the guy who opened the door fit waitress NancyLou's description. Medium height, slim build, dark hair, mermaid tattoo on his bare arm. I don't have to try hard to look little-old-ladyish, but I put some extra effort into it and gave him a grandmotherly smile.

"We're looking for a young man who was working at the

137

Hideaway down in Eureka," Mac said. "We think he rides a bike like that one parked out back."

The guy stepped back as if he was going to deny bike ownership and any connection with the Hideaway, so I said, "We seem to be in some trouble, and we just don't know what to do. We're hoping maybe he could help us out."

He looked us over, hesitated a long moment, and then pulled the door back so we could come inside. I felt a smidgen of guilt for playing the helpless-little-old-lady card, but you work with what you have. He clicked the remote on a TV showing some daytime game show and motioned us to an undersized sofa. He opened the small refrigerator. "Can I get you something to drink? I think we have root beer and Pepsi."

All I could see on the refrigerator shelves was a long hunk of salami and cans of Coors and Budweiser, but perhaps if he dug far enough he'd find soft drinks. That looked, however, as if it would take a major excavation, and I shook my head. Mac gave him our names. He didn't respond with his own name, and Mac finally said, "You are Ron, aren't you? Ron Sweeney?"

"This must be about Renée Echol, right?" He sounded resigned.

"We're the ones who found Renée's body out there at Kate's Kabins. Apparently that puts us under suspicion in her murder."

"I suppose NancyLou at the Hideaway gave you my name, didn't she? Nice lady." He dropped into a chair across from the sofa. "But I hope she isn't giving my name out to just anyone who asks. I didn't think she knew I was here in Orick."

Mac didn't go into how we heard about Orick. "You knew Renée outside of just telling the police she'd been in the Hideaway with a bearded guy?"

"Well, yeah, sort of." He squirmed as if the admission made him uncomfortable. "I do a little yard work to pick up extra money now and then, and I met her that way. She was, you

138

know, *older*, but she was fun, and she liked riding around on my bike with me. She said she was thinking about getting one of her own."

"Did she talk about her work?" I asked.

"Not much. But she was excited about some property she was figuring on buying, although I don't know what it was or where."

"It was that old resort site, Kate's Kabins. Where we found her body," Mac said. "She had an option to buy it."

"Yeah? We were out there a couple times on the bike, but she never mentioned anything about buying it."

"We wonder if she was in partnership with an investor on the purchase because, from what we've heard, the ocean frontage made it rather pricey."

"You think this investor could have killed her?"

"We're at least wondering who he is." Mac gave him a disarming smile. "Although, to be honest, we wondered about you too, at first. Someone heard a motorcycle going out there, maybe the night she was killed. You have a motorcycle."

"Me and how many thousands of other guys?" Ron retorted. "I'm not the greatest guy in the world, I admit that. I've outrun the cops a few times on my bike. I got cold feet and walked out on a girl the day before we were supposed to get married. But I've sure never *killed* anyone. What I'm doing right now is trying to hide out from whoever did kill her."

"You think the killer is also after you?"

"A week or so before Renée was killed, I got a phone call right there at the Hideaway. It was some guy telling me to stay away from her. I didn't take it seriously. Just kind of, you know, blew him off. But when she turned up dead, I figured maybe I'd better cool it for a while. So I came up here to stay with my buddy for a while."

"But why would he come after you after she was dead?"

"When she was first reported dead, I figured the guy who

called me had probably done it. So I wanted to do the right thing and went to the cops about seeing her in the Hideaway with that guy, thinking maybe it was him. But they didn't arrest anyone, so then I got to thinking, maybe, whoever he was, he was still on the loose and he'd decide to come after *me* next. Or maybe he didn't kill her, but he thought *I* did, and was mad enough about it to take me down. I had no idea what kind of psycho I might be dealing with, and I don't have any ambitions toward being a dead hero."

A rather convoluted story, but the possibilities had obviously scared him enough to put him into hiding. "But you don't know who the caller was?"

"I figure it must have been the guy who was in the Hideaway with Renée or her ex-husband."

The ex-husband again! Mac and I exchanged a surreptitious glance. "Did you ever meet the ex-husband?"

Ron shook his head. "I think Renée was careful we didn't meet. She said he had a temper like a bull with porcupine quills stuck in his butt, but I think she still had a thing for him. Or maybe she was afraid of him. I dunno."

Busy woman. When did she have time to sell real estate, with all the men in her life?

"An ex-con, isn't he?" Mac asked. "Some connection with drugs?"

"He might have been involved with drugs, all right, but what he got sent up for was stealing a safe. He and a buddy blew out the back side of a building and hauled the safe out with a forklift. A rental forklift! Can you imagine that? Took guts, but a little short on brains, know what I mean? That's how they got him, I think, tracking down the rental. Renée didn't even know he was out of prison until he showed up at her house one day."

"Does he have a parole officer? Or a job?" I asked.

"Beats me. I think he was staying with a buddy somewhere

140

around McKinleyville. I know he rides a Harley. I saw it there at Renée's house a couple times. An older Screamin' Eagle Softail that he'd stashed somewhere before he went to prison. A real classic." Ron might be wary of the ex-husband, but he definitely admired his bike.

And the ex-husband was another motorcycle-ish guy, now living in McKinleyville. That was another small town between the dinosaur park and Eureka. The local airport was located there. So now we were back to Duke having heard a motorcycle on the road going out to Kate's Kabins.

"What's the ex-husband's name?" Mac asked.

"Ric. Richard, I think, but Renée said he always went by Ric."

"Could you give us a description of him?"

"Like I said, I never actually met him, and the only time I accidentally saw him up close he was wearing a helmet and motorcycle leathers."

"Do you think he could have killed Renée?" I asked.

"I think she was maybe afraid of him, but, like I said, she still seemed to have a thing for him."

"Do you think he's still around McKinleyville?" Mac asked.

"I don't know. And I'm not about to go digging around to find out." With a sharp glance between us, as if he suspected we might have digging in mind, he added, "You might think twice about doing it too."

"Why didn't you just pick up and leave the area instead of coming up here to Orick?" Mac asked.

"At first I thought they'd figure out right away who killed Renée, probably her ex or that guy I saw her with in the Hideaway, and I wouldn't have to hide out for long. I thought I could just keep a, you know, low profile until they arrested the killer and then I'd go back to regular life."

"No one around Orick seems aware of your presence," Mac assured him.

141

"I don't leave the trailer much, and I sure don't go hoggin' around on the bike. But if you found me so easy, someone else could too. Someone a lot more dangerous."

"We could be dangerous, but you let us in," I protested.

Ron laughed. "My grandma might be dangerous too. She might smother you in cookies or drown you in hot cocoa. Anyway, I'm thinking what I'll do now is what my little brother used to say. Make like a missile and blast off."

Mac stood up and I followed his move. "We certainly thank you for talking to us. You've been very helpful. And we'll keep your warning about staying away from Renée's ex-husband in mind."

***

We picked up another local newspaper on the way back to the motorhome. I gave a little gasp when I saw the photo of two items on an inside page. One was a gun, the other a nondescript cap. No printing or emblem identified the cap, but I'd know that grease stain on the visor anywhere. The stain had never been more than an unidentifiable blob to Mac, but I'd always seen the unmistakable shape of Donald Trump's head in it.

"That's your cap!"

Mac stopped the pickup at the edge of the convenience store's parking area. He studied the photo with me. "Yeah, I guess it is. I thought I'd just misplaced it, but I must have lost it in the swamp."

We read the article together. A K-9 dog and handler working the scene of the murder had found the cap among reeds at the edge of the swamp, the gun later found in the water nearby. Tests were currently underway to determine if the gun was the one used in the murder. Already determined was the fact that it was an older, unregistered weapon, ownership unknown. I was relieved they didn't identify it as a Glock. We'd never actually seen Duke's weapon since the murder.

"I guess I'd better go in and identify the cap they found as mine."

"And tell them we don't know anything about the gun."

"I wonder if they'll believe that." Mac looked at the newspaper photo again.

The long-barreled gun didn't look as if it had been in the water long. It wasn't rusty or corroded. The make, Ruger, was written in the metal on one side, and something was scratched on the handle.

"It looks like the kind of gun an old geezer like me would own."

Yes, it did. And those scratches looked like initials. MM.

MAC

It was getting late by then, and we decided to wait until the following day to go to the sheriff's office about the cap. I kept wondering, if a gun is unregistered, how do you prove it *isn't* yours? And if it was the gun that killed Renée . . .

We met Brian at the dinosaur park gate at 10:00 the next morning, Tuesday. I had my camera, of course. Ivy had a notebook and a couple of pens. We were both wearing old jeans, hoodies, gloves, and rubber boots.

"It's a pretty good climb," Brian said. He carried a new-looking shovel and was wearing jeans too, as if he were prepared for digging. But I was apparently mistaken about his doing any digging because he handed the shovel to me before he unlocked the gate.

"Kathy thought you should have this in case you want to dig up treasure or bodies or anything. It's never been used. She bought it thinking I was going to dig up a garden space for her." His smile said, *Think again, Kathy.*

The long-handled shovel looked big enough to disinter a dinosaur. I told Brian to thank Kathy for her thoughtfulness in sending it along.

We followed the winding path upward through the park, Brian puffing before we'd gone far. At the Tex the Rex figure, which was quite imposing even with a few teeth missing, he climbed over the picket fence. I followed and then helped Ivy over too. We climbed farther up the hill, struggling through brush and blackberry vines.

Brian couldn't immediately lead us to the old hole Duke had dug. We went up and down and back and forth on the hillside, and he had to stop and rest several times, once putting a hand on his heart. I remembered Ivy saying she'd seen a lineup of pill bottles on their kitchen counter, and I guessed now that they were Brian's. She picked up a few interesting rocks along the way. Our movements stirred up forest debris underfoot, and twice she went into sneezing spells.

Once, while he was resting, Ivy and I climbed higher and reached the top of the hill where the far side ended in a cliff. Not really a high cliff, maybe eighteen or twenty feet, but below lay a wicked jumble of sharp rocks. We could also see the burned remains of Kate's Kabins and the swamp off to the south. Going back down the hill, we caught up with Brian again and then the old saber-toothed tiger Duke had told us about, a rather formidable encounter when you're not expecting it. I heard something in the brush. I paused and spotted a flicker of movement between heavy branches.

"What is it?" Ivy whispered.

Ghost goat? Live goat? *Cougar?* The shovel wasn't much defense, but I held it out in front of me and stepped between the noise and Ivy. Silence followed, but not exactly a comforting silence. More like a waiting-to-pounce silence. After a long moment, I whacked the shovel against a nearby tree trunk, then hit it twice more, hard, the impact vibrating up my arm and rattling my teeth. Good thing I still have my own teeth. False ones might have flown through the air like some alien denture attack.

A larger crashing noise followed my whacks, but now it was moving away from us. I lowered the shovel.

"You scared it off," Ivy said.

"Our hero." Brian smiled, but his tone was more mocking than appreciative. "Must have been a scared deer or goat. A cougar is the only thing really dangerous out here, and they don't make *any* noise when they sneak up on you."

We struggled around in the brush for several more minutes, Brian getting ahead of us at some point. Ivy and I both stopped short when we heard a crash louder than anything before. A blast of angry profanities followed. Definitely not a ghost goat. We pushed through a wall of rough branches, and there he was.

Brian had found the hole. Brian was *in* the hole. Floundering like a beached fish. Ivy winced at a second blast of profanity.

"Don't just stand there!" Brian yelled. "Help me get out of here!"

I dropped the shovel and grabbed his hand. With his feet clambering on the root-tangled side of the hole and Ivy helping by grabbing a fistful of jacket, he finally scrambled up to solid ground. Below him, muddy water puddled the bottom of a still-impressive hole. Brian wasn't as wet and muddy as I'd been after my dip in the swamp, but he was even madder. He glared as if he'd like to shove us both in the hole, apparently blaming us for his condition.

"I've had it," he muttered and started down the hillside. "This is a waste of time." He stumbled over a protruding stone, picked it up, and slammed it back to the ground. I won't accuse him of targeting my foot, but a half inch closer and I'd have toe troubles.

"I need to get some photos," I said.

He flapped a hand toward the hole. "Help yourself."

It's rather difficult to *stomp* down a steep hillside, but Brian managed to do it. On a comparative scale, I'd say he was less noisy than a dinosaur but considerably louder than a ghost goat.

I wished I'd taken photos while Brian was still in the hole, but we made do with me clambering down into the hole and Ivy snapping several shots of me to show depth and width of the excavation.

I'm embarrassed to admit we kind of lost our way going back down the hill and floundered around in bushes and skunk cabbage for some time before we finally found the trail again. Closer to the gate, I spotted a vehicle parked out by the triceratops. A car with a familiar word and emblem blazed on the side, a familiar officer standing beside it.

I had that cannonball-in-the-belly feeling that I knew who he was looking for.

Chapter 13

MAC

Deputy Hardishan looked our way as I closed the gate behind us.

Brian wasn't exactly my idea of an exemplary hero figure worthy of imitating, but this looked like a good time to apply his system of preemptive action. I hurried over to the deputy.

"Glad you're here! We were planning to come in to see you today. That cap in the picture in the newspaper? It's mine. I lost it when I fell in the swamp out there."

"I remember you were covered with mud," the deputy agreed. "But you didn't mention anything about losing a cap or a gun in the swamp."

I noted he'd tied the gun and cap together, and I hastened to untie them. "In the general confusion of falling in the swamp and finding the body, I didn't even realize I'd lost the cap. But I don't know anything about the gun. That isn't ours. We've never had a gun."

Deputy Hardishan didn't say anything more about the gun, but his skeptical look didn't offer any assurance that he believed me. He glanced at the jungled hillside behind us, and I uneasily wondered if he was thinking we may have buried other incriminating evidence there.

I offered a hasty explanation. "I'm doing another article on the treasure that's supposedly buried somewhere in there."

"Dead bodies are buried there too, according to the old tales. So, if you find any, let us know." He returned to the more important current situation. "But if you're looking to get the cap back, it's not going to happen anytime soon."

"You consider it *evidence?*" Ivy asked. That was exactly what they considered it, of course, although the deputy just raised his eyebrows and didn't answer Ivy's question. She tried another one. "Have there been any more reports of Renée being seen after the waiter saw her in the restaurant?"

The door to Brian and Kathy's apartment suddenly opened and Brian stepped out. Apparently we'd wandered on the hillside long enough for him to do a quick shower and change of clothing. He was in slacks and jacket now, headed for the Porsche. He stopped short when he saw Deputy Hardishan, then continued on toward the car in what I saw as a determinedly casual saunter.

"Mr. Morrison," Deputy Harishan called. "I need to talk to you again."

Brian stopped. "I told you everything I know when I was in the office yesterday."

"Not quite *everything*," Deputy Hardishan said, a meaningful edge to his voice, and I had the sudden epiphany that Brian, not the two of us, was the main focus of today's visit from the law. Although the deputy still turned and gave us a hard look. "I also may need to talk to the two of you again later."

So we weren't off the hook, but apparently we were dismissed for the moment. Not giving the deputy time to change his mind, but not wanting him to think we were overly anxious to get away, we did our own casual saunter to the pickup. Once inside, we looked back to where Brian and the deputy stood by the car. Kathy came out and tucked her hand under Brian's arm. Woman Standing by Her Man. I also spotted Sheila's car parked over by Duke's trailer.

More discussion and then Brian motioned Kathy to go back inside. She seemed reluctant to go, and he actually gave her a little boost. He didn't appear to be under arrest, but he got in the car with the deputy, and they drove away. Kathy stood at the door to their apartment, clutching the knob with both hands behind her and watching the departing car.

"I wonder what that was all about."

"I'll go over and see if she's okay," Ivy said. "If she needs help or anything."

Ivy emptied the rocks in her pocket into the plastic bag of beach rocks she'd earlier picked up at the cove and headed toward Kathy still standing at the door. I knew she had to be as curious as I was about the little scenario we'd just witnessed, but, knowing Ivy, I also knew she wasn't going to Kathy simply out of curiosity; she was concerned about the woman.

IVY

I halfway expected Kathy to scurry through the door and leave me standing outside like a stray cat, but she just stood there. I couldn't tell from her expression what she was feeling. Bewildered? Dismayed? Angry?

"Is anything wrong?" I asked. "Can I do anything to help?"

Her gaze finally focused on me. "No. Everything's fine," she snapped. "The deputy had a few more questions to ask Brian, that's all, and Brian told him he'd rather do it at the station than here." She straightened her sagging shoulders. "People call in with the most absurd ideas when there's a crime, you know."

"The sheriff's office got a tip about something?"

"It's all such a ridiculous waste of time. That's why Brian said he'd rather do the interview at the station instead of here. So it wouldn't waste my time as well as his. Brian is always so thoughtful. He knows I have things to do."

A rather lengthy comment, and it made me think of some old saying about *methinks the lady doth protest too much*, especially when she added, "I'm reorganizing the kitchen cabinets."

Yes, that was so important. We all need to keep our spices and boxes of cereal organized.

"Alphabetical?" I inquired politely. "Or by size of container?" She just glared at me, and I added, "Everything's

149

okay, then?"

"Everything's fine. I told you that. Brian has already been very helpful to the law officers, you know. Telling them about his lunch to talk investment properties with that woman who was killed, which was apparently the last time anyone saw her."

I had the impression the deputy hadn't spelled out what the tip was about, at least to Kathy, but she probably suspected it was about Brian's non-business relationship with Renée. Which was no doubt why Brian preferred to be interviewed at the station rather than at home.

So, who had the tip come from? There must be various people who knew about Brian and Renée's affair and might alert the sheriff's office to it, people I didn't know. But the one name I did know, *Sheila*, jumped into my head and stuck there like a piece of gum under a movie seat.

"Have you heard from your nice friends since they left?" Kathy asked. "I forget her name. Mildred? Marvella?"

A deliberate change of subject, and an equally deliberate mangling of Magnolia's name. Kathy knew perfectly well what Magnolia's name was. Being recognized by Magnolia had been an obvious knee-rattling shock for her, but now she was trying to give the impression that she barely remembered this former neighbor.

"Magnolia," I said.

"Oh, yes, of course. Magnolia! So nice to see her again. Does she keep in touch with neighbors back in Missouri?"

"They still own their home there, so they go back occasionally. But neither of us really stays in touch with anyone. The neighborhood has changed, and most of the people we knew are dead or moved away."

I thought I caught a slight relaxing of Kathy's shoulders, as if she was relieved to hear that. She gave an elaborate sigh. "Isn't it sad how things can change so quickly? I didn't live there long enough to get attached to the neighborhood, and I was so busy taking care of Andy, of course, that I never really got to know anyone. But I do remember it as a lovely street."

"Well, I know you have work to do, so I won't keep you from it. But if there's anything I can do—"

"Thank you. You've already done enough, I'm sure." She smiled sweetly, as if she was really grateful, but I caught the snarky undercurrent.

So, what did that mean? I'd already "done enough." Did she think that tip to the authorities had come from us?

Back at the motorhome, Mac remembered he'd dropped the shovel up by the hole Brian had fallen into. He wanted to retrieve and return it, of course, but we decided that could wait until later. We'd both had enough hill climbing for one day. He took BoBandy out for a short walk instead.

I wanted to talk to Sheila and find out if she knew anything about Renée's ex-husband, but she wasn't home from Duke's yet. Then another curiosity intervened. I was almost certain Kathy had been relieved when I said that neither Magnolia nor I kept in close touch with neighbors back in Missouri. Why? I dug in my purse for the information about Magnolia's friend back in Missouri that I'd scribbled on a scratch pad.

I had to locate a phone number to go with the name, a rather lengthy process since I'd never done it on the cell phone. Even after I had the number I didn't expect to reach Franny Lisbon right away, but after only two rings a woman answered with a cheery hello.

"Hi. Is this Franny Lisbon?" Hastily, to forestall an immediate hang-up because I probably sounded like a telemarketer, I added, "We've never met, but I'm a friend of Magnolia's from there on Madison Street, and—"

"Oh yes, Magnolia! I haven't seen her since—" She broke off as if suddenly realizing that volunteering information that Magnolia was away from home was a bad idea. "But they're coming home soon. Maybe today! I always keep a close watch

151

on their place for them. And this is—?"

I knew Magnolia and Geoff wouldn't be home today, but I appreciated Franny's attempt to rectify her slipup on giving out information about an empty house to a stranger. "I'm Ivy MacPherson. Although I was Ivy Malone when I lived on Madison Street, across from Magnolia and Geoff. That was before you moved to the area, so we've never met. They came up to our wedding in Montana."

"What color was Magnolia's hair?"

At first I thought it was just a friendly question, but then I realized she was checking me out. If I really was Magnolia's friend, not some stranger planning house burglary, I'd know about Magnolia's ever-changing hair color. "It was a lovely orchid for the wedding, but she'd changed to royal purple when I saw her a few days ago. They'd been in Idaho on one of her genealogy trips and were headed for Arizona."

Franny chuckled. "That's our Magnolia, isn't it? She must have the widest array of hair colors and the biggest family tree on the planet."

Okay, that took care of the formalities. I was properly identified, and perhaps I'd given Franny a tidbit or two so she could maintain her status as local gossip queen. "Why I'm calling is, I wonder if you remember a neighbor over on Jefferson Street, Genevieve Higman. Her husband's name was Andy, but he died, and she moved away."

No hesitation from Franny. She instantly yanked Genevieve out of a mental file of old gossip. "Yes, I remember Genevieve. I didn't know her well, but I've wondered what became of her."

"So you don't know where she went when she moved away?"

"No. She just disappeared after her husband died. It was a little strange. Rude, actually, now that I think of it. I mean, I used to take her cookies or an occasional casserole. I even sat

152

with Andy a couple of times when she had errands to run. And then she just up and left without a *word*." It sounded as if my asking about Genevieve Higman had revived an old grievance about the woman.

"I suppose the job of taking care of someone twenty-four seven can become overwhelming."

"Yes, I suppose so. I don't think they'd been married too long, and she'd spent several years taking care of an ailing mother before him. I do believe she *was* rather overwhelmed. I hope she's getting along okay."

Not married long? I'd thought, from the way Kathy talked, that she and first husband Andy had been married a long time. But perhaps, from her age, I'd just assumed that. Did any of this change my suspicions about that first husband's death? Or just raise more questions?

"She sold the house?"

"They were just renting."

"Was it a happy marriage, do you think?"

If the question surprised her, she gave no sign of it. "I suppose so, at least as happy as was possible in her husband's condition." Franny hesitated before her voice lowered to a confidential level. "I probably shouldn't say anything . . ."

I hesitated too. *Probably shouldn't say anything* was undoubtedly a signpost on the pathway to gossip. Maybe I should just back out of the conversation . . . But for me, of course, this was *investigation*, not gossip. Although there sometimes seems a rather fine line between the two.

"But after one of the times I sat with Andy, a friend told me she'd seen Genevieve coming out of a motel over on the other side of town. Genevieve had told *me* she had to go to the doctor's office and get a bill straightened out. So I, you know, *wondered*. I mean a *motel*, in the middle of the afternoon?"

I made one of my brilliant comments. "Umm."

"But she was alone, my friend said." Franny paused before

adding in a virtuous tone, "So probably she was just visiting out-of-town friends after she'd been to the doctor's office. Or something like that."

"Did she ever mention other family?"

"Just that mother who died. Cancer, I think it was."

"Her husband died of a heart attack, didn't he?"

"Yes. He'd had heart trouble for quite some time, although we didn't know that right away. He was out and around a time or two when they first came, but he became bedridden rather soon."

"Maybe they moved to the area for better medical treatment for him?"

"Could be. Although he certainly got a lot worse after they came here. She had enough medications lined up on the counter to start a pharmacy of her own. Poor guy. And he'd gotten so terribly thin. I hardly recognized him. But Genevieve took devoted care of him," she declared. "I can certainly say that for her."

"When you were sitting with Andy, did you talk to him?"

"Not really. Genevieve had said he'd probably sleep most of the time, and that's what he did. Though one time when he woke up he was quite agitated and kept asking for Evie. I mentioned that to Genevieve, and she said Evie was his sister. Who'd died years ago."

"How sad. Did he ever seem afraid?"

"Afraid? No. He just wanted his sister Evie. And her long dead. So, poor guy, it wasn't just his heart that was bad. His mind was failing too."

I was fairly certain Franny suspected Genevieve may have had a relationship going on outside of devotedly caring for husband Andy, but I didn't catch any hint of suspicion about her hurrying his death along. And if she did have that suspicion, I was also fairly certain she'd mention it. Franny was not a zipped-lip keeper of secrets.

"You know, this is really odd," she said suddenly.

"Odd?"

"I hadn't thought about Genevieve for a long time, but now you're the second person to ask about her within the last few days."

Another repetitive echo from me. "The second person?"

"Yes, it was, let's see, a week ago Thursday that a man came to the house inquiring about her. Although his inquiry was of a more, oh, *official* nature I guess you'd call it."

"You mean law enforcement?"

"No. He was a private investigator."

A private investigator? I was startled. Did someone else have suspicions about Genevieve? "Did he say why he was looking for her?"

"Not specifically, but I think, from little things he let slip, that it was about an inheritance. I'm very observant about things other people might not notice," she explained as if she were sharing a confidence. "Why are *you* looking for her?"

Because I suspected she may have killed her first husband back there in Missouri. Because I suspected she and/or her current husband may have killed a woman here. I didn't want to blurt out such tabloid-worthy accusations, but neither did I want to manufacture some pie-in-the-sky story. The truth and I sometimes have an uncomfortable relationship, but it seems to be a permanent relationship, not one I can toss away like old pantyhose. So I dodged an explanation and tried a different route.

"I think I'd like to talk to this private investigator. Did he leave a card or any way to get in touch with him?"

"Yes, he did. But you haven't said why *you* called to ask about Genevieve."

I couldn't tell if she was really concerned about my motives or just curious enough to push the issue. "I've recently had some unexpected contact with Genevieve out here on the West

155

Coast. Magnolia was here and talked to her too." I didn't mention how *not* glad to see us Genevieve/Kathy was, but I did say, "We were both a bit concerned about her. She uses her middle name now, and she's remarried and seems happy enough, but—" I broke off and searched for a *but* that didn't include suspecting she was a killer. "But I'm sure an unexpected inheritance would be most welcome," I finally added brightly.

"The thing is, after the man left—" Franny's voice dropped to that confidential level again. "I hate to say this because he certainly seemed *nice* enough, but I wondered afterward if it was some kind of scam."

"Scam?"

"You know how they're always warning you about people on the phone pretending to be a grandson or an IRS agent or something. I happen to know Genevieve came into a big insurance payoff when her mother died. That happened before Genevieve and Andy moved here, even before they were married, I think."

"You did mention they hadn't been married long."

"Anyway, I've wondered if this man who was looking for her was trying to pull some crooked scheme to do her out of that insurance money. I have no idea what kind of schemes crooks try to pull, but he just didn't *look* like a private investigator."

"That's why dishonest schemes work. Honest people can't figure them out." I hesitated, feeling a little guilty because my mind quickly tossed up a possibility. What did that say about me? "I've heard about a scheme to get a victim to pay a finder's fee before they'll provide information about collecting an inheritance. But then, after the victim pays, the con man is long gone. Because there never was any inheritance."

"Oh, how *awful*. Preying on someone like that. You can't trust anyone anymore, can you?"

156

"In what way didn't he look like a private investigator?"

Franny's sudden laugh sounded self-conscious. "I suppose those of us who've never met a real private investigator get our ideas about how they look from movies or TV. Handsome and suave, but tough underneath. And very attractive to women, of course."

"So what did this man look like?"

"He was kind of, well, *chubby*. Our street is on a bit of a hill, you know, and by the time he got up the steps to my door he was *puffing*. He wore glasses that he had to keep pushing back on his nose, and his hair was in a comb-over style to cover a balding spot."

A fairly observant woman, Franny Lisbon. "Not exactly a James Bond or Magnum PI type, then," I said.

"No, but don't get me wrong—he didn't look scruffy or sleazy. He wore a very nice suit, and his handkerchief was clean when he got it out to wipe his forehead. If I were guessing, I'd say he looked more like an accountant than a private investigator. But we shouldn't stereotype people on the basis of how they look," she added as if chastising herself. "And he did have a *marvelous* voice, very deep and manly."

"Maybe his not looking like a private investigator enables him to be a very good private investigator," I suggested. "Kind of throws people off guard."

"Yes, that could be."

Although it also occurred to me that an accountant might well be able to come up with a nifty inheritance scheme.

"I certainly wouldn't want Genevieve to miss out on an inheritance if there really is one, just because I thought the private investigator didn't look right. There was that other detective on TV who always wore an old raincoat that looked as if he'd slept in it."

"Columbo?" I suggested.

"Yes, that's the one. Do you intend to contact this man?"

157

"I'm not sure. What did he want to know about her?"

"The main thing, of course, was that he wanted to find out where she was now. But he also wanted to know how well I'd known both Genevieve and Andy. How long they lived on Jefferson Street, and did I know where they'd lived before that. Did she seem to be taking good care of her husband and was he ever in a nursing home. Oh, and *pictures*. He wanted to know if I had any photos of her or her husband."

"Do you?"

"No, of course not. I mean, Genevieve and I weren't good enough friends that we'd take *pictures* of each other. And it would be kind of creepy, wouldn't it, me taking photos of Genevieve's ill husband?"

"I wonder if the private investigator talked to anyone else in the neighborhood?"

"I know he talked to someone who gave him my name and told him if anyone in the neighborhood would know anything about Genevieve, it would be me." She sounded proud of the local referral. "Will you contact him?"

"If he's a scam artist, I wouldn't want to let him know where Genevieve is. But, like you, I wouldn't want her to miss out if there is a real inheritance."

"Hold on a minute and I'll find his card."

I don't know what I expected a private investigator's name to be, but Megalthorpe wasn't it. Roger Megalthorpe. Well, probably just more of the TV influence making me expect something a little more dashing and detective-ish sounding. She gave me a phone number off the card.

"So will you contact him?" she asked again.

"I'll have to think about it. It's hard to know what to do. But I do appreciate your talking to me. I wonder if there was insurance when Genevieve's husband died."

"I have no idea. And, of course, I *wouldn't* know, the way she scooted out of here after he passed away." She paused, annoyance with Genevieve surfacing again. I expected her to ask where Genevieve was now, and I tried to detour the question.

"Genevieve apparently has unhappy memories of her husband's last days there on Jefferson Street. She didn't seem to want to do any reminiscing with Magnolia and me."

"I can understand that. I was thinking I might drop her a card if I had her address, but sometimes it's better just to leave the past in the past, isn't it? Maybe that's how she felt when she didn't tell anyone goodbye."

We chatted a few minutes more about how Madison Street had changed and what Magnolia and Geoff were doing. I inquired about her pot-bellied pigs, and she said she'd lost that skirmish with city authorities; the pigs now had a country home.

"But I have a miniature goat now. Her name is Gretchen and she lives in the kitchen most of the time. I really need her. There have been a couple of break-ins in the area, and I'm teaching her to wake me if she hears any strange noises."

She sounded gleeful, and I suspected the city officials may have met their match in Franny and her guard goat. "Right," I said, and we ended the conversation with our mutual assurances that we'd like to meet in person sometime.

After the conversation ended, I sat there wondering what to do with these unexpected bits of new information. About Kathy, of course, not the guard goat. Did I want to contact Roger Megalthorpe? He'd surely want an address for Kathy, how he could get in touch with her, and who knows what else. How much information was I willing to give him?

Although I also had to wonder, how much information could I extract *from* him?

I'd talk to Mac before deciding anything, of course. That's another of the nice benefits of marriage. There's always someone to talk things over with. And there's no one I'd rather

159

talk with about anything than Mac.

Chapter 14

IVY

When Mac and BoBandy came in from their walk, I told him what Franny Lisbon had said about the private investigator back in Missouri. Over lunch we discussed both the scam possibilities and these new facts about Genevieve/Kathy. That she and the first husband hadn't been married long. That she'd earlier received an apparently considerable amount of insurance when her mother died. That she may have had a mysterious motel liaison with some unknown person back in Missouri. That she'd scooted off with nary a goodbye to anyone after her husband died.

We decided the first step would be to investigate the investigator and find out if he really was a legitimate PI. If he wasn't, then we could be fairly certain this was some scheme he'd cooked up. Using the cell phone, we looked up private investigators back in Missouri and there he was: Megalthorpe Investigative Services, with the same phone number Franny had given me.

Okay, we'd call Roger Megalthorpe. But, at least at first, it would be more to get information from him than to tell him anything. The first thing we needed to know was why he was trying to locate Widow Genevieve.

I tried an immediate call, but it went to voice mail and I didn't want to leave a message. So we drove on into Eureka, and after an afternoon shuffling between the library and the newspaper, which had been publishing since the mid-1800s, Mac had both facts and legends for his article. There had actually been several long-ago stagecoach robberies in the area, and the old tale about buried pirate treasure was retold in a couple of history columns. Plus we found more information about the old hermit and his goats, including various goat sightings over the years. Mac figured he had enough information for a lighthearted article for the magazine, and I had the side benefit of an old-time recipe for applesauce cake that I found in the column next to a blurry picture of what might be a ghost goat. Or it might just be a piece of an old hermit's long underwear hanging on a branch.

We'd been back at the motorhome for only a few minutes, and Mac was still in the bedroom, when Sheila came over. I wasn't surprised. She must have seen us at the dinosaur park when she was at Duke's trailer. She handed me a carton of frozen applesauce she'd made from her own homegrown apples and managed to make fidgety small talk about the weather until she apparently decided she could get down to the real business of this visit.

"I saw you were there when that deputy hauled Brian off. Is he under arrest?"

"No. He voluntarily accompanied the deputy to the station to answer some questions. I think they were investigating a tip that had come in."

"An anonymous tip?"

"I don't know."

"Was it from a man or a woman?"

"I don't know that, either."

Sheila jumped to her own conclusions. "Someone told them about Brian and Renée!" She sounded elated. "I wonder who?"

"I'm afraid Kathy thinks it was us." I'd been tempted to come right out and ask if Sheila herself had called in the tip, but she'd already made a preemptive claim to innocence with her question about who might have done it. I tackled a different subject that made me curious. "I had the impression earlier, when you said you thought Duke needed a better cell phone for emergencies, that you thought he might be in some danger."

"That's right. I'm afraid Duke might need to call nine-one-one sometime and that old phone would be about as helpful as a pet rock. I guess it's no secret there's no love lost between Brian and me." She wrinkled her nose as if just the name gave off an offensive odor. "I don't trust him. And I happen to know something that gives me a big reason not to trust him."

"Something concerning Duke?"

"Oh, yes. Duke didn't have any money to actually hire Brian to run the dinosaur park, so he added a—oh, what do you call it? A codicil, that's it—he added a codicil to his will that if anything happened to him while Brian was still managing the dinosaur park that they could buy it from the estate at half whatever the county has the property appraised at. I'm pretty sure Brian suggested it. Duke's nephews will then share whatever is in the estate."

"Brian can buy the entire property or just the dinosaur park?"

"I don't know. I never actually saw the codicil," she admitted.

"But you think this puts Duke in danger?"

"Accidents happen." She emphasized *accidents* with that little jiggle of fingers indicating quotation marks around the word. "Renée's death certainly proves Brian is capable of murder."

"There is that old qualification, 'Innocent until proven guilty,'" I pointed out.

She dismissed that detail with a shrug. "What I can't understand is why the sheriff's office hasn't figured out yet that he *is* guilty. And I don't think he'd hesitate to kill again if he thought he could gain something from it."

"It seems unlikely he'd let the park go so badly downhill if he really wanted to *own* it."

"Seems that way," she agreed grudgingly. "But I still think he wants it."

"Why?"

"I think he and Renée had some big scheme in mind. Maybe she pulled a fast one on him, something underhanded and sneaky, and got that option on buying Kate's Kabins for herself. And it made him so mad he killed her."

"What about Kathy?"

"Oh, I don't think *Kathy's* capable of murder. Although, if dear old Brian told her to put a little poison in Duke's chocolate chip cookies, she'd probably reach for the carton of arsenic. Anything to keep Brian happy," she added with a disdainful snort.

"I meant, do you think Kathy is in danger from Brian?" Although Sheila's snarky comments made me think that if Kathy was doing alphabetical in her kitchen reorganizing, maybe arsenic would be right up there in first place on the shelf.

Sheila considered the possibility of danger to Kathy for a moment, then shook her head. "I don't think so, not now that Renée is dead."

"In other words, you think Kathy might earlier have been in danger because she stood in the way of Brian being with Renée, but now she's safe."

"At least as safe as anyone can be, married to a shyster like Brian."

"What makes you think he's a shyster?"

"When they first came here, I think they were looking for a good place to hide out. I think he'd been involved in some business thing that went up in flames, and people who lost money were after him."

"What makes you think that?"

"Just kind of reading between the lines on what Kathy has said. I have a good intuition about such things, and I am going to get Duke a better cell phone."

She was gone before I realized I hadn't asked her about Renée's ex-husband.

164

***

Given the time difference between California and Missouri, we decided to wait until morning to try calling PI Megalthorpe again. We were curious about whether the deputy had brought Brian home, or if the interview had led to his actual arrest, but, short of peeking in windows or knocking on their door and inquiring, we didn't know how to find out. Mac spent the evening working on the new article about the buried treasure. The photos I'd snapped of him in the hole turned out great, and Mac planned to use one of them for the magazine article. I used Sheila's applesauce in my newfound recipe for applesauce cake.

Mac isn't tied to standard cereal or bacon and eggs for breakfast, so in the morning we had applesauce cake, dense and moist and delicious, and scrambled eggs for breakfast, then sat on the sofa together to call Roger Megalthorpe. This time, after going through a pleasant receptionist, he came on the phone with a brisk, "Megalthorpe." He didn't sound like a chubby man with a comb-over hairdo, and I remembered Franny had mentioned his "marvelous" voice. He sounded quite detective-ish, confident but on guard, a guy who might have a gun in a concealed holster under his jacket and maybe another strapped to his ankle.

I gave my name, identified myself as a former resident of Madison Street, and put the phone on speakerphone so Mac could also hear. "I understand you're trying to locate Genevieve Higman."

"Yes, I've made some inquiries about her. Thank you for calling, Mrs. MacPherson. You have information about Mrs. Higman's current whereabouts?"

"Possibly."

After a brief pause, perhaps waiting to see if I'd offer details, he added, "I'm authorized to offer remuneration for the information."

165

Mac and I looked at each other in surprise, and then Mac's cell phone rang. He hesitated about answering, and I knew he was reluctant to leave this conversation, but after looking at the name of the caller he took the phone into the bedroom and slid the accordion door shut.

I wasn't interested in remuneration, but I was, as always, curious. "How much remuneration?"

"That depends on the quality of the information," Megalthorpe replied smoothly.

"I understand this concerns an inheritance?"

"Inheritance? No." He sounded surprised. "What makes you think there's an inheritance?"

I didn't explain about Franny Lisbon's powers of observation, which may have been running on low voltage the day she talked to Megalthorpe. "Why are you looking for her, then, if it's not an inheritance?"

Another hesitation, as if he were calculating how much to tell me. "It's a rather odd situation."

"I presume that's why you're investigating it."

"Yes. Well. My client is from out of state. He had an uncle he hadn't seen or heard of for a number of years. His family has dwindled because of several recent deaths, and he decided to try to connect with this uncle. He traced the uncle as far as a care facility here in Missouri where he was basically bedridden with heart trouble and an increasing dementia along with a loss of memory. But a very nice old guy, the staff says. Not at all combative or unpleasant."

"And this involves Genevieve Higman how?"

"The uncle has disappeared. He never had any visitors, the staff says, until a brother showed up and started visiting him regularly. Then the brother one day became quite agitated about what he considered ill treatment of his brother, raised a big fuss and threatened to sue, and finally said he was taking his brother home to care for him himself. He physically picked up the man and carried him out to his car and drove off. Didn't bother with the man's clothing or anything else."

"I can't say I blame this man for taking his brother away, if the brother was being mistreated or neglected. In fact, his concern and quick action are rather admirable. But, again, how does this involve Genevieve Higman?"

"I'm getting there. An aide there at the nursing home thought the brother's actions were rather, well, exaggerated for a rather minor offense. They'd merely neglected to bring the man the glass of milk he asked for at lunch, which apparently made *him* quite agitated. Anyway, the aide jotted down the license plate number of the brother's car. They had the man's old file in their archives, and I traced the vehicle license number back through the Department of Motor Vehicle's records. The car was registered to Genevieve Higman."

"How . . . odd."

"Yes." He let me contemplate that for a moment, then added, "The care facility made a cursory investigation to find out where their patient had been taken but didn't turn up anything and let it drop."

"That seems a bit careless. Maybe unethical. Or even criminal."

"I suspect it was a case of 'let sleeping dogs lie.' They didn't want to chase the brother down just to find themselves tangled in a lawsuit about careless or incompetent care of a patient. I'll have to say, this isn't exactly a higher-class establishment. There's a rating system for such institutions, and this one ranks near the bottom of the scale. They have various bad marks for lax patient care and financial irregularities on their record. So apparently they decided to just sweep this one under the rug."

"They didn't know anything about the brother who made off with their patient, then?"

"No. No one asked for identification when he was just visiting, of course, and the man's file didn't have any information about a brother. One older employee said the visitor was always very solicitous about his brother. Read to him and brought him socks and a bathrobe, sometimes cookies or other goodies. She wasn't able to give a description other than fairly heavy and probably dark haired, but she thought his name may have been Art. But my client says his uncle didn't have a brother named Art or Arthur or anything near that."

"And this man who disappeared from the nursing home, his name is—?"

"John Anderson. A rather generic name, which has made it harder to find out much about him. I need to talk to Genevieve Higman and find out why her car was used to remove Mr. Anderson from the nursing home, and who was using the car. And if she knows where Mr. Anderson was taken or is now."

John Anderson. An odd thought occurred to me. "Did John Anderson have a sister?"

"No. There were a couple of brothers, but they died before he did."

"Was Mr. Anderson married?"

"He was, but his wife was also dead before he entered the nursing home."

"Do you have her name?"

"Let me see. It's probably in here somewhere . . ."

Silence then, except for Mr. Megalthorpe muttering and mumbling to himself, plus a noticeable burp. "Sorry. I've been having some stomach problems." Another delay and then he said, "Yes, here it is. Evelyn was his wife's name. After several falls while living alone he apparently realized he could no longer care for himself and arranged for his own admission into the care facility. By then he already had heart problems, but the loss of memory and drift into dementia came after he was in residence there."

Evelyn . . . Evie? Franny Lisbon had heard Genevieve Higman's husband calling for "Evie." And a vehicle registered

168

to her had removed John Anderson from the nursing home. Which meant what?

"By the way, you mentioned that Mrs. Higman had remarried—"

"No," I said sharply. *Tricky, Mr. Chubby Detective.* He'd tried to use a sly gimmick to mislead me into giving him information I *hadn't* offered. "I don't believe I mentioned anything about Mrs. Higman's current marital status."

He asked the question bluntly, then. "*Is* she remarried?"

I still wasn't certain how much information I wanted to give him, and I used that handy-dandy line law officers often find useful when they don't want to tell you something. "I'm not at liberty to discuss that at this time."

Big, non-detective-ish sounding sigh. "Very well, then. But if she is remarried, it might be interesting to check her new husband's fingerprints."

"Are you accusing Genevieve or—" I broke off because I'd almost slipped and said *or her husband* of something. I backtracked and limited the question. "Are you accusing Genevieve of something?"

He tossed the question back to me. "What would I be accusing her of?"

Good question. This all seemed murky as mud soup. "Has anyone ever tried to collect on a life insurance policy for John Anderson?"

"So far as I know, Mr. Anderson had no insurance. With his wife already deceased and his finances limited, he probably didn't feel any need for insurance. We don't, of course, at this point know whether he's dead or alive."

Megalthorpe wasn't accusing Genevieve of trying to pull some insurance scam, then, on John Anderson's life. Then he added another comment.

"But there was considerable insurance on Andrew Higman's life. Which was paid to his widow, of course."

So Genevieve had collected insurance on both her mother and her husband. A tidy little do-it-yourself retirement plan? Perhaps sufficient to provide a new husband with a Porsche?

"I'm willing to make a trip to wherever Mrs. Higman is now," he added. "She's apparently using something other than the Genevieve Higman name, because even with considerable effort I haven't been able to find any information under that name."

I had no doubts now about Roger Megalthorpe's legitimacy as a private investigator, but I still wasn't about to jump into complete cooperation. "Suppose I tell Genevieve about talking with you and let her call you."

"It would be best, under the circumstances, if you didn't take Mrs. Higman into your confidence about anything we've discussed." He sounded alarmed. "And I would remind you, there is remuneration involved for information."

"Kind of like a bounty."

"If you want to put it that way."

"I'll have to think about all this and get back to you."

I tapped the cell phone to disconnect the call before he could say anything more. I figured I'd gotten more information from Private Investigator Megalthorpe than I'd given him, which was my intent in calling him. But this information I'd acquired from him took off on a totally new tangent unrelated to my suspicions.

Or did it?

Chapter 15

MAC

Ivy was still sitting on the sofa holding the phone when I returned to the living room. Her nice eyebrows were scrunched in thought.

"Did the private investigator have any helpful information?"

"I'm not sure. At the moment I don't know quite what to think."

She filled me in on what the private investigator had said, and I could see why she was puzzled. PI Megalthorpe was certainly suggesting some peculiarities back in Missouri.

"We could just ask Kathy if she knows anything about a John Anderson," I suggested.

"Mr. Megalthorpe was quite specific about not wanting anything shared with Kathy. Whom he still knows only as Genevieve, of course. I didn't tell him what name she was using here."

"We aren't obligated to go along with what Megalthorpe wants," I pointed out.

Ivy nodded. "Right. But I think he's concerned that if she knows he's looking for her, she'll take off for parts unknown."

Would Brian and Kathy actually do that? Kathy had certainly been jittery about Ivy and Magnolia showing up from her past. "We know about Husband Number One, Andy," I mused. "We know about Husband Number Two, Brian. But now we seem to have an extra man in the picture. Was he another husband?"

"I knew a woman years ago who signed up for a class in taxidermy hoping to meet a man," Ivy said. "Stuffing dead animals to find a husband seemed a little desperate to me. But

171

kidnapping a husband out of a care facility? That's definitely over the top."

"Did the private investigator say when this happened? Was it before or after Husband Number One died?"

"We didn't get into that. By the way, what was your call?" Ivy asked.

"I'd left my name and number at the library, and the librarian gave it to that old guy she'd said used to live out in this area. He had a lot to tell me about stagecoach robberies and buried treasure and ghost goats."

I started adding this new information to the notes on my laptop and had just gotten to the tale about a treasure hunter being butted off the cliff on the back side of the hill by what he claimed was a ghost goat, when we had another visit from the law.

"Mr. and Mrs. MacPherson," Deputy Hardishan said when I opened the door. He sounded unexpectedly hearty. "I have some good news for you."

"You've found Renée's killer?" Ivy asked.

"No, but I think you'll still find it good news."

"Good news is always welcome," I said.

I invited him inside, but he said he had only a few minutes to spare. "I just wanted to let you know that the owner of the gun we found in the swamp turned up. He had a photo of himself and the gun that showed the initials scratched on the handle."

"Which you'd thought could be initials for Mac MacPherson. You thought I'd lost the gun after killing Renée with it, and then when I went back to look for it I fell in the swamp."

He didn't admit I was right, but he did murmur, "Very astute, Mr. MacPherson. But the initials turned out to be MM for Mason Myers, and it was not the murder weapon. He and a couple of friends had been target practicing out by the swamp a couple months ago, and he lost the gun then."

"So now you know we were telling the truth about not owning the gun." I resisted an I-told-you-so crow. "That should take us off the list of suspects."

"Until the killer is in custody, no one is eliminated as a suspect."

"Is Renée Echol's ex-husband among the suspects?" I asked.

With law-enforcement expertise, he answered my question with another question. "You have information about the ex-husband of the victim?"

He sounded interested, but the question didn't give us a clue about whether an ex-husband was news to him or if they were almost ready to slap handcuffs on him.

"No, not really," I said. "We understand he rides a classic old Harley. I believe a motorcycle was heard going out to Kate's Kabins around the time Renée Echol was killed."

"There are a few of those old bikes around." Pleasant. Uninformative.

Characters in mystery novels always seem to have a friend in law enforcement who helpfully supplies them with inside information. What did we have? An officer who'd make an artichoke look like a loudmouth.

"What we've never been able to understand," Ivy said, "is why we *are* suspects. We didn't have any motive to kill Renée."

"A motive isn't actually necessary to establish guilt. Killers have been convicted with motive still unknown. But you asked questions about the Kate's Kabins property at a couple of real estate agencies. Renée already had it tied up. She had what you wanted."

That sounded to me like a wild-eyed guess at a motive, and sometimes wild-eyed guesses are right. Although this one wasn't.

"You think we could have murdered her over *Kate's Kabins?*"

Ivy sounded aghast.

Deputy Hardishan pointed out a hard truth. "People have been killed for less. Unpleasant things happen in the heat of an argument. Perhaps Ms. Echol antagonized you concerning her coming ownership of the property and you reacted impulsively. But you're not top-of-the-list suspects," he added in a kindly tone, as if that should be a comfort.

"Who is top of the list?" Ivy shot right back.

He shook a reprimanding finger at her as he also shook his head.

"What about Brian?" I asked.

"Mr. Morrison wasn't held after his recent questioning."

"But you must have had an interesting tip to make you question him again," Ivy persisted.

"We'd like to further question the man who called in the tip," Deputy Hardishan admitted.

"He told you about a relationship between Brian Morrison and Renée?" I asked.

I was fishing, of course, but Deputy Hardishan wasn't biting. He smoothly produced that ever-popular, conversation-ending line. "You know I'm not at liberty to discuss details of the case at this time."

Right. We were as apt to get details from a ghost goat in an email as we were to get details from Deputy Hardishan.

The deputy left, and I went back to my notes for the magazine article. Ivy settled down to read a mystery on her e-book reader with Koop on her lap. But then we had another visitor. This time it was a thin young woman with dark shadows around her eyes and a toddler in her battered old car. She was apologetic about bothering us but said she was looking for Sheila because she had some baby clothes to sell and knew Sheila bought items for her secondhand store. Since Sheila wasn't around, soft-hearted Ivy helped her out by buying them.

I raised my eyebrows after the woman was gone and we

were the owners of two bulging sacks of baby things.

"Something you aren't telling me?" I inquired.

"The Lord gave Abraham and Sarah a surprise bundle rather late in life," she said. "The Lord is in the miracle business, you know."

I tried not to feel a bubble of panic. Babies are wonders, sweet and precious, every one a true miracle of life. But— sleepless nights, spit-ups, diaper changes! *Lord, I thank you for all your blessings and miracles. I thank you for bringing Ivy and me together. But I, uh, hope this isn't a miracle you have in mind for us.*

Ivy recognized my panic. "No miracle in the offing. So you can stop with the sweaty palms and twitchy eyelid." She sounded a little huffy. "I'll take the baby things to town and donate them to the Salvation Army or Goodwill."

I was relieved, and yet I have to admit to a certain regret that Ivy and I didn't get together early enough in life to have a surprise bundle of our own. Did Ivy ever have that same regret? But she was off on a different subject now.

"You know, Deputy Hardishan did unintentionally give us one interesting bit of information beyond telling us about the gun," she said thoughtfully.

"Which was?" I couldn't think of any interesting information, but perhaps I was still distracted by miracles and baby things.

"I thought it was probably Sheila who gave them a tip about Brian and Renée's affair, but the deputy let slip that the tip came from a *man.* So who do you suppose that could have been?"

"Mr. Ex-husband?"

"That'd be my guess. I doubt Ron Sweeney would be volunteering any more information," Ivy agreed. "Y'know, I've been thinking."

"Uh-oh." She rewarded me with an eye roll for that snarky comment on the dangers of her thinking, and I hastily amended it. "Thinking about Renée's ex?"

Ivy made one of her not-unusual, across-the-universe jumps in thinking. "The private investigator seemed to think that fingerprints of Genevieve's new husband, if she had one, might be interesting."

"Wouldn't the sheriff's department have taken Brian's fingerprints and checked them out already?"

"Brian hasn't actually been arrested, just questioned. As we were. They haven't fingerprinted us, so he probably hasn't been fingerprinted either," she pointed out. "They no doubt tried to get fingerprints at the old cabin where we found Renée, but apparently they didn't get any prints good enough to need our prints for comparison. But if we could get Brian's fingerprints to Megalthorpe, he could have them checked out."

"Checked out for what?"

"Criminal record. Wanted fugitive. Identity. Whatever. Maybe Brian Morrison isn't his real name. Maybe Kathy doesn't really know who she's married to. Maybe there's another Mrs. Morrison somewhere."

"We'd have to be pretty sneaky to get them," I said. "Brian was touchy about just having his photo taken. He'd probably go into orbit if we tried to get his fingerprints."

"So what sneaky way could we get his fingerprints on something?"

We tossed suggestions back and forth, but we apparently weren't sneaky-minded enough to come up with anything workable. Then Ivy had an idea about fingerprints that already existed. The shovel! I'd been wearing gloves when I carried it when we searched the hillside, but Brian's hands had been bare when he held it before handing it over to me. His prints might still be on the handle. Was the shovel still out there on the hillside where I'd dropped it?

Although I saw a small complication. "Can you mail a shovel?" With a really long handle?

176

"We'll worry about that later," Ivy answered in her best put-it-off-until-tomorrow fashion of *Gone with the Wind* Scarlett. However, because Ivy is a practical woman, she also added, "First we have to get the shovel."

We worked out a simple plan. We'd drive over to the dinosaur park, retrieve the shovel, and ship it to the private investigator at the address on his website. Then we'd buy another matching shovel for the Morrisons.

***

Over at the dinosaur park, our timing was good. Brian's Porsche wasn't in the carport, and Kathy's old Honda was also absent. I hadn't locked the park gate when we came out behind Brian, so we should be able to get back inside. We parked by Tricky the Triceratops and hurried to the gate. I was wearing gloves, and I'd brought a long strip of plastic to wrap around the shovel handle to protect fingerprints on it.

Problem #1: Brian had at some time come back and locked the gate. Maybe he'd even climbed up and retrieved the shovel.

That was a worrisome thought, but, after a brief consideration, I doubted he'd climbed the hill again. The rundown park was evidence he wasn't a man to exert himself if he could avoid it.

But the locked gate ended nicely simple Plan A. We stood there trying to think of a workable Plan B.

"You could boost me over the fence," Ivy suggested.

I might, but no way was I going to have Ivy struggling alone through trees and brush and encountering anything from a ghost goat to a cougar. I tweaked her idea. Plan B. I'd climb over the fence. Ivy would park the pickup down the old road toward Kate's Kabins where it would be out of sight if Brian and Kathy returned. She'd wait for me there. I figured I could climb the hill, retrieve the shovel, and get to the pickup in no more than half an hour.

Ivy didn't like this plan; she saw various possible pitfalls.

Maybe I should have listened to Ivy.

IVY

The first problem with this latest plan was that the fence wasn't climber friendly. The chain links were too close together for a foothold, and a nasty twist of barbed wire that wasn't visible at casual glance curled around the top.

We moved on to Plan B-1.

Mac parked the pickup under some overhanging branches close to the fence. He climbed on top the cab and, using a board from the back of the pickup, eased over the barbed wire and onto a branch. After he retrieved the shovel, he'd climb the tree inside the fence, get out on the branch, and drop to the ground outside the fence. Then he'd join me where I was waiting with the pickup. The plan wasn't exactly at a James Bond level of cool, but it sounded workable.

Mac got across the fence. But then came a complication. The board slipped, and a protruding nail snagged the seat of his khaki pants. The rip wasn't deep enough to reach his skin, but it was big enough to expose a generous expanse of Hawaiian-print boxer shorts. That was one of my first surprises about Mac after we married; I would have assumed . . . if I'd thought about the subject at all, that is . . . that he was a plain shorts kind of guy. Not so. His shorts wardrobe consisted of everything from this Hawaiian print to red plaid to a surprising dance of pink dolphins on black.

It looked to me as if the rip must be letting in a fair amount of cool air, but Mac didn't seem to notice. He turned and waved just before he disappeared in the tangle of vines and brush, and the last I saw of him was a red flash of the hibiscus on his shorts. I started to call out to tell him, but then I decided it didn't matter. Only a few goats, ghost or otherwise, would see him and his hibiscus there on the hillside.

I got in the pickup and cautiously edged it across the parking lot. Sheila's car was parked at Duke's trailer again, so I circled the gift shop, hoping to avoid notice by them. Which I thought I could, unless they happened to be looking out the window. I eased out to the road to Kate's Kabins and followed it to a dip and curve where I could park and not be seen by anyone in the trailer. The chain-link fence ended a few feet from my parking spot, where the hillside turned into a cliff. Then I waited.

I kept checking my watch. Eleven minutes. Fourteen. Twenty-two. Toenails grow faster than time moved as I waited. My imagination, however, raced at warp speed. I envisioned Mac trapped in the hole Duke had dug. I saw him sinking in a heretofore unknown patch of quicksand in the creek. And maybe ghost goats did exist. In homicidal herds. Gleefully using Mac's Hawaiian-print shorts for target practice.

At twenty-six minutes I got out of the pickup. At twenty-nine minutes I paced a few steps up the road. At ten minutes past the half hour I worriedly headed back to the dinosaur park on foot. I edged around the corner of the fence and crept along it toward the spot where Mac had entered the park, again hoping to avoid attention from Sheila and Duke in the trailer. Then I stopped short.

Someone was at Brian and Kathy's door. Someone doing something with the lock and glancing around with the stealthy movements of a burglar. *Sheila?* Yes, Sheila. What was she doing there? It was obvious, with the cars still gone, that Kathy and Brian weren't home. Was she trying to get inside to look for something that would incriminate Brian in the murder?

Finally, after a rattle of the doorknob with gloved hands, she apparently gave up and ran across the parking lot and back to Duke's trailer. I waited until she disappeared inside before continuing my own stealthy journey along the fence. I was still curious, but there was a bigger problem at the moment.

179

A few feet from where Mac was supposed to use a branch to get over the fence I saw why he'd never made it to the pickup. He had the long handle of the shovel safely wrapped in plastic to protect fingerprints, but beside him was the branch on which he was planning to cross the fence. Broken. He was sitting on the ground rubbing his knee, his expression pained.

"What happened?"

"Branch broke. I hit my knee on a rock when I fell."

Then, to add one more complication, the Porsche zipped around the gift shop and pulled into the carport. Brian got out and immediately spotted us.

He stalked up to where I stood and Mac sat on opposite sides of the fence. "What's going on?"

My mouth, trapped between truth and various unlikely stories, clamped shut. Then Brian spotted the plastic-wrapped shovel.

"Hey, you found the shovel! I figured we must have dropped it up there somewhere, but I didn't have time to go after it. But you didn't have to go to all this trouble to retrieve it. You could have waited until I got home and unlocked the gate."

I dodged the real explanation for our retrieving the shovel, which was at odds with his interpretation. He also, fortunately, wasn't asking for an explanation about why the handle looked as if Mac had tried to bandage it with plastic. "Mac hurt his knee," I said.

Mac floundered to his feet, gingerly keeping his weight off the bad knee.

"Can you walk over to the gate?" Brian asked. "I'll get it unlocked so you can come out that way."

Mac hobbled along the inside of the fence, hibiscus waving like a red flag. Brian had the gate unlocked by the time we got there. He reached for the shovel as soon as Mac stepped through the gate.

"Thanks." With a smirk at Mac and a wink to me, he added, "You might check out that rip in your pants before you head to town or anywhere. That's some pretty flashy underwear you've got there."

Mac twisted to look at his exposed hibiscus, and Brian jauntily headed toward the carport with the fingerprint-covered shovel. The grand climax to our plans A, B, and B-1.

"I'll go get the pickup," I muttered. Mac, now holding the rip together with one hand, slumped down beside the gate to wait for me.

Sheila came out of Duke's trailer just when I reached the corner of the fence. She stopped short, apparently startled to see me. What I wanted to do was ask what she'd been doing at Brian and Kathy's door, but then I decided, since she hadn't seen me then, that it might be more prudent not to let her know I'd seen her.

"Mac hurt his knee. I'm going to get the pickup so I can take him home."

I figured that statement raised more questions than it answered . . . how had Mac hurt his knee and why was the pickup hidden around the corner? . . . but Sheila didn't ask for an explanation. She said, "Duke's knees are acting up again, so he took a couple of pain pills. He's sleeping now. I've been cleaning the refrigerator."

"Good. Tell him we'll stop by again one of these days." I hurried off before Sheila could ask questions.

I retrieved the pickup, helped Mac into the passenger's side, and we made a hasty exit.

No shovel. No fingerprints.

On the bright side, we didn't have to figure out how to wrap and send a long-handled shovel.

Chapter 16

Back at the motorhome, Mac changed out of his ripped pants, and we put ice and then antibiotic ointment on his swollen and scraped knee. He didn't want a doctor, of course. There must be a line in some secret Male Code that says real men don't see a doctor for anything less than a near-death emergency. Which doesn't mean they don't want a fair amount of pampering, of course.

I fixed his favorite meat loaf for dinner, gave him a couple of ibuprofen and a freshly baked brownie, and he stretched out on the sofa while we watched an old John Wayne movie on DVD. Koop usually curls up on my lap, but tonight he went into Comfort Cat mode and settled down on Mac's stomach. BoBandy snuggled up to his leg. By morning the swelling had gone down, the sun was out, and he decided he was in good enough shape to wash the pickup. At lunch he came in with the bag of rocks I'd left in the pickup and asked if I wanted to keep them.

I peered in the plastic bag. Outside of their natural environment, shiny beach rocks tend to dull into a just-another-rock look that makes me wonder why I picked them up. Mac pointed to a larger, darker stone. "That doesn't look like a beach rock."

"It's the one Brian almost smashed into your toe when we were looking for Duke's treasure hole. I picked it up because of its unusual shape."

I jiggled the sack to change the stone's position and better show off what looked like Barbra Streisand's profile along the flat edge.

"What unusual shape?" Mac asked.

Mac has many marvelous talents and abilities but seeing the faces I often see in various objects isn't one of them. Sometimes I find this frustrating, but now that I looked more closely at this bumpy-edged stone, maybe the Streisand resemblance wasn't all that great. "Never mind. Just toss 'em."

Mac grabbed the bag, but then he stopped and looked in it again. "Can they get fingerprints off a rock?"

"Fingerprints?"

"Brian had hold of that stone . . ."

Yes! I'd read that fingerprints weren't easy to retrieve off rock, but I'd also read about a case in which fingerprints from a rock that had been thrown off a freeway overpass and killed a motorist had been used to identify the perpetrator, so they must be able to do it sometimes. I'd been wearing gloves when I picked up the rock, so mine wouldn't be there.

Using a section of the plastic bag so he wouldn't get his own fingerprints on the rock, Mac withdrew it and set it carefully on the table. The stone was smooth, flat, and greyish. Just another rock. Streisand had disappeared. But if Brian's fingerprints were on it . . .

Mac tilted his head as he eyed the stone. "What do you think?"

I nodded. Worth a try! And easier to mail than a shovel.

***

We packed the stone in a new plastic bag and a square box that had held some pickup part Mac had bought. A rock probably didn't need padding, but I padded it with crumpled newspaper anyway. I blacked out the printing on the box with a marking pen and got Megalthorpe's address off his website. We took the package into the Trinidad post office. The clerk inquired about contents, but he didn't appear startled by my "It's a rock" answer. Although he did raise his eyebrows when I sent it by express mail, the fastest and most expensive way possible. He said the package needed a return address, so I

183

used the numbers on Sheila's mailbox. When I asked, I also found that Sandy's package had arrived at General Delivery. I couldn't wait to get back to the motorhome to open it, of course, so I tore into it right there in the pickup. We both stared at the contents.

"They'll look great on you," Mac said.

I've seen jeans like this on other women. Ordinary on the front, but with backside pockets glittering with metal studs and glass crystals and metallic embroidery. This design was graceful and swirly, with glittery points around the swirls. I tilted my head to study the design. Surely the swirls and points couldn't be what they looked like to me . . .

"I think that's the style now," Mac offered. "At least they don't have ragged holes like I'm always seeing."

I have jeans with holes in them, but that's because they're worn out, not because they acquired fashionable—and expensive—holes in a jeans factory. Now sunlight struck one of the glass crystals and shot a beam like a laser out the window. I hastily stuffed the jeans back in the tissue paper in which Sandy had wrapped them before some passing motorist became a casualty.

I appreciated Sandy's gift, of course. She and her friends probably wear jeans like these. But glitters and twinkles on *my* backside—? I've sometimes wondered if it doesn't occur to Sandy that her gifts might be a wee bit over-the-top for an LOL or if she knows and is determined to drag me into twenty-first-century fashion anyway.

The thong panties she'd once sent were surprisingly comfortable. The toe rings worn with shoes were fine. But neither of those items were openly *visible*, and the glittery design on these jeans would light up my backside like a Christmas tree. Actually, that's what the design looked like. A Christmas tree. With an octopus twined around it.

We didn't find a place for the baby things in Trinidad, so

we drove on down to Eureka and donated them at a Salvation Army store. I also picked up a nice nut chopper at a bargain price.

Back at the motorhome, Mac's knee was hurting again so he stretched out on the sofa. I stuffed the jeans in a drawer. I texted PI Megalthorpe to tell him an item with possible fingerprints was on its way, although I still didn't give him an identifying name for Brian. I also texted Sandy a thank-you for the surprise gift without mentioning how startling a surprise it was. She texted me right back saying she'd been planning to send me something else that was popular now, but *Then I saw the jeans and they were so "you."* She also sent a couple of photos of that other current fad. *Personally, I think they're kind of gross,* she wrote, *but maybe I'll try them sometime.*

Hairy fingernails. The girls were using snippets of fake fur glued to fake fingernails, and one girl had even managed to use bits of her own hair. The photo showed her hairy-fingernailed hand alongside her hair. A matching ensemble.

Hairy fingernails vs. glittery jeans? *You made the right choice, Sandy.*

I can always wear the jeans on some dark and moonless night.

***

On Saturday Mac's knee was better, and we spent time wandering around McKinleyville. We weren't exactly *looking* for Renée's ex, but this was where Ron Sweeney had thought Ric Echol was staying. We saw lots of motorcycles, but none that matched the photo of the Harley Screamin' Eagle that Mac had found on the internet. We did see the town's 160-foot totem pole in a shopping center, watched people flying enormous kites on Clam Beach, and ate great clam chowder and cornbread at a café with an oversized balloon of a laughing crab near the front door. When we got home, Sheila was just changing the sign on her garage sale from Open to Closed.

She wasn't at church the next morning, where we heard a rousing version of "When the Saints Come Marching In." The pastor preached on Psalm 46:1, "God is our refuge and strength, an ever-present help in trouble," which is a glorious truth that I've experienced over and over in my life.

Sheila was unloading items from her SUV when we got home. A small microwave, a ruffled lamp, and several cardboard boxes of stuff. She'd apparently been making the rounds of other yard sales to resupply inventory for her own. We waved but didn't stop.

After lunch we decided to drive out to the cove and see if the crime scene tape was still up at Kate's Kabins, but along the way we spotted Duke sitting in his tree chair and turned off to say hi. Which reminded me I wanted to check on the internet for the availability of a special gift I'd like to give him before we, hopefully soon, took off for our delayed honeymoon in Arizona. Duke was wearing slacks and a sports coat today, more dressy than his usual old work pants.

"Going somewhere?" Mac asked.

"Sheila said she didn't feel like opening up her yard sale this afternoon, so we're going down to Eureka for pizza. Might even take in a movie."

"How're the knees doing?"

"Doin' fine. Sheila's pills really kill the pain."

I hated to say anything if the pills were really helping him, but— "Doctors usually say we shouldn't take pills prescribed for someone else." And what did Sheila have that required strong pain pills?

"Yeah. Right." Duke snorted his disapproval. "They want you to come in and pay big bucks for an office call. Say, I've been going through some old photos to see if I had anything that might be useful when you're writing about treasure and stagecoach robberies." He stood up and grabbed his walker. "Come on inside and I'll show you what I've got."

186

"I'll wait out here," I said. "I've been wanting a chance to try out the chair."

Mac and Duke went inside the trailer, and I sat in the padded tree chair. It had a nice, springy feel. I thought it liked being sat on. I looked across to Brian and Kathy's place. Brian usually parked the Porsche in the carport, but it was out in the parking lot today. Maybe it had gotten a few specks of dust and he was planning another wax and polish job? It was some distance from Kathy's car, as if Brian didn't want his glossy pet infected with something the old Honda might have.

I was looking at the cars and idly wondering if Kathy ever resented the difference between the classy Porsche and her own modest vehicle when—

What happened first? The flash? The boom of explosion? The flying car parts?

The flash blinded me, and all I saw for a moment was a sunburst of blazing light. I covered my ears and jumped out of the chair. Something thudded to the ground in front of me. I blinked several times before I could see that the thudding something was a piece of car. Red. More car parts fell, hitting the parking lot like metallic rain. Mac ran down the ramp from the trailer, Duke and his walker skidding behind him. The boom of the explosion echoed in my ears. The door to Brian and Kathy's place flew open and Brian stood in the doorway as if blasted into immobility. Mac grabbed me around the shoulders and dragged me back just as something crashed into a nearby tree. An SUV came out of nowhere, and Sheila jumped out.

Flames roared around what was left of the topless, sideless vehicle. The engine lay on its side a few feet away. Tires blazed, and one blew out with a bang. Then another explosion. The gas tank? More flying car parts. Black smoke. A throat-choking, nose-burning smell.

For a few moments we were a frozen tableau, and then

187

everyone moved at once. Brian jumped out of the doorway and ran toward his blazing Porsche, arms outstretched as if to embrace its melting frame. He was yelling—or groaning, some kind of anguished noise. Kathy came out with a cell phone to her ear, apparently calling for help. Sheila stepped out from behind her SUV. Duke said, "Holy cow!"—an expression I haven't heard in some time.

"What happened?" Sheila asked. She, in her plaid cape and perky purple hat, didn't look nearly as shaken as I felt.

"I was sitting here looking at the car and it blew up! Foom!" I threw my arms in the air. "Just like that, it just . . . *blew up!* Like a bomb hit it. If Brian had been in it, he'd have been blown up too!"

Brian circled the engine and the largest piece of flaming vehicle remaining. Smaller, scattered car parts littered the parking lot. That acrid scent of burning plastic and rubber smoked the air. I coughed when the shifting wind blew a cloud of dark smoke our direction.

Sheila waved smoke away from her face. "Of course he wasn't in it."

In the distance I could already hear a siren. The rural fire station wasn't far away. "What do you mean?"

"Don't you see what's going on here? What Brian's doing?"

All I saw was a mangled, blazing car, smoking car parts scattered like bits of a metallic barbecue, and Brian standing there with an incredulous, disbelieving look on his face. He was apparently too shocked or dazed to realize he was standing dangerously close to the burning car. Didn't he feel the heat of the flames? If another tire blew—

Mac ran out and pulled Brian away just as another tire did blow. Car parts embedded the wall beside Kathy and Brian's door like some haphazard attempt at street art sculpture.

Feeling dazed myself, I repeated the question to Sheila. "What do you mean?"

"They must be close to arresting him for Renée's murder. He's getting desperate. So now he blows up the car to make it look as if someone tried to kill him too." She sounded exasperated with my denseness, as if anyone should see the obvious. "A diversionary tactic. Don't you see?"

I hadn't had much time to think, and the explosion still plugged my ears, but this thought wasn't even lurking on some distant mental horizon. Brian blowing up his own beloved Porsche? Surely not.

And yet, if he wanted to divert attention from his own guilt, make it look as if whoever killed Renée was after him too . . .

"But Brian was careful not to actually get himself hurt or killed, of course." Sheila thrust her arms through openings in the cape and crossed them over her chest. She leaned back against the front of her SUV. "Just watch his act when the authorities get here."

"How would he do it?" I asked. "I mean, the car was just sitting there all by itself. No one was even around it. I was looking right at it."

"I don't know." She uncrossed her arms and her narrowed eyes studied Brian. "I don't know anything about explosions. A remote control device of some kind? You can just bet your booties he did it somehow!"

I don't know anything about explosives either, but I have had a smidgen of scary experience. Several years ago, back in Missouri, someone planned to blow up my old Thunderbird by rigging dynamite under the car. It was supposed to go off and blow both me and the Thunderbird to smithereens when I turned on the ignition. What saved me was that the car wouldn't start that morning. *Luck* some people said; the good Lord looking out for me, I figured.

But that must not be how this explosion was set to go off because Brian had to have started the car before he backed the Porsche out of the carport. Why didn't it blow up then, with

189

him in it? That's assuming someone else had rigged the explosion and was trying to kill him, not what Sheila was suggesting. Could someone else have set off the explosion using some kind of timer or remote control device?

From how far away did remote control devices work? No one in the immediate area had jumped out of a tree and raced off when the explosion blew. Or at least I hadn't seen anyone. A timer, a ticking clock sort of thing? That was hardly practical. How to know when to set it for? If that was the system that had been used with the intent to kill Brian, it hadn't worked, obviously. Brian was still here.

Could he have done it himself by using a remote control device from inside the house, where he was safely away from the exploding car?

Did Brian know how to do something such as that? It would surely take some technical know-how. But I remembered Kathy saying he'd opened up his computer to fix something inside it. That surely took some electronic expertise. Could he use that same kind of knowledge to set up an explosion? I wouldn't poke into the internal workings of our laptop any more than I'd try a self-appendectomy.

A fire engine arrived first. Mac came back to where I was standing. The firemen had the blaze cut back considerably by the time deputies arrived a few minutes later, though that acrid scent was still strong enough to make my eyes water. I don't suppose every deputy and law officer in the county came, but a haphazard tangle of official vehicles, both state and local, soon crowded the parking lot. An ambulance also arrived. Another fire engine. A county road maintenance dump truck showed up. Then an old motorhome. Two pickups that looked as if they'd been four-wheeling in the mud, plus a muddy, barking dog. A motorcycle with a sidecar attached.

Nothing like a good explosion to draw a crowd.

No feds yet, but I figured they'd show up soon. The Bureau

of Tobacco, Guns and Explosives, or something like that.

Brian stood in the midst of the vehicles and officers, arms waving wildly. "Someone tried to kill me!" he yelled.

"See? What'd I tell you?" Sheila crossed her arms over her chest again.

"They destroyed my car! They tried to blow me up!" More arm waving and then a despairing slap of hands against his bowed head.

"Give the man an Oscar," Sheila muttered. A moment later she determinedly headed toward a deputy. She was giving him her wild theory about Brian rigging the explosion himself, of course, how he'd set it up as a way to divert attention from his own guilt in Renée's murder. But Sheila didn't look like some wild-eyed fanatic spouting he-done-it gibberish. Except for one fairly subtle pointing toward Brian, her arms were controlled as she talked to the deputy, her expression earnest and intense.

Maybe what she was saying wasn't just a wild theory . . .

Kathy had come out and put her arms around Brian, apparently trying to comfort him. He pushed her away and went back to raving about how he'd backed the car out of the carport just a few minutes earlier. How he'd left the engine running while he went back inside, just for a minute, to get the wallet he'd forgotten. Then the explosion.

"Someone tried to kill me!"

Brian kept circling the burned car as he raged at a full bellow, stopping here and there to stare into someone's face as if expecting to find the culprit looking back at him. Was that possible? I've heard of arsonists returning to the scene of their crime to watch the flames. Was the person out there watching right now? How about that motorcyclist with the sidecar?

I searched the faces of onlookers, but since most of them were law officers of one type or another, finding a guilty person among them didn't seem likely. However, I noticed that an officer was taking photos of the burning Porsche, and he also turned the camera to get photos of the crowd, including us. I hadn't seen or heard the motorcycle leave, but it was gone now.

More officers had gathered around Brian. He sounded convincing. Loud, excited, distracted, scared, angry, the way someone who'd just escaped an attempt on his life would sound.

"If I hadn't gone inside I'd be dead! Someone tried to kill me!" he repeated.

I couldn't hear what Sheila was telling the officer, but it occurred to me that this could be Sheila's own diversionary tactic. Trying to make them believe Brian had blown up his own car because *she'd* done it. She'd mentioned a remote control device to set off the explosion. Maybe she had one right there in her SUV and had set it off as she was driving over here.

I stopped my headlong rush down that trail of thought. No logical sense in it. Sheila didn't like Brian; she'd made that plain enough. But kill him? Why?

I also couldn't believe she knew enough about explosions or remote control devices to set this up. What ordinary citizen did? Although someone could be hired to do almost anything. Did Sheila know a blow-up-a-car kind of person? Maybe. Some rather scruffy types showed up at her garage sales. I'd seen a couple of guys who looked as if they might be anything from terrorists to serial killers. But that was unfair, of course. Judging someone on the basis of looks always is. What one of the scruffy guys had actually bought was a rather battered old Barbie doll for his little girl.

I suddenly wondered if Brian realized Sheila was talking to the deputy about him. How would he react if he did notice it? He'd surely be furious, and if he'd already killed once . . .

I was thinking so hard I didn't even notice Deputy Hardishan approaching until he spoke. "Well, if it isn't the nice

192

couple who always seem to be around when there's a disaster on the menu. What are you doing here?"

"We just happened to be visiting Duke." Mac motioned to Duke still standing with his walker at the foot of the ramp to his trailer door.

"Just coincidence, of course," the deputy said.

"Do we look like demolition experts?" I grumbled.

"No, but—"

I could see the good deputy was lining up a mental list of criminals who didn't look like the killers, arsonists, or terrorists they were, so I was glad when Mac interrupted.

"Any idea yet what kind of explosive was used?"

"Not yet. Something smaller than a nuclear bomb but bigger than a firecracker. Any suggestions?" A facetious question at best. Maybe even a bit snarky.

"We can give you a statement of what we saw," Mac said. "But that's about it."

"We'll be in touch." A threat or a promise from the deputy? Probably both.

"We aren't planning to leave the area in the immediate future," I offered.

"Good." He didn't even smile to suggest he realized I was being just a teensy bit snarky myself about his previous demands that we not leave.

So far Duke hadn't said a word, but now he clumped off with the walker toward Kathy. She was standing next to her old Honda. Her gaze never left Brian, and she seemed oblivious of anyone else.

Suspicious ol' me, I briefly wondered if Kathy might have tired of Brian's affection for, as she'd once put it, this hunk of "four wheels and expensive insurance" and decided to get rid of it. Without injuring Brian, of course.

I discarded that thought almost immediately. Kathy might wish Brian would treat her as well as he treated the Porsche . .

193

. maybe she'd like a little waxing and polishing too . . . but I couldn't really think she'd figure a way to destroy something that meant so much to him.

Now Duke gave Kathy an awkward hug and they talked a minute before he clumped back to where we were standing.

"Does Kathy have any idea who might have done this?" I asked.

"She thinks it's just a terrible accident."

Accident? Another thought that had never entered my head.

"She said Brian had the spark plugs changed recently and maybe one of them was defective. Or maybe the mechanic accidentally did something when changing the oil at the same time."

Mac and I exchanged glances, as we often do. A defective spark plug or an oil change causing an explosion like we'd just seen? Even with my limited car expertise, that sounded about as likely as blaming the bad car fairy.

Sheila returned without comment on her conversation with the deputy, but apparently she was satisfied with his reaction, or we'd be hearing about it. The deputy she'd spoken with was talking to a state police officer now.

"Looks as if the excitement here is over. They ought to be arresting Brian very soon now. Shall we head on into town for pizza?" she said to Duke.

I thought he was reluctant to leave, but after a hesitation he nodded, and she helped him into her SUV and put his walker in the back seat. Was she driving off with an incriminating remote control device in her vehicle? No, if she'd had one, she'd have tossed it out before she got here.

The Porsche was a misshapen chunk of hot leftovers now, tires all blown and burned. A warped piece of metal that had fallen near us looked as if it might be what was left of a license plate. A couple of officers appeared to be questioning Brian.

Were they about to arrest him?

Kathy went over to support Brian with an arm around his waist. This time he didn't push her away; he didn't even seem to notice her. A few official cars left. An officer got rid of the onlookers in the motorhome and pickups. No one tried to stop us when we got in our pickup and drove off.

We weren't escaping, of course. Local law enforcement knew where to find us. I suspected they also had license numbers of the other onlookers.

Back at the motorhome, my ears were still ringing. The sight of an exploding vehicle isn't as *ghastly* as a dead body, but this scene seemed branded on my brain cells. I managed to fix a pot of coffee, and we discussed the various possibilities. A spark plug accident. An unknown culprit trying to kill Brian but somehow miscalculating and destroying only the Porsche. My previous experience with an explosion rigged to be set off by the car ignition, and how that didn't apply here because the car hadn't exploded until it was just sitting there with the engine idling.

"Of course there are no doubt other ways to rig an explosion," I said.

Mac nodded. "Sheila's theory of Brian putting explosives in the Porsche himself and setting it off by remote control from inside the house."

"Will the investigators give any credence to that theory?"

"Maybe. Especially if they really are close to targeting him for the murder." Koop had climbed up to drape himself around Mac's neck, and Mac stroked the stubby-tailed end of Koop's orange body.

"I wonder if they searched the house after we left."

"For a remote control device?" Mac said. "They'd need a search warrant, wouldn't they?"

"Not if Brian thought he'd hidden it well enough and gave them permission to look."

We both gave that a few moments' consideration.

"I don't think he did it," I finally said reluctantly. "I guess I'd *like* to think he did it as a way to make them think whoever killed Renée was after him now," I had to admit. "Because by now I definitely think he killed her. But I don't think he caused today's little incident."

"Because?"

"Because the Porsche meant too much to him. Because I don't think he just looked or acted devastated about it being destroyed. I think he *is* devastated."

"He could have done it but still be devastated that he had to do it," Mac suggested.

I nodded. Made sense to me.

"So, if you don't think Brian himself did it, who did?"

Chapter 17

IVY

We discussed that while we drank more coffee. The obvious possibility, of course, was what Brian either actually believed or what he wanted the authorities to believe: that the person who'd killed Renée had also set the explosion and tried to kill him. But we both still thought Brian had killed Renée, either because of her romantic involvements outside her entanglement with him, or because she'd double-crossed him some way by getting the option on the Kate's Kabins property for herself.

But if he hadn't killed her, if someone was out to get both Renée and Brian, why? Had they been working together in some scheme to get both Kate's Kabins and Duke's property, and this collusion had angered someone enough to kill them both? Someone who also had designs on the properties? As a side issue in there, had Brian actually planned to arrange some "accident" for Duke and obtain the property through the wording of that codicil on Duke's will?

Or had someone been angry enough with Renée and Brian about their affair to try for double murder?

I clunked a palm against my head as a supporting thought jumped into my mind. How could I have let *this* slide by? "Renée's ex! Remember? Ron Sweeney said he'd gone to prison after blowing up the back side of a building to get to a safe. An *explosion!*"

"I'll see if I can find anything on the internet."

***

Near dark, Deputy Hardishan showed up. Mac opened the motorhome door and greeted him. A wind had come up, and he had to brace his arm against the door to keep it from slamming shut. "Well, if it isn't our favorite lawman."

"Wouldn't want you to think I was neglecting you."

He came inside. This time he didn't separate us, and we went through the afternoon's events together, starting with how I'd been peacefully sitting in Duke's tree chair. Old, dry leaves flew by the windows while we talked. He asked the expected questions and scribbled our answers in his notebook. He was beginning to feel like, if not exactly an old friend, at least not an enemy. We asked a few questions too, although we didn't really expect answers. Had they found anything to indicate what type of explosive was used or how it was set off? Gasoline? Dynamite? C-4?

"You know about C-4?" Deputy Hardishan lifted an eyebrow, a talent he hadn't before exhibited. I was a bit envious. That one-eyebrow lift is a technique I've never been able to master.

"Not really. I've just read about it. Do you have any suspects?"

"Suspects other than yourselves, you mean?" he asked.

I couldn't tell if the smile that came with the comment meant *Of course you nice folks aren't really suspects* or if he was trying to put us off our guard with a little cop humor. But all he said was, "You know I can't discuss that."

"Is it illegal to blow up your own car?" Mac asked.

The deputy hesitated, squinting as he apparently ran Mac's question through some mental check list. I noted he didn't ask why Mac asked that particular question. "I suppose, under certain circumstances, it wouldn't necessarily be illegal. If it's on private property . . . and no illegal explosive is used . . . and it's not done for insurance purposes . . ."

Insurance hadn't even occurred to me. I'd been so concentrated on Sheila's theory that Brian had done it to divert suspicion in Renée's murder away from himself that any other motive he might have hadn't entered my head. I wouldn't think

Brian and Kathy needed insurance money, but who knew?

But Deputy Hardishan's offhand remark about an insurance payoff did suggest that they were seriously considering the possibility that Brian had set the explosion himself, for whatever reason.

"Are you checking on recent purchases of explosives locally?" I asked.

"You think we should do that?" The deputy sounded interested, but I could tell he was gently teasing me for even asking the question. This was already on their schedule.

"The explosive wasn't necessarily purchased here, of course," Mac said. "It could have been brought in from anywhere. Especially if it was C-4 that was used."

"Experts who know more about explosives than we do will be here tomorrow. The federal Bureau of Alcohol, Tobacco, Firearms and Explosives. We'll be working with them, of course."

The deputy stood up, our question and answer session apparently concluded. At the door he turned and asked another question. I couldn't tell if it had only then occurred to him or if for some reason he'd been saving it. "We understand Renée Echol's ex-husband is in the area. You happen to know anything about him?"

"We heard he was staying somewhere around McKinleyville and that he rides an older Harley. One of the classic models, not something beat-up and decrepit. An ex-con, I think. He might have a parole officer who'd know something."

"His parole officer is down south, and Echol isn't exactly keeping in close contact with him."

So, Ric Echol's name, if not the man in person, was familiar to them. "That's why you're looking for him?" I asked. "Parole violation?"

"Just let us know if you have any contact or hear anything about him."

The law had suspicions about Brian, but I was reasonably certain now that he wasn't their sole suspect in the explosion. Ric Echol was on their radar too and not just for parole violation. They undoubtedly knew about his experience with explosives.

After the deputy left, Mac got on the laptop to see if he could find out anything about Ric Echol's explosion and stolen safe, and I started spaghetti for supper. Before I had it ready, he called me over to the laptop.

"I haven't been able to find anything about that particular explosion, but did you know that right here on the internet you can buy books that tell you how, and show you with illustrations, to use 'commonly available' ingredients to make an explosive?" He sounded mildly shocked. "Or you don't even need to buy a book. There are sites with instructions right there. Look at this one."

I looked and read the first line: *Boil ten cups of urine.* A startling instruction in itself. Someone could make an explosive starting with *urine?* But the amount of that ingredient was also rather startling. Ten *cups* of urine?

"You're saying that even with no experience someone could make an explosive device?"

"It's like a recipe. *We* could probably do it."

Probably. Although we'd have to save up for that first ingredient. "You're thinking Brian found a good exploding-Porsche recipe?"

"I know you don't think he did it, but Kathy says he spends a lot of time on the computer. If I can find this stuff, he certainly can. Although we don't know anything about his background or past. Maybe he's an explosives professional and doesn't need internet recipes."

We already knew Brian had at least a minimal electronic ability, perhaps enough to rig a remote device to set off an explosive. If he could also mix up that explosive himself, there'd be no incriminating trail to show he'd bought something.

But I still didn't think he'd done it. I don't like Brian. I don't like the way he tried to run us out of the dinosaur park parking lot. I don't like the way he treats Kathy. I don't like the shabby affair he carried on with Renée. I also thought he'd killed her. Not your all-around nice guy.

I just didn't think he'd set the explosion. Was that LOL intuition? Mine is notoriously iffy. But I thought Brian was simply too devoted to that Porsche to destroy it. His pride and joy. Not all that admirable in itself, being so attached to what was basically just a shiny thing with wheels, but his attachment to that shiny thing was enough to make me think he didn't do it.

Or was that just stubborn thinking, a refusal to admit I was wrong? Let's face it. I've been wrong before. Could I even be wrong about Brian being the killer? Being unlikeable, even unfaithful, didn't necessarily mean he also committed a murder.

Then Mac surprised me. "But I don't think he did it, either."

"The murder or the explosion?"

"You're having second thoughts about him being a murderer?" Mac sounded surprised.

"I'm not sure," I had to admit. "Innocent until proven guilty and all that, you know. But, okay, why don't *you* think he set the explosion?"

"The same reason you think it. Too attached to that vehicle. Plus the fact that I have confidence in what *you* think."

I kissed him on the top of the head and decided there was no need to point out times my mental workings had hovered around pet rock level. "How about Ric Echol, then?"

Mac nodded. "I'm open to the possibility that he did it, although at this point I have no idea how."

"We could try to find him. Help out law enforcement."

201

"Finding him might be a little like grabbing a tiger by the tail."

True. I gave this some thought.

Maybe it was time for a different line of thinking. "Deputy Hardishan doesn't like to mark anyone off his suspects' list, but I think we're far down as both explosion and murder suspects. Maybe we should just leave all this to the sheriff's department and the Bureau of Alcohol, Tobacco, Firearms and Explosives and head for Arizona."

Mac didn't hesitate before nodding. "I doubt they need any help from us. In fact, I'm sure they'd rather not have any help from us."

Over spaghetti we made a decision: we'd leave in the morning. Even though I didn't think Brian had set this explosion, I wasn't hardwired to risk my neck to try to exonerate him from guilt. We didn't listen to a weather report before going to bed. Maybe we should have.

The wind increased in intensity during the night. Mac was already awake when I woke to the sound of wind rattling things I was fairly certain shouldn't be rattling. The walls shuddered under the assault, and then rain started pounding the roof and battering the windows. Koop was already in bed with us, and BoBandy jumped up to join us. The wind increased in fury, far more than anything we'd yet experienced here. We both got up to peer out the window. Sheila's yard light illuminated trees bending as if they were bowing to royalty. A chunk of black plastic she'd been using to keep weeds down in a flower bed flew over the garage.

Mac was concerned about the trees close to the motorhome. He turned on the lights, put a jacket on over his pajamas, and slipped his feet into rubber boots so he could go outside and check. I put on a robe and watched him moving outside, his head turned upward to look at the nearby trees. Koop jumped from the dinette onto my back and scooched

202

down into my arms. BoBandy squirmed close to my legs.

Mac came back inside just as Sheila's yard light and the motorhome lights went off. A power line must have gone down somewhere. Maybe a tree had fallen on it.

"I think we'd better move away from these trees," Mac said.

We both dressed in the dark. Moving an RV isn't a major production; RVs are meant for moving, and we intended to head for Arizona in the morning anyway. But water and electrical hookups have to be disconnected, stabilizing jacks raised, and movable stuff put away. Not a quick and easy job in the dark in the middle of a wind and rain storm.

Mac was just headed for the door to go back outside when the hardest gust yet blasted the motorhome. It almost seemed to *lift* it. Could a motorhome blow over in a hard-enough wind? I grabbed the kitchen counter for balance.

The motorhome didn't blow over. But something landed on the roof. No, more than landed— A smashing, ripping, tearing crash. As if one of the dinosaurs over at the park had taken flight and crash-landed on us. With it came a strange draft of cold air and an equally strange, raw scent that didn't smell like cozy motorhome interior. I fumbled for the flashlight that was usually on the bench seat of the dinette and flashed the beam at the ceiling.

The broken end of a huge branch protruded into the room. It had smashed right through the roof like some alien visitor from outer space. Rainwater dripped around it. We both just stood there, momentarily too astonished to move.

"Holy cow," Mac said. It seemed an appropriate comment at the moment. He reached up and touched the sharp end of the branch.

We both went outside. After that oversized gust, the wind had diminished a fraction. I hoped it was a my-work-is-done-here diminishing. Mac aimed the flashlight beam at the top of the motorhome.

The branch sat there like some monstrous growth sticking out of the roof. But when it bounced and flopped in the wind, it looked more like a predator trying to drill or eat its way inside. Parts of the big branch trailed over the windshield. The flashlight beam showed a raw slash on a nearby tree where the heavy branch had split off the main trunk.

"Can we still move the motorhome?" I asked.

"We're going to try. Hopefully before anything more comes down."

Using the flashlight, we got the electrical and water hookups undone and raised the stabilizing jacks. Mac gave a couple of huffs while we were doing it. He still had an occasional twinge from the knee he'd injured trying to get over the dinosaur park fence. Inside, I didn't bother trying to put things away. We weren't going far. Not with a monster-sized branch growing out of the roof.

Mac got the engine started and the headlights on. He had to peer through the stuff hanging over the windshield, but slowly, very slowly, we moved away from the trees and into the open space beside Sheila's garage. The wind might not be blowing as hard as that explosive gust that had dismembered the tree, but it was still blowing steadily enough to make the motorhome feel as if it might take flight any moment. Mac shut the engine off and we just sat there in the dark, shaky but thankful it wasn't either of us punctured by the broken branch.

We didn't go back to bed. I heated water on the propane stove and made tea, and we sat at the dinette, drinking tea and listening to the branch sound as if it were galloping across the roof. BoBandy, barking and growling, ran back and forth between the bedroom and sofa. Mac and I dozed off and on while leaning against each other at the dinette.

Daylight eventually filtered through the branch-draped windshield. The wind was still blowing, but it wasn't whipping the branch into a gallop. The room was cold. Without electricity to run the fan on the furnace, the heat had shut off. We were still dozing lightly when a hammering on the door fully wakened us.

"Are you okay?" Sheila gasped when Mac opened the door. She was less nattily dressed today: dark fleece leggings, an oversized coat, and a knit green hat pulled down over her ears, hair sticking out like tufts of red straw.

"We do seem to have a roof problem," Mac said. "I don't think it's a do-it-yourself job. We'll have to get to a repair shop."

Sheila peered inside. "I'll say. But you're going to have to get that thing off the roof before you can go anywhere. I'll call Pastor Mike at church. He'll know someone with a chain saw who can help."

I went back to the house with her. I hadn't been inside her double-wide before. It was quite roomy and nice, three bedrooms. The decor was heavy on knickknacks. Two glass hutches of figurines and antique dishes, and more odd items stashed here and there. A stuffed racoon. An old Underwood typewriter. Two lava lamps. Everyone to their own taste, of course.

Sheila called the pastor and he said he had a chain saw and would be over as soon as the wind let up enough that he could get on the motorhome roof. She suggested we have breakfast with her, then remembered she didn't have electricity for her kitchen range, so I invited her back to the motorhome where I could cook on our propane-fueled stove. Her house hadn't suffered any real damage from the storm, but bits of broken branches scattered both yard and roof, and one gutter drooped at the corner.

Mac switched the generator on to provide electricity for the furnace fan, and the interior of the motorhome warmed quickly. While I fixed breakfast, Mac turned on our battery-operated radio and got a weather report saying a storm had struck all up and down the coast, wind hitting over a hundred miles per hour someplace up in Oregon. Sheila slapped her thighs with her hands and said she'd about had it with this kind of weather and might just take off and visit her daughter in Las Vegas for a few days.

The pastor and another man I remembered seeing at church arrived in an old, mud-streaked pickup about an hour later. Pastor Mike was wearing jeans and, under a rain jacket, a sweatshirt that said *Will preach for food*. Rain was falling now, but not pounding, and he climbed the metal ladder on the back end of the motorhome and wielded the chain saw with the expertise of someone who sawed logs as well as preached sermons. Within a few minutes he had the branch cut into several chunks, and the other man stacked them in a pile. They decided the section of branch actually going through the roof would be best left in place rather than pulling it out and leaving a gaping hole for the rain to come through.

After finishing with the motorhome, the two men cleaned off Sheila's roof and fixed the gutter. They didn't hang around after they were done; another parishioner needed help with a couple of broken windows. Mac tried to pay them, but they wouldn't take anything, so all we could do was thank them profusely. Before they left, Pastor Mike gave us the name of a shop in McKinleyville where we might get the roof repaired.

Mac called the shop and they said bring the motorhome in and they'd get to it right after they replaced the metal roofing that had blown off their own building. I called our insurance company and got a claim for repairs started. On the way out the driveway, with Mac driving the motorhome and me following in the pickup, I stopped and went in to tell Sheila we might not be back for a few days.

"This isn't going to be a fifteen-minute repair job. We may have to find someplace in town to stay for several days."

"You don't need to do that. Just come back here in the

pickup and stay in that room over the garage. The refrigerator isn't working, and, with the electricity out, neither is the kitchen stove, but maybe you could get by with an ice chest for a few days. I have an old Coleman camp stove in my garage sale stuff you can use. I think everything else is okay. We can go out and take a look at it if you'd like."

I ran back out to tell Mac and it took us about thirty seconds to decide we didn't need to look. The room would be fine. With both a cat and dog, finding a motel or other temporary living quarters in town might not be easy. I ran back in to thank Sheila for her generous offer and tell her we'd be back later.

***

Windblown debris scattered the highway on our drive down to McKinleyville. We were right about the repairs taking several days. They couldn't just yank the branch out and patch over the hole. They'd have to replace a whole section of roof. We wouldn't be blithely taking off for Arizona as planned. They faxed the repair estimate to the insurance company. They did, fortunately, have an indoor storage area where the motorhome could sit until they could work on it. We got clothes and personal belongings out of the motorhome, plus dog and cat food, battery radio, BoBandy's leash, and Koop's cat carrier, and emptied the contents of the refrigerator into an ice chest. We were back at Sheila's by midafternoon.

She came out with the key to the garage. "This is another reason I don't like to rent the place. The inside stairs are the only access to the room, and I don't like people traipsing through the garage with all my yard sale stuff in there. I guess I should have outside stairs built." She smiled. "Although I don't think you two are going to steal the Tarzan books or elephant-head nutcracker out of my garage sale stock."

I doubted the over-the-garage room was legal without some different exit in case of emergency, but we weren't worried about legality at this point. The room was modest, the slanted ceiling low, but the décor didn't include any stuffed dead animals or ancient typewriters, and it was certainly acceptable for our needs. Small kitchen stove, refrigerator, TV, and microwave, none of which worked without electricity, of course, but Sheila brought up the two-burner Coleman stove. The tiny bathroom was shower only, no tub, but that was fine. With no electricity to run the pump on the well, there was no water available for showers now anyway. Koop prowled around and found a window ledge acceptable as an observation post. BoBandy could also look out the window by standing on his hind legs.

The last thing Sheila said before handing me the garage key was, "I called Vivian and I am going down to visit her for a few days. She says the sun is shining there. So you can kind of look after the place, and Duke too, while I'm gone, okay?"

"We'll be glad to," Mac assured her.

"And if anyone comes looking for my garage sale, tell them it'll be open when I get back. And I expect Brian to be under lock and key in jail by then too!"

Sheila didn't waste time. I didn't think she'd leave so late in the day, but she was packed and gone within a couple of hours. She said she liked driving at night.

"So, what are we going to do while we wait for repairs?" Mac asked after I'd fixed ham and eggs on the camp stove for supper.

"We might see what we can find out about Ric Echol." Before Mac could remind me of the dangers of tiger-tail catching, I added, "We don't have to try to *grab* him or anything like that. If we find out anything, we can just tell Deputy Hardishan where he is, and let them take it from there. The deputy almost *asked* that we do that."

"Sometimes you can make the most outrageous ideas sound reasonable," Mac muttered.

Chapter 18

IVY

Sometime in the night the electricity came back on. We must have left the light switch on when we'd tried it while the electricity was off, and we woke in the middle of the night with the light glaring like some all-seeing eye overhead. Ever-protective BoBandy gave a couple of warning barks to the invasive light. Unexcitable Koop opened one eye, stood up and stretched, and went back to sleep.

We eventually went back to sleep too and slept later than usual the next morning. Unpredictable weather had decided on sun today, and it was a beautiful, windless day. All the appliances, except the refrigerator, were working nicely. Although the water heater hadn't been turned on to begin with, so there was no hot water. Mac did a manly cold shower, but I settled for more of a toe-dip rinse. We had scrambled eggs and toast but no coffee for breakfast. Coffee wasn't a refrigerator item and so we hadn't brought it from the motorhome. We had plenty to eat, but breakfast without coffee felt unfinished, like missing the end of a movie.

We'd also forgotten Koop's litter box when we left the motorhome in the shop. I found a cardboard container in Sheila's garage, and Mac dug up dirt to make a back-to-basics box for him. I was hoping we'd hear from Private Investigator Megalthorpe. The laptop was another item we hadn't brought, but he could call, or we could pick up email with our cell phones. He should have the rock by now, but I didn't know how long checking for fingerprints might take. Of course, if the rock didn't reveal anything, we might never hear from him anyway.

After breakfast we decided to go over and check on Duke.

First glance showed broken branches on the ground around his trailer but no damage to the trailer itself. A dark rectangle of burned asphalt scarred the parking lot and, in spite of the storm, a faint acrid scent of burned Porsche lingered. What was left of the car was gone, no doubt hauled off for analysis by the experts. I expected the old Honda would now have moved up to residence in the carport, but it wasn't there either.

Kathy came out of Duke's trailer as we started up the ramp to the door. She was wearing a ruffled apron over leggings and a sweatshirt with a colorful spray of flowers on the front.

"How're you doing?" Mac asked.

"We didn't have any damage to the building from the storm, though Brian says there may be trees down in the park. Our electricity came back on sometime in the night."

"Brian's . . . okay?" My subtle way of asking if he'd been arrested since he didn't appear to be around.

"He's feeling terrible, of course, about what happened to the Porsche. He's been talking with the insurance company on the phone, but you know how hard dealing with insurance companies is. Like pulling wisdom teeth." Her mouth pulled down into a frown. "I made a batch of whole-grain cookies and just brought some over to Duke."

When the going gets tough, the tough bake cookies.

"Brian drove down to Eureka in the Honda this morning," Kathy added, apparently in response to Mac's glance at the empty carport. "He's thinking perhaps we should get a lawyer."

"To deal with the insurance company?" Mac asked.

"I-I don't know why, I can't *imagine* why, but I'm almost sure the people investigating the explosion think Brian may have blown up the Porsche himself. Can you imagine them thinking *that?*" Kathy tried for indignation, but her voice wobbled, and she had to blink back tears. "After the explosion they even wanted him to come into the sheriff's office to take his fingerprints. He refused, of course."

210

"He did? Why?" Mac sounded so innocent asking that question, but I knew what he was thinking. The answer to *why* Brian didn't want his fingerprints taken was because they'd reveal something incriminating about him. More than ever I hoped we'd hear from PI Megalthorpe soon. I also had to wonder why law enforcement wanted Brian's fingerprints *now*. They surely couldn't get his or anyone else's prints off the barbecued remnants of the Porsche. Were they zeroing in on him on Renée's murder?

Kathy planted her hands on her hips. "Why did he refuse? Because honest citizens shouldn't have to give their fingerprints when they haven't *done* anything," she declared righteously. "I refused too."

"Did they want your fingerprints also?" I asked.

"I just wanted them to know I wouldn't do it either. If they did want them."

Yes, definitely the poster girl for Stand by Your Man.

"Do you still think it was an accident?" I asked. "Spark plugs or something like that?"

"I thought it was. But now . . . I don't know. It's terrible to think, but maybe someone *was* trying to kill Brian."

"We understand they may be looking for the dead woman's former husband," I said.

"Really?" She brightened. "Maybe he's the one who did it! Actually, I talked to him once. I saw him coming out of that woman's house in Eureka and followed him to a bar in McKinleyville. This was before she was killed, of course."

We stared at her, mutually flabbergasted. Kathy, stalking Renée's ex?

"He wasn't a pleasant man. He seemed to blame both Brian and me for—" She broke off and then ended with a vague wave of hand. "For . . . things." Then she clutched her apron and drew her shoulders in with a kind of combination shiver-shudder.

I felt mildly indignant for her. Ric Echol was blaming Kathy for not being a good enough wife to keep her husband from chasing after *his* ex-wife? Unless there was really some more sinister reason she'd talked to him. Maybe she'd thought the two of them could figure a way to break up Brian and Renée's relationship?

Mac had a more practical thought. "Where was this bar?"

"On a side street somewhere in McKinleyville. The Office. I thought that was a peculiar name for a bar. But then I don't know much about bars."

"Have you told the sheriff's deputy that you talked to him?"

"No. Maybe I should. But I can't go anywhere right now. Brian has the car. And I have a new chocolate soufflé recipe I want to make before he gets home anyway."

When the going gets really tough, maybe the tough up the ante to soufflés.

Kathy scooted on over to their apartment, and we went up the ramp to Duke's trailer. We told him about our windstorm disaster and that we were staying in Sheila's garage room temporarily. I noticed the handgun and holster were hanging by the door now, along with his overloaded key ring. He said Sheila had been by to tell him she'd be gone for a few days. He didn't seem disturbed by the prospect of her absence. Maybe she'd pushed for a let's-get-married-in-Vegas trip. We talked about the explosion. Mac asked if he had any thoughts on what may have caused it.

"Probably what Kathy said. An accident."

"Sheila had another theory. You probably heard her."

Duke snorted. "That woman has more theories than Carter has liver pills."

Another old saying I hadn't heard in a long time. Younger people probably have never heard it.

"Say, you folks don't happen to be going into town, do you? With Sheila gone, I need to pick up a few groceries."

"We thought we might run into McKinleyville. We need groceries too. Want to come along?"

"Great!"

We'd brought BoBandy along, so the little pickup was crowded with three people and a dog, but BoBandy draped his rear end across Duke and his front end across me, and we managed. We certainly wouldn't make him ride in the back of the pickup.

In McKinleyville, Duke directed us to Safeway, where we bought groceries to last as long as we thought we'd be in Sheila's room, and Duke got groceries for himself and the cats. Afterward he said, if we had time, he'd really like to get a haircut, so we took him to a barbershop. I thought we'd be better off *not* looking for Ric Echol, but we did have some spare time, and Mac used his phone to locate The Office.

We found it a few blocks away, a generic-looking, concrete block building next to a martial arts academy. It bore no resemblance to an office. We sat at the counter, which had a dagger and some initials carved into the wood. I felt we should order something, but I had no idea what. Mac took care of it with a request for two glasses of 7Up.

"We're interested in a classic old bike we heard someone around here rides," Mac said when the bartender brought our drinks. "A Harley Screamin' Eagle Softail."

The bartender gave the counter a swoop with a rag. "You looking to buy a bike?" He sounded as skeptical as if Mac had asked about availability of a used flying saucer.

"Just interested," Mac said. He's kind of stuck with the truth, same as I am.

"Yeah, there was a guy used to come in rode an old Eagle. But he doesn't come in anymore."

"He left the area?"

"Nah. Well, I don't know. Maybe he did. But he kept pickin' fights with other customers, so we told him he wasn't welcome

213

here anymore."

"Were the police ever called?"

"We took care of it ourselves." He unexpectedly grinned and pulled a baseball bat out from under the counter. "Meet Shorty. He's our friendly persuader."

I was persuaded. I hadn't planned to start a fight with the two guys at the other end of the bar, and I certainly wasn't going to do so now.

"You happen to know this guy's name or where he lives?" Mac asked.

"I'm not that nosy."

"Did he usually come in alone or with someone?"

"Usually him and another biker."

Interesting information, but not helpful enough to win us any points with Deputy Hardishan. We finished our 7Ups and by then it was time to go back to the barbershop and pick up Duke. He looked quite spiffy, with a beard trim as well as a haircut. He insisted on taking us to lunch at a place called Billie's Burgers, where we had great burgers and Duke flirted with the buxom older woman for whom the eatery was named. Somehow I doubted he'd have any trouble finding another girlfriend if Sheila abandoned him permanently for warmer weather.

Back at Duke's trailer, we helped pick up the broken debris under the trees. Kathy's old Honda was back but not in the carport. Apparently that was reserved for the ghost of Porsches past. Neither Kathy nor Brian came out to talk to us. We could see through the dinosaur park gate that broken branches and windblown debris littered the pathway.

Back at Sheila's place, we discovered a couple of cans of peaches had fallen out of one of Duke's sacks of groceries in the pickup, but we decided we'd wait until later to take them to him. He'd bought bananas and apples so wouldn't be needing the canned peaches right away.

214

We started cleaning up the yard at Sheila's place, stacking broken branches on the pile the pastor's friend had started. By then, the knee Mac had injured when he was trying to retrieve the shovel from the dinosaur park was bothering him, and he stretched out on the sofa with BoBandy snuggled up beside him. He used his cell phone to peruse the internet for the gift we wanted to get for Duke, but I felt very much at loose ends. Accompanied by Koop, I wandered down to Sheila's garage sale area and studied an assortment of mismatched wine glasses. Someone knocked on the door while I was there. It was a young man who wanted to talk to Sheila about some incense sticks. Koop took one sniff at him, hissed, and bounded back upstairs. Koop isn't shy about expressing his aversion to smokers, and this man had a definite smoker aroma. I told the man this wasn't one of Sheila's regular yard sale days, but I did show him her giant-sized cup of incense sticks. He merely seemed impatient and actually swatted at them. I had to grab the cup to keep them from tumbling over.

"No, no. I want the Golden Temple. The *Golden Temple.*" He snapped his fingers, apparently annoyed that I didn't produce the incense by snapping my own fingers. "Maybe she left a package for me?"

I cautiously peered in a couple of drawers, but I wasn't sure I'd give him a package even if I found one. "I don't see any package."

He stormed back to his nice Lexus and roared off. I thought his reaction was rather excessive for something as minor as a missing stick of incense. What was so special about the Golden Temple scent? When I went back upstairs, Mac said he'd ordered the gift for Duke.

Sheila called that evening. I told her about the young man and she muttered something uncomplimentary about "that jerk." She asked if the electricity had come on and if Duke was okay and if we'd heard anything more about the explosion of

215

the Porsche. She finally said the weather in Las Vegas was lovely, but her daughter was such a messy housekeeper that she thought she'd come home in a few days. "I found three socks and a mummified pork chop under the living room sofa," she stated, and I could practically see her nose wrinkle in disapproval.

Okay, maybe a little messy, I agreed. But I wasn't sure three socks and a mummified pork chop were any worse than a stuffed raccoon. I also figured guests peering under sofas deserved whatever they might find.

The next afternoon we decided it wouldn't hurt to do a little more checking on Ric Echol. We thought if he'd gotten himself blacklisted at one bar he'd undoubtedly found another, so Mac used the internet to get a list of local bars and taverns.

We went to a couple of sophisticated lounges connected with nice restaurants, a couple of rough places that looked as if a beer belly was required for admittance, and several others in between. At each one, Mac used the starting point of asking if they remembered a customer with a Harley Screamin' Eagle. We got a couple of maybes but no specifics.

We were also becoming way more familiar with bars, taverns, lounges, and beer joints than I ever wanted to be. Although we met some friendly people. A bartender suggested I try a "Pink Lady," and when Mac went to the restroom, a sociable guy wanted to buy one for me. I politely declined, but it seemed like a nice offer, except for the look that went with it. But I decided I must be mistaken. Who leers at an LOL? We talked with a young man whose wife had just left him and taken their dog and boat with her. We commiserated with him, although I suspected part of their marriage problem may have been that he sounded as if he missed the dog and boat more than the wife.

We also found one bar where the bartender said a biker had been in asking if an older couple in a Toyota pickup had been in there looking for him.

Ric Echol had found out we were looking for him, and now he was looking for us? *Uh-oh.*

By that time we were both fairly well saturated with 7Up, and it seemed a good time to abandon our tiger-by-the-tail search, at least temporarily.

The next day we chose a different project.

MAC

"We came over to see if Brian needed help with cleanup out in the park," I said when Kathy answered my knock on their door. We'd decided encountering a few ghost goats and a cougar or two might be preferable to searching for a man whom Ron Sweeney had rather crudely but perhaps accurately described as having a temper like a bull with porcupine quills stuck in his butt.

Kathy clapped her fingertips together. "Oh, that's wonderful! Brian is lying down. He isn't feeling well, so I know he'll really appreciate you doing the cleanup. There are a couple of rakes out in the carport."

Apparently our offer to "help" had morphed into an offer to *do* the cleanup. Was Brian not feeling well because he was still mourning the Porsche? Although I was more inclined to think he was just allergic to work he knew was out there.

"Have you heard anything more about the cause of the explosion?" Ivy asked.

Kathy rolled her eyes. "They don't tell us *anything.*"

"Did Brian find a lawyer yesterday?" I asked.

"He talked to a couple of them, but they wanted ridiculous retainers. Would you like some peanut butter cookies? I just made a fresh batch."

"Sure," Ivy said. Ivy is a great cook, but she never turns down goodies someone else has made.

217

"Come on in and I'll put them in a bag for you."

We'd no more than stepped inside and closed the door than we heard a vehicle outside. Kathy looked out a window and her response was almost melodramatic. A gasp. A drop of cookie. A touch of chest.

We couldn't see why she was gasping, but a moment later someone knocked on the door. Kathy didn't move to open it, so I made a questioning motion in that direction. She didn't respond, and I cautiously opened the door. I wouldn't have been surprised to see a Harley Screamin' Eagle and a bearded biker sporting porcupine quills, but what I saw were two cars emblazoned with Sheriff on their sides and four armed officers. The one in front had some official-looking papers in his hand.

"Mr. Morrison?"

Before I could say anything, a deputy I recognized said, "That's not Morrison." Deputy Hardishan stepped up to the door. "What're you doing here, MacPherson?" The question had a definite touch of how-come-you're-always-around-when-something's-happening? suspicion.

A flippant *We've got to stop meeting like this* came to mind, but more prudently I managed to say, "Just, uh, visiting."

Kathy apparently overcame her qualms and pushed her way in front of me. "I'm Mrs. Morrison."

"We're here to serve a search warrant and search the premises," the first officer said. He handed her one of the papers.

Kathy momentarily looked as if she might do a maidenly faint, but then she reversed that to an attacking-mama-bear stance. "*Search?* Search for *what?* This is outrageous!" She shook the paper at him without looking at it. "You can't just come into our home and start digging in our things!"

"It's all in the warrant, ma'am, so—"

"No. Definitely not. My husband is ill. You'll have to come

218

back some other time. We'll talk to our lawyer and see . . . see what he says about this infringement on our rights." She tried to thrust the paper back at him, but he blocked it with an uplifted palm.

I knew her protest wasn't going to work. They didn't have a lawyer, and even if they did, I also knew that with a search warrant the officers could definitely come in and search. Brian, dressed in a robe and needing a shave, blundered out of the bedroom.

"What's all this about?" he demanded. He grabbed the paper from Kathy and studied it. "You're looking for a *gun*? There's no gun in here. Go ahead and look." He tossed the paper as if it was confetti and stalked back toward the bedroom.

Kathy, following Brian's arrogant disdain, left the paper on the floor.

"Please come back out here, sir," the officer said. "You may remain on the premises while the search is conducted, but you may not interfere in the process."

I thought for a moment Brian might just slam the door and barricade himself inside, but after a moment he turned and stalked back to the living room.

"After the search is completed, you will be furnished with a list of items removed."

"What I'm going to do is sue you," Brian stated.

"That's your right, sir, but right now we *are* going to conduct our search."

Ivy and I looked at each other. No one was paying any attention to us. We could apparently leave if we wanted, but we weren't being kicked out. Were we leaving? Ivy answered that by unobtrusively dropping to the sofa and patting the space beside her. Curious may not be Ivy's middle name, but curiosity is embedded in her genes. Okay, I was curious too. Would they find a gun? Brian sat in one of the blue recliners, yanked the lever to raise the footrest, and folded his arms across his chest. Kathy perched on the edge of the other recliner. The paper still lay on the floor.

The officers spread out to the kitchen and bedroom and the computer area concealed by a folding screen. It didn't seem like an appropriate time for small talk and we all sat there in silence. I kept thinking Brian would order us to get out, but apparently his mind was on other things.

I've heard law officers aren't necessarily neatniks about doing searches, and, from the clunks and thuds issuing from various places, I guessed that was true. A deputy filled the kitchen counter with items from the cabinets as he searched them. Apparently, he didn't feel obligated to return everything to its proper place. The search seemed to go on and on. We had to stand aside when they removed the sofa cushions to search under them. They also moved the sofa itself to look underneath. No socks or old pork chops under Kathy's sofa.

Finally Deputy Hardishan came out of the laundry room carefully carrying a cardboard box. A second officer followed with a plastic bag holding a box of powdered laundry soap and a third bag holding a small box with printing on the side. I thought it looked about the right size for a box of shells.

The officers had apparently found what they were looking for because a few minutes later Deputy Hardishan handed Brian—where he was still glowering at them from the recliner—a paper. Brian grabbed the paper and suddenly roared to life. He leaped out of the recliner, yanking himself upright on one foot when his other foot snagged on the footrest.

Chapter 19

IVY

The caught foot and flailing arms lent a certain Three Stooges aspect to Brian's fury, but then he jerked the foot free and lunged toward the closest officer.

I don't know what he had in mind, but three officers instantly formed a formidable line of defense. They didn't draw guns, but for a moment I thought they might. Brian, apparently realizing he was outnumbered and outgunned, backed off. But not silently.

"I'm gonna sue you! I'll sue for every cent this county has! I'll sue every one of you personally for every cent you have!"

I wondered what had prompted the search. Law enforcement doesn't serve a search warrant on a hey-let's-dig-around-and-see-if-we-can-find-anything-interesting basis. A search warrant has to be for a specific item or items, and a judge has to approve and sign the warrant. So they'd had information from somewhere. Would a search warrant be issued on the basis of an anonymous call? I doubted that.

Obviously, they also couldn't arrest Brian simply on the basis of finding a gun, or they'd undoubtedly have done it. Just owning a gun is no crime, and I doubt there's any law against gun storage in a soap box if that's what you find appropriate. The gun would have to be tested to determine if it was the murder weapon and checked for fingerprints. The soap box no doubt would also be checked for fingerprints as would the box of shells for the gun.

"Where did the gun come from?" Kathy asked, her voice almost a whisper. She seemed dazed.

"Where did they find it?" Brian asked.

"In the laundry room."

Brian headed that direction. Kathy followed. So did I. They didn't seem to notice. Good. Being an invisible LOL sometimes comes in handy. Peering between them through the door of the laundry room, I saw powdered soap scattered across the top of the washer and spilled on the floor.

"They must have found it in that soap box the deputy took," Brian said.

"But how did it get there?" Kathy ran a finger through the spilled soap powder. "The box was sitting down there on the floor, way back in the corner. It was almost empty. I always use that liquid kind now." She pointed to a large plastic jug of a bargain brand on top of the dryer.

"Somebody put it there," Brian growled. "Just like I told those dumb cops, somebody *planted* it there. Who's been in here?"

"No one!"

I figured that included Brian. I doubted he even knew how to turn on the washer. Both of them suddenly seemed to become aware of me behind them and turned to glare. I could also see their minds churning around a ridiculous impossibility. Me, or maybe Mac, planting a gun in their soap box.

I launched a counterattack. "I didn't even know you had a laundry room! You need to look for someone who had the motive, means, and opportunity to get inside the apartment. Maybe someone who knows how to pick a lock to get inside."

"Weren't you two going to do some cleanup out in the park?" Brian growled. His glare said we were shirking our duty.

"Yes, I believe so."

"I'm going to go lie down again." Brian planted a hand on his stomach, and he really did look as if he didn't feel well. Which is how I presumed he would feel if he figured the sheriff now had an incriminating gun to make a murder charge stick. He stalked back toward the bedroom.

Kathy wiped her hands on her apron. "I believe I'll clean

up the kitchen. They left a terrible mess." She put a finger to her chin with a distracted air when she added, "I think I'll make some raisin cookies." I noted that she didn't repeat her earlier offer of cookies for us.

We exited the house and picked up rakes in the carport. And then realized we didn't have a key to the gate. Not inclined to go back and ask for it, we returned the rakes and got in the pickup where BoBandy was waiting. Cookie-less, we drove home to Sheila's place.

"So, what do you think?" Mac asked when we were sitting in our room with coffee from the jar of instant we'd bought in McKinleyville, and I was wishing I'd bought ingredients to make cookies. By now I had a real yearning for cookies. Peanut butter. Raisin. Chocolate chip. Anything.

I gave Mac's question a moment's thought and then gave the obvious answer. Except it came out a question. "Brian shot Renée and then hid the gun there?"

"You believe that?"

"Hiding the murder gun right there in the house doesn't seem too smart. Wouldn't he have been more likely to get rid of it?"

"But you don't think it's his gun anyway."

I had to nod. No, I didn't think it was Brian's gun. I didn't like Brian any better today than I ever had, but my dislike still didn't make him a killer. I didn't doubt the gun found in their soap box was the murder weapon, but I still doubted it was Brian's gun.

I wished I could wrap it up neatly in my mind with a simple sequence: Brian killed Renée. The gun was Brian's. He'd hidden it in the soap box. End of story. But, like a book with pages missing, I just couldn't make this fit.

"How about Kathy?"

"I suppose she'd hide a gun somewhere if Brian told her to, and the soap box would be a logical spot for her. But I think the gun was a big shock to both of them."

"Their surprise could have just been an act," Mac pointed out.

"Would Brian have told them to go ahead and search if he knew the gun was hidden there in the house?"

"He could have thought he'd hidden it so well they'd never find it. Another preemptive strike because he figured they were going to search no matter what he said," Mac said. "What do you think about his claim that someone planted the gun there?"

"Who could have gotten inside to plant it? Kathy keeps the outside door locked even when she's right there at home."

"A biker with a criminal past might know how to pick a lock and get inside."

Yes indeedy. But if Ric Echol knew how to pick a lock, would he have gotten himself sent to prison for blowing up the back side of a warehouse to get to a safe inside?

The uneasy thought occurred to me that Ric Echol might have greater success finding us than we'd had finding him. Hopefully, he didn't have a big supply of leftover explosives on hand.

***

The next morning we were outside doing more cleanup work, Mac being careful of the knee that was still giving him occasional twinges, when a car drove in beside Sheila's house. A stocky man got out and went to her door. He received no answer to his knock, of course, and he drove on back to where we were working.

"Mrs. Weekson is away for a few days," Mac said when the man got out of the car. BoBandy ran up to sniff him. Koop was off hunting in the grass. He isn't much for eating what he catches, but he likes to bring us gifts. "We're looking after the place for her, but her garage sale won't be open today."

"Actually, I'm looking for an Ivy MacPherson." The man gave me a speculative look. I didn't jump to identify myself to

224

an unknown visitor.

Up close, he wasn't just stocky; he was chubby. He also had a few strands of hair in a careful comb-over on his otherwise balding head. A nice suit. Identification dawned. He couldn't be, but—

"You drove all the way out here from Missouri?" I gasped. Or maybe it was a squeak.

"Actually, I flew to San Francisco and drove up from there in a rental car." He motioned to the midsize Ford behind him. "I stayed in Eureka last night. I can see you know who I am."

"Private Investigator Megalthorpe." I couldn't tell if there was a gun in a shoulder holster under that nice suit, but now I did recognize that melodious voice.

"Exactly."

"But how did you know—" The return address on the rock we'd sent him, of course.

"I believe I mentioned I was willing to come out here—?" True. But we hadn't expected him to show up in our driveway unannounced. "And the matter did seem rather urgent once the lab notified me of what they'd found. Could we sit somewhere and talk about the rock?"

We invited him to our upstairs residence. He got a briefcase out of the car and brought it along. I offered coffee, specifying that it was instant, and he accepted. He didn't get right to the point, which I presumed was PI technique. He chatted about seeing storm damage and inquired if such storms were common in the area and how long we'd lived here. Mac didn't elaborate on our living arrangements or mention the motorhome, just said, "Not long."

I heard Mac's impatience, which was how I felt. *Get on with it, Mr. Private Investigator.*

Megalthorpe mentioned that he and his wife usually vacationed in Florida, but they might have to try a vacation here sometime. "Beautiful area." Finally he got down to the point of this visit. "About that rock you sent me. Might I inquire how you acquired it?"

"Why don't you just tell us if the rock showed any fingerprints. Presumably it did, or you wouldn't be here," Mac said.

"Yes. Well. I took the rock to a reputable lab in the area. Getting fingerprints off rock surface isn't easy and can't always be done. But they did indeed get fingerprints off your rock. I don't know what name he's using now, but the fingerprints are those of Andrew Higman."

He made the statement so casually that it took a moment for the information to sink in. When it did, I was stunned and yet not really surprised, if that's a possible combination.

"Kathy's . . . Genevieve's dead husband," I said.

"Not so dead, apparently," Megalthorpe pointed out. "But *someone* is definitely dead. Mrs. Higman had a body cremated."

"What did she do with the ashes?" I asked.

"Unknown."

"How did they have Higman's fingerprints to compare with the fingerprints on the rock?" Mac asked.

"How about if I start from the beginning with what I know? In trying to find what became of John Anderson, my client's uncle, I've done considerable research on the Higmans."

We both nodded. Now I really wished we had some cookies.

"Genevieve, whose last name was Smith before she married Andrew Higman, was a bookkeeper for many years. She never married in those younger years and spent several years caring for her mother in her mother's final years. She received a considerable insurance payoff when her mother passed away. Not long afterward she married Andrew Higman."

Megalthorpe didn't spell out a connection between the insurance money and the marriage, but he obviously thought there was one. Older woman, anxious not to drift into her later years still single; devious man, willing to marry for available money. And, since then, a woman willing to do almost anything to hold onto the husband she'd snagged?

"Did you find out anything about how Genevieve and Andrew met?"

"No, I can't say that I did." Megalthorpe sounded regretful.

"But you investigated Andrew Higman's past?"

"Yes indeed. An interesting, if somewhat checkered, past. Mr. Higman first made a considerable amount of money selling a large parcel of commercial real estate in New Jersey that he inherited from his father. He spent it, as the saying goes, like a drunken sailor, and rather quickly lost the remainder of the money in another real estate deal. His wife at the time divorced him. He was then involved in several get-rich-quick schemes where it was difficult to tell if he was the con man or the man being conned. At one time he was caught in the middle of a mining stock fraud, for which he served time."

"And his fingerprints went on record," Mac said.

"Right. That was before he and Genevieve got together. After their marriage, the Higmans invested Mrs. Higman's insurance money in a soft drink business in Alabama and lost it all. At some time in there, Mr. Higman developed a heart problem and was under a doctor's care at the time they rented a small home in an area where you, Mrs. MacPherson, formerly lived. But Mrs. Higman, perhaps cognizant of the payoff she'd received when her mother died, had taken out a rather large insurance policy on her husband soon after their marriage."

"Before he developed heart problems," Mac suggested.

"Yes. And she, rather fiercely I'd say, managed to hold onto the policy through the ups and downs of their financial situation." Megalthorpe paused and cleared his throat. "I am, I should advise you, now working with the insurance company on this case."

"An insurance company willing to finance a trip out here?"

227

"Well, yes. But what I have to say from here on is not proven fact. Merely my educated speculation on the matter." He lifted his eyebrows in a questioning gesture to make sure we understood that. He hadn't, I noted, mastered that difficult one-eyebrow-raised technique. Or maybe it's a genetic trait, although I think grandniece Sandy may have it and no one else in the family does.

Mac and I both nodded.

"I believe the Higmans, aware of the troublesome fact that even though Mr. Higman had heart problems and they couldn't collect on his insurance unless he actually died, conceived a plan to make it possible to collect without Mr. Higman actually having to go through the unpleasant process of dying."

"They moved to what was for them a new city in a new state, and they made sure everyone knew Mr. Higman had heart trouble," I said as details scrolled through my mind. "Mr. Higman managed to find a male patient in an adult care home, a man with heart trouble and dementia. He befriended this man and eventually took him to his home where Mrs. Higman passed him off as her husband, who had become bedridden. Apparently, because they were new in the area, also doing this successfully with a doctor who had never met the real Andrew Higman. So, when this man—"

"John Anderson, I believe," Megalthorpe put in.

"Then when this man died, he died as Andrew Higman, not John Anderson."

"Exactly. And Widow Higman collected on Andrew Higman's insurance. She did, of course, by then have a legitimate death certificate with that name on it."

"That's not an easy scheme to pull off," Mac said skeptically.

"True. But it appears they did pull it off. Mr. Higman, or, rather, the man whom Mrs. Higman was passing off as her husband, had a heart attack and died in the ambulance on the way to the hospital. With his heart problems already on record, there was no autopsy, and his death certificate shows acute myocardial infarction as cause of death."

The same death certificate grandniece Sandy had located for an Andrew Higman.

"Wouldn't x-rays or other medical records look different for two different men?" Mac questioned.

"All I can think is that the Higmans somehow managed to keep incriminating earlier records away from the new doctor."

"But now, with fingerprints proving Andrew Higman is still alive, the insurance company is unhappy that they paid off on a death that wasn't really the death of their insured," Mac said.

"Yes, that's their suspicion. Although there is another serious matter involved here."

"Andrew Higman's—or, more accurately, John Anderson's—death," I said. "Was it a natural death, and the Higmans just waited until it happened, or did they tire of waiting for him to die and hurry it along?"

Megalthorpe nodded. "There are various substances that might induce a heart attack, particularly in a man who already has heart trouble. And, with a man already known to have heart trouble, there'd be no suspicion that it wasn't a natural heart attack. As I said, there was no autopsy. The fact that Mrs. Higman had him cremated quickly isn't necessarily suspicious, of course. Many cremations are done quickly. But she *did* have it done quickly, and cremation would do away with the body ever being autopsied or tested for any substance he may have been given. She then, for all practical purposes, disappeared."

"She and the still-alive, real Andrew Higman took the money and ran," Mac said.

"With new identities," Megalthorpe agreed. Identities which, at this point, he still didn't know.

I tied all this in with the limited information Kathy had

given about her past with Brian. An indefinite marriage date. Perhaps Brian had said they need not do it again because they were already married, even if their names were different. Although they'd had a honeymoon in Tahiti. On insurance money from Brian's "death"? Money that had also been used to purchase a Porsche? But since then they'd apparently lost most or all of that money in another of Brian's get-rich-quick schemes and had been living in the little travel trailer when they arrived at the dinosaur park. I thought of that array of pills on Kathy's kitchen counter. Brian's pills for a heart condition, I was now reasonably certain. And now Brian, apparently working with Renée, had some new scheme going with the Kate's Kabins and the dinosaur park properties. Except Renée was dead, and he may have killed her . . .

My head reeled with the effort of trying to keep everyone straight in this complicated situation. A dead Andrew Higman and a live Brian Morrison. Genevieve Higman back in Missouri and the Kathy Morrison of now.

Mac had another thought.

"But isn't it rather difficult to change identities and get all the paperwork necessary for a new life? Would Br—I mean Andrew, be able to do that?"

"From what I understand, buying a new identity isn't all that difficult if you have the right connections, which Andrew Higman probably did, given his criminal record. I think the going rate is about three thousand dollars, and for that you get a phony birth certificate and everything else you need. Of course, simply having papers for a new identity isn't infallible. It takes some diligence to pull it off, but Mr. and Mrs. Higman seem to have been successful at living quiet, inconspicuous lives under the new identity in this area."

Except Magnolia came along and identified inconspicuous Kathy Morrison as Genevieve Higman. And now there was also the matter of a dead woman in a burned cabin and an

230

exploded Porsche. Which were hardly inconspicuous.

"What you want from us, then, is the name the Higmans are currently using," Mac said. "And exactly where they can be found."

"That's why I'm here, yes."

"It doesn't sound as if there's any way to prove murder in the death of John Anderson," I offered. "The heart attack may, in fact, have been quite natural."

Although the thought also occurred to me that I might not be so eager to eat Kathy's cookies after this.

"That's true. I was at more or less of a dead end and about to close the case as unsuccessful when I received your call. Now I believe we can at least prove insurance fraud because Andrew Higman is definitely alive and Mrs. Higman collected on the insurance policy for his death. Unless you somehow managed to acquire the fingerprints of a dead man?" Megalthorpe's question was not without facetiousness. He was getting a bit impatient with us.

"We need a little time to talk this over," Mac said smoothly.

"Yes, of course. I understand." Then, with a note of alarm, he added, "You're not thinking of going to the Higmans and discussing this with them, are you?"

"Are you planning to go to the local law enforcement authorities and discuss this with them?" I asked.

"I believe it would be more appropriate to start with the authorities in the area where the crime—or crimes—were committed, although we'll need the cooperation of local authorities here, of course. Although I am concerned that the Higmans may disappear again and probably do a better job of it this time if they know the authorities are definitely after them now. But I can't do much if I don't know the names they're using now."

I doubted that. He was, after all, a private investigator, quite a good one I thought, and he had the area pinned down now.

231

I figured he'd guessed we were staying not far from where the Higmans lived. I tried to think back and remember if I'd given him any clues when I first talked to him on the phone or if we'd said anything today.

"I do have a photo, if you're interested," he added.

"I thought you didn't have a photo. You were asking Franny if she had any photos."

"That's true. What I have is an old newspaper photo. I thought a current and clearer photo might be helpful. Would you like to see what I have?"

Megalthorpe opened his briefcase and drew out a photocopy of a newspaper photograph of a man with his hands cuffed behind him. He was considerably younger than the Brian Morrison we knew. Beardless. At least fifty pounds lighter. Lean, dark-haired, and good looking. The caption identified him as Andrew Higman, headed for incarceration after conviction on the stock fraud scheme. Megalthorpe also produced a photocopy of a driver's license for Andrew Higman, also with a photo, again beardless. A private investigator has resources that grandniece Sandy doesn't have.

Would I have identified Brian Morrison as the man in the photos if I didn't already know fingerprints identified them as the same person? I doubted it.

Megalthorpe then produced a copy of a driver's license for Genevieve Higman. Her hair was different then, a mousy brownish color, a mousy style. But I could recognize the Kathy Morrison of now in it.

"As I've mentioned before, I am authorized to offer remuneration for the current name and whereabouts of both Mr. and Mrs. Higman." The lifted eyebrows again.

"Mr. Megalthorpe, we are not interested in remuneration," Mac said firmly.

The private investigator's sharp look swiveled between us. "But I think you are interested in justice. Mr. and Mrs. Higman

232

have definitely committed insurance fraud and may have committed murder."

So why weren't we rushing to give Megalthorpe the information he wanted? Not because we doubted his information was correct. Not because we doubted Megalthorpe himself as a private investigator. But there was the matter of Renée Echol's death. And an explosion of a Porsche. With this new information, it seemed rather more likely the Morrisons were deeply involved in both.

"Hardishan?" I whispered to Mac, and he nodded.

"You'll be around for a few days?" Mac asked the private investigator.

"I plan to be, yes."

"Leave us your cell phone number and we'll be in touch."

"When?"

"At the appropriate time."

Chapter 20

IVY

Before he left, Megalthorpe also gave us the name of the motel where he was staying in Eureka. He asked about a good place to eat there and we recommended the Hideaway. After he left we discussed the situation briefly, and then Mac tried to call Deputy Hardishan. The woman on the phone at the sheriff's office said he was unavailable at this time and would we like to talk to someone else?

We looked at each other and, with the silent communication that is so nice when you're comfortably married, agreed on no. We'd had our rough spots with Hardishan, but we felt we could trust him. We needed advice on whether to give Megalthorpe full information about Brian's and Kathy's names and whereabouts or give the information to the local sheriff's department and let them work with law enforcement in Missouri.

Mac left our names and number and asked that Deputy Hardishan call or come see us, that it wasn't an emergency, but we had a matter we needed to discuss with him as soon as possible. Mac called the repair shop and found, not unexpectedly, that our motorhome wasn't ready yet. We took BoBandy for a walk before dark and then spent the evening watching an old Steve Martin movie on DVD, one of us occasionally coming up with a comment or question about Kathy or Brian. I really wished we had a cookie to go with the hot chocolate I made to accompany our Bible study before bed.

The next morning we'd just finished breakfast when we heard a car pull up beside the garage. If Sheila were here, this would be a garage sale day. I could just ignore the potential customer but, peering out the window, I saw what looked like the sad woman from whom I'd bought the baby clothes. I went down to open the side door and tell her I could help with a few dollars without her having to sell any more of her meager possessions.

It wasn't her, however. This woman was also thin and about the same age, but she was better dressed and driving a newer car. She said she'd seen a frilly lamp here earlier and wanted to look at it again. I told her the garage sale wasn't really open, but I glanced around and spotted a frilly lamp with an eleven-dollar price tag on it. The woman stepped inside and offered eight. It really was a gosh-awful lamp, and Sheila always bargained on prices, so we haggled a bit and she finally paid ten dollars. I put the money in a drawer for Sheila, and I felt rather pleased with myself. Maybe being a yard sale haggler was my real calling in life?

I did not, however, intend to actually open Sheila's garage for business even if this was Saturday, and when Mac came downstairs we decided to take the cans of peaches we'd found in the pickup over to Duke. Just as we were going out the door, a motorcycle roared up beside the garage. I can't tell one motorcycle from another except by color and sometimes size, but Mac can. His forehead creased in a frown, and my intuition . . . a suddenly screamin' intuition . . . kicked into gear.

"Is that a Harley Screamin' Eagle?" I whispered.

"I think so."

"Let's just close the door and—"

Too late. The motorcycle rider had spotted us. A big man, black motorcycle jacket, heavy black boots, and a black helmet that gave him a vaguely Darth Vader look. He took off the helmet and hung it on a handlebar. Tangled dark hair shot with a few streaks of steel gray, same with the beard. Sharp blue eyes. Good-looking, in a tough, mess-with-me-and-you'll-be-sorry kind of way. My heart and stomach did an uneasy square dance.

Had Ric Echols somehow found us?

I tensed, waiting for hostile questions. *What were you two doing asking nosy questions about me all over McKinleyville?* And when we had no satisfactory answers to that question—

His heavy eyebrows drew together as he looked at us. With recognition? Surely not. He may have heard we were looking for him at the bars and taverns, but we hadn't actually encountered him. Did we fit some generic description of an older couple in a Toyota pickup looking for him? Oh, yes. But he couldn't see the pickup. Blessedly, it was out of sight on the back side of the garage. We'd parked it there because Mac had been planning to wash it again, and the closest faucet was back there.

"Garage sale open today?" the biker finally asked. The question didn't sound particularly friendly, but neither did it sound like a trick to trap older folks.

"No, Mrs. Weekson isn't here today," Mac said. "And we were just—"

I know Mac had started to say *just leaving,* but if we got in the pickup and drove off, Ric would see it and do a flash-bam *Bingo!*

"Just going back upstairs," I interrupted hastily.

"I'll be back."

Warning? Promise? Threat? Any one of those was enough to make me feel a tap dance of dinosaur toes up my back.

He turned and headed back to the bike. It was also black, decorated with a flame-shooting dragon that I could recognize if I saw it again. But then I had to question myself for speed-labeling him Ric Echol. He *looked* menacing, but he wasn't *doing* anything menacing. He could be someone else entirely. Maybe simply a nice biker with a fashion sense hung up on basic black.

But then he gave us another speculative look as if again thinking we might be the people he was looking for. Well, maybe not specifically looking for today, because he was apparently on a garage sale run at the moment, but—

An SUV pulled into the driveway and parked near the door of Sheila's double-wide. Sheila's SUV. *Great timing, Sheila! Welcome home! We're so glad to see you.*

I called to her when she stepped out of the SUV. "Hey, Sheila!"

She walked toward us. "Were you looking for my garage sale?" she said to the biker. "It's usually open on Saturdays, but I've been away, and it won't be open today."

"I just came out to pick up something for a buddy. Golden Temple." He lifted those heavy eyebrows questioningly. Sheila wasn't saying anything, and he added, "Golden Temple incense? It soothes his bad back."

Sheila gave him an inspection deep enough to x-ray his gall bladder. "I'm sorry, but Golden Temple is no longer available."

"No longer available?" Even a tough, bearded biker can look dismayed, and this one did. "You mean just not available today or *permanently* not available?"

"Permanently not available."

Mr. Hot-Tempered Guy in a Lexus was certainly going to be unhappy about that. But why did I suddenly feel as if Sheila and biker guy were speaking some other language? Sheila didn't seem inclined to try to sell him a different scent and there were lots of incense sticks in that big cup in the garage.

"Who did you say your buddy is?" Sheila sounded wary.

"I didn't say, but it's Bowser. Short guy." He held a hand at chin height. "Rides a Harley Low Rider."

Did that mean something to Sheila? It didn't to me, of course. Bowser sounded like an innocent enough name, as if he were a friendly, shaggy-dog type of guy. But maybe Bowser in this unfamiliar language meant something different too.

"The Bowser who works at the plant nursery near the airport?"

"Yeah, he fills in there once in a while."

"Okay, you tell Bowser that Golden Temple isn't available. Permanently."

"Because I came in place of Bowser, is that it?" The biker's tone went surly, and the question sounded like an accusation.

Sheila offered no explanation, just a glance at me and a sharp repeat of her earlier statement. "Golden Temple is no longer available. Permanently."

Ric—if he was Ric—momentarily looked as if he might contest that statement with a big fist, but he finally slammed the helmet on his head and threw a leg over his bike. It was facing toward the pasture, so he had to make a tight circle to head back out to the road. And in making that little circle he went a few feet beyond the garage. Where our Toyota pickup was in full view.

I clutched Mac's hand and dragged him inside, slamming the door behind us. Mac *oofed* and grabbed his knee. He'd been having trouble with it ever since that day at the dinosaur park when the broken branch dumped him on the ground.

"I'm sorry! I didn't mean to—"

Mac waved off my apology. "What's he doing now?"

I peered through the small window draped with a towel. I thought for a moment the guy was going to jump off the bike and come right through the door after us. But, with Sheila standing there looking at him, he apparently decided against that approach and roared down the driveway to the road. Even inside the garage, we could hear the bike skid around the corner and then accelerate to what sounded like supersonic speed as he headed for the highway back to town.

Would he come back with a gun . . . maybe the gun with which he'd killed Renée? No, the gun that had killed Renée was the one found in the soap box in Kathy and Brian's laundry room. Even if test results hadn't come back yet, I was sure of it. That was why it had been planted there, to incriminate Brian.

Planted by Ric?

I determinedly stopped the mental babble and opened the door cautiously. Sheila was still standing there, her back to us as she listened to the bike in the distance.

"That Golden Temple incense seems really popular," I said.

"Yeah. Well, I wouldn't have sold him any even if I had enough to sell. He looked kind of phony to me."

Phony? A phony *biker*? Meaning she thought he was really a mild-mannered shoe salesman just pretending to be a bad-boy biker? Or was she thinking something different, such as undercover, as in undercover cop? But surely a garage sale business selling a few knickknacks and the occasional pocketknife or frilly lamp wasn't enough to warrant investigation by an undercover cop.

"Ric hasn't been here with his Bowser buddy before?" I asked. I was surprised at his coming here, given the hostilities between Sheila and Renée. From what Ron Sweeney had said, there had still been something going on between Ric and his ex-wife, so it seemed unlikely Ric and Sheila were friendly enough even for garage sale haggling. Of course, maybe this wasn't Ric. Or maybe he hadn't known it was Sheila his buddy had been buying Golden Temple from. I was babbling to myself again.

My question did bring a sharp turn from Sheila. "*Ric?*"

"Wasn't that Ric Echol, Renée's ex-husband?"

Sheila's mouth did a startled drop and something like realization dawned in her widened eyes. Her gaze shot back to the road.

"So that's how——" Then she shook her head, dismissing the biker. "I have no idea who that was. I heard Renée's ex was in the area, but he came sometime after our friendship went kaput." Then, even with Renée dead, she couldn't avoid a dig at her ex-friend. "Although that guy looked like the kind of lowlife she'd have been married to."

I changed the subject. "By the way, I sold that ruffled lamp in your garage sale things for ten dollars. I hope that's okay. The money is in the drawer."

Sheila looked delighted. "You got ten bucks for that ugly old thing? Great! Maybe I'll have to hire you on garage sale days."

"Did you have a good trip?" I asked.

"It was okay. I need to get my stuff unpacked. I want to go over to Duke's later and fix him a good dinner. He probably hasn't had one since I've been gone. I brought some T-bone steaks in an ice chest."

I didn't mention that I doubted Duke had been underfed. He'd bought a good supply of groceries when we went to town, and he'd really enjoyed that great burger at Billie's place. "Did you know that several deputies from the sheriff's department came out and searched Kathy and Brian's place a couple days ago?"

"Really? Duke didn't mention that when I talked to him on the phone. Did they arrest Brian?"

"They found a gun in their laundry room, but they didn't arrest him." I had no intention of yet telling her the other startling information we'd learned from Megalthorpe about Brian and Kathy.

"Why not? If they've got the gun that—" She gave a shrug. "Well, I suppose they have to run tests on it to prove it's the gun that killed Renée."

"Probably."

"But you'd think, after the explosion and now the gun that they'd do *something* about Brian instead of just standing around with their hands in their pockets. I wasn't exactly fond of Renée, as you know, but I do think her killer should be brought to justice. Have they figured out yet that Brian blew up the Porsche himself?"

"We haven't heard anything more. Well, we were on our

way over to Duke's to return some canned peaches he left in the pickup, so—"

"If you don't mind waiting until later, we could all have dinner together. I have plenty of steak."

Sounded good to me. But— "You don't mind our being there at your . . . reunion dinner?"

"It's not like I've been gone for months. C'mon," she urged. "We never did get to have dinner together that first time we planned to."

I looked at Mac, who so far hadn't participated in this conversation. "Sure. Sounds great," he said.

We went back upstairs, where we had a nice surprise. The shop called. Our motorhome was repaired and ready to go! We immediately drove to the shop. Mac climbed up on top to inspect the outside roof, and we both scrutinized the inside. A great job! Mac drove the motorhome, and I followed in the pickup back to our place at Sheila's. He temporarily parked beside the garage, and we got out and inspected everything again. It almost felt like a reunion with a long-lost friend.

By then, however, Mac's knee pain had escalated to a full-time ache, so we decided to delay moving back into the motorhome. We'd stay in the over-the-garage room one more night. He took some ibuprofen, and I put a pillow under his leg on the recliner. I started to run over to tell Sheila we wouldn't be going to dinner at Duke's after all, but Mac stopped me.

"You go and enjoy a good steak. I'll probably sleep most of the time you're gone anyway." Ibuprofen did tend to make him sleepy. "If I get hungry I'll eat some of that leftover meatloaf."

I fixed a plate with meatloaf and leftover mashed potatoes and carrots that he could just pop in the microwave. I felt a bit guilty leaving him home alone, but sleep was probably better for his knee than sitting cramped up in Duke's little dinette. I also have to admit I was looking forward to a T-bone. Mac was

241

asleep, with both BoBandy and Koop snuggled up beside him on the recliner, by the time I grabbed my jacket and cell phone and Sheila and I headed over to Duke's in her SUV.

It was almost dark by then, though a full moon was coming up over the hills to the east, a few clouds turning the sky into a moonscape that made me wish I had some artistic talent and could paint it. *Nice going, Lord!* He provides these tidbits of beauty all the time, but we're mostly too busy to notice.

We had a little more information to give to Deputy Hardishan about Ric Echol now, but he still hadn't called. We also, wanting to talk to Hardishan first, hadn't called Megalthorpe yet. I had the cans of peaches in a bag to return to Duke; Sheila had the ice chest in the back seat. Tonight, she was wearing a long black sweater over black leggings. No hat tonight, but a turquoise clip held her hair back, a silver concha belt cinched her waist, and a scarf decorated with brilliant zigzags of color swirled around her neck. Lots of pizzazz that made me feel even more dumpy than usual in my sweatpants and shirt. Though they were purple.

At Duke's trailer, we carried our supplies inside. Duke hadn't missed the peaches, but he was glad to see them. Sheila gave him a hug and he hugged her back, but he was looking over her shoulder at the ice chest, and I had the feeling he was more interested in the steaks than in the fact that she was home. His right knee was giving him trouble tonight. He kept raising his leg and shaking it as if trying to loosen a stiffness in the knee.

Sheila also noticed the knee lifting. "Old men and their knees," she grumbled, but it was an affectionate grumble. I'd told her about Mac's recently acquired knee trouble, though not how he'd acquired it. "Do you still have your pain pills?" she asked Duke.

"No, I used them all up. You got some more with you?"

"I'll bring them over tomorrow."

242

She also had a surprise gift for him tonight. A new cell phone. "The number's different than your old one, but it's all activated and ready to go. All you have to do is start using it."

She confiscated his old phone, ceremoniously gave it a burial in the trash can, and took a few minutes showing him details on working the new one. He experimented by punching in random numbers until someone actually answered.

I don't know who it was, but Duke said, "This is Ghost Goat Space Adventures. Are you interested in reserving a space ride for Mars next year? Ten percent off for early booking."

I've often heard how gullible people are, but apparently this one wasn't *that* gullible because the voice said, "Sure. Sounds great! And I can give *you* an awesome deal on buying a private island in the Bahamas."

Duke just grinned and punched the Off button.

I shook my head and grinned back.

Sheila used the broiler in Duke's little oven to do the steaks. I made a salad and she did quick baked potatoes in the microwave. She'd brought chopped mangos for dessert. "Kathy talks about eating healthy, but she's always feeding him those cookies that are enough to put a dinosaur on a sugar high," she whispered to me as she put the mangos in the refrigerator until we were ready for them. I was sorry Mac would miss the dessert. He loves mangos.

I offered the blessing, not something either Sheila or Duke ever did, I was sure, but they bowed their heads, and Duke said a hearty *Amen* before he picked up his fork. The steaks were tender and juicy, and Sheila entertained us with stories about quirky people she'd met on her visit to Vegas.

"And then there was my daughter. Sometimes I wonder about her." Eye roll. "Would you believe I found a *paper clip* in the vegetable soup she made?"

I knew the daughter had three kids, a job, and a husband who apparently thought sitting around and drinking beer was an acceptable occupation. I was surprised the daughter had the time or energy to make soup, with or without paper clips.

My next thought was that maybe Sheila should have been a little more helpful and made soup herself. Then she wanted to know all about the search of Kathy and Brian's place. I tried to give her an abbreviated account, by now wanting to get back to Mac, but she kept asking questions. Did the officers in the search group make any comments about what they found? Did they say why they'd decided to search Brian and Kathy's place? If Brian claimed it wasn't his gun, how did he explain it being in their laundry room?

"He said someone must have planted it there."

"Sounds like something he'd say," Sheila scoffed. "Who did he try to make them think did it?"

She was cutting the last of the meat off the bone for Duke when she asked the question. It sounded like a casual question; she was absorbed with the steak cutting. And yet at that moment a memory rose in my mind like the triceratops in the parking lot unexpectedly roaring to life.

That day when Mac was going over the dinosaur park fence to retrieve the shovel with Brian's fingerprints on it. Sheila doing something with the knob or lock on Brian and Kathy's door when they weren't home. Trying to get inside to look for evidence, I'd thought at the time.

I looked at the key ring on a hook beside the holstered gun at Duke's door. Keys galore, keys past and present. A key to Brian and Kathy's door, which had once been Duke's home, was surely among them.

Sheila hadn't been trying to get inside to look for evidence Brian had killed Renée. She was locking the door after she'd already been inside *planting* evidence.

And if she had evidence to plant, the gun that killed Renée, that meant—

My mind reeled as facts rearranged and fell into place in my mind. There were gaps. Why had she done it? How had she gotten Renée to go out to the old cabins? Where had she gotten a gun?

That last question answered itself. Her garage sales. She bought or traded items as well as sold, an underground highway of items that might be legitimate, such as baby clothes or fishing gear. Or maybe less legitimate. Like guns.

I looked at Sheila. She was looking back at me, and I was aware of a sudden graveyard silence. Her hands were still on the knife with which she was cutting the steak.

"Awesome steak!" I said enthusiastically. "And cooked just right. Sheila, you're a great cook!"

"Sure is," Duke agreed, and I realized he hadn't a clue that something ominous had just happened between Sheila and me.

Sheila, however, now that the moment was past, also acted as if nothing had happened. "I have more steaks in the freezer at home. We'll have to do this again when Mac can be here," she said warmly.

My mind raced. Even if she was acting innocent, she knew that I now knew what she'd done. Somehow, without revealing her real identity, she'd tipped off the sheriff's department that the gun—the murder weapon she'd put there—was in Brian and Kathy's place, and she'd done it adroitly enough, probably while she was on the road to Vegas, that they were able to use the information to get a search warrant.

Get away from her, my mind yelped at me. *Now!*

"It's such a nice evening with the moonlight and all, I think I'll just walk home tonight," I declared with manufactured brightness.

And as soon as I got away from the trailer, I'd call—who?— 911? Was telling 911 that I knew who'd planted a murder gun in Brian Morrison's laundry room an emergency? After what had passed between us, it would definitely be an emergency if Sheila caught up with me on my moonlight hike.

245

Heavy woods lined the road all the way between the dinosaur park and home, woods that might contain anything from stray muggers bedding down for the night to wandering ghost goats, but those woods could also provide a hiding place if I needed it. I slid out of the little dinette and stood up.

But Duke said, "You don't want to be out there walking in the dark. Used to be it was safe around here no matter the time of day or night. But I don't think that's so anymore."

"That's true," Sheila said. "Sit down and have some of the mango I brought for dessert. I'll drive you home. We can take some mango to Mac too."

She sounded so calm, so totally nonthreatening. I had a momentary twinge of doubt. Had I read something into that brief moment that passed between us that wasn't really there? Maybe. But I settled for that old adage, *Better safe than sorry.*

"I'm really too full for mango." I patted my stomach. "It was a wonderful dinner, Sheila, and there's no need for you to interrupt your evening for me. I can walk."

"Nonsense. It's much too far for you to walk. I need to run back to the house and get some pain pills for Duke anyway. I don't like to see his knee hurting him like it is tonight."

But if I got in the SUV with Sheila, she could take me . . . where? Anywhere. And do what with me? If she could use a gun on a former friend and plant that gun to throw blame on someone else—

Do not get in the car with her.

"Really, I'll enjoy the walk. And I need the exercise after that big dinner." I patted my stomach again.

"Well, okay, if you really want to."

Her easy capitulation surprised me. It might emphasize that I was wrong about her. Or it might merely emphasize that she was a clever schemer with some other nefarious plan in mind. The earlier tap dance of dinosaur toes escalated to an ominous stomp. I hadn't brought a purse, but I picked up my jacket, felt the reassuring weight of my cell phone in the pocket, and pretended nonchalance as I sauntered the four steps to the door. Once outside, I dropped the pretense and made a headlong dash for escape. I could run to Brian and Kathy for help. I'd gotten to the edge of the trees around Duke's trailer when the door opened behind me.

"Hey, wait up," Sheila called. "You forgot the carton of mango chunks for Mac." She was already headed down the ramp toward me.

Another moment of doubt. Was I totally wrong about Sheila's involvement in Renée's murder and in planting the gun to make Brian look guilty? My notoriously busy imagination in overdrive? Here she was, remembering that Mac was home alone with a bad knee, thoughtfully sending him nice mango chunks, and I was acting as if the carton she was holding out to me might hold bat tongues in arsenic.

The plastic carton was in her left hand. I warily reached out and took it. And then, before I could even say thanks, she pulled her right hand out from behind her.

A holster. Not empty.

"Where'd you get that?" I asked. As if that were relevant at the moment. What was relevant was that it took her about two seconds to yank the gun out of the holster—Quick Draw Sheila—and point it at me. She let the holster fall to the ground.

"Duke keeps his gun right by the door, as I'm sure you've noticed. I told him I heard something outside and better check since you were out here all alone."

I decided all I could do was play dumb. Dumb was what I felt anyway. I'd earlier had some minor suspicions about Sheila, but I'd gotten hung up on suspicions about both Brian and Ric Echol. Why hadn't this great epiphany about Sheila hit me earlier? Before I was looking down the barrel of a gun.

"I appreciate your concern." I clutched the carton of mango

chunks. "Do you hear anything now?"

She cocked her head to listen. Or pretended to. "No, I don't think so."

I didn't hear anything either. Just a big silence of me and Sheila alone out here in the night. A gun doesn't make any noise until it's actually shot, but my ears rang with projection of a lethal boom. In spite of nervous sweat puddling in my armpits, I held to my pretense that this was a normal, friendly situation.

"Thanks again for a lovely dinner." I lifted the plastic carton. "And the mango for Mac. Well, I'd better get started. Perhaps we'll see you in church tomorrow."

"I'll walk a ways with you. There are all kinds of unexpected dangers in the night, you know. Ghost goats. Cougars. Dinosaurs. The gun may come in handy."

Yeah, right. But I knew I was looking straight at the biggest danger in this night. Had she smiled at Renée the same way she was smiling at me now? "That's very considerate of you, but there's no need for you to—"

Sheila's pretended concern for me took an impatient nosedive. "C'mon, get walking. Straight ahead to the gate." She motioned with the gun.

Why go to the gate? It was padlocked shut, and she didn't have a key—

But, of course, she did have a key. At the gate, under the dim glow of the lone yard light in the parking lot, she opened her left hand and there, like some magician's trick, was Duke's loaded key ring. I had a moment's hope. It would take two hands to get the padlock open. She'd have to set the gun down—

No, she didn't. With alarming dexterity, she managed to keep the gun pointed at me with her right hand, maneuver the padlock up tight against one of the gate posts with her hip, and then ram the key into the lock. The padlock opened, and she

248

yanked the chain free with her left hand. Another yank on the gate and it swung with an *open sesame* smoothness.

I looked around for a knight in shining armor, but all I saw was the gloomy triceratops with a toe missing.

I made another pretense at not understanding what was going on. I wrapped my arms around myself. "Brrr. It's really chilly out here. Don't you want to go back and get a jacket?" And give me time to do a disappearing act.

"I'm fine."

"There's a lot of debris from the windstorm on the trail. I don't think it's a good time for a walk in the park."

"Walk," she said.

"You look as if you know how to use a gun," I said in the most conversational tone I could manage. "That's very reassuring, out here among the ghost goats and cougars and all. Though I'm not sure how effective bullets would be on ghost goats."

Did my laugh sound as phony to her as it did to me? Apparently it did, because what she said was, "Cut the small talk, Ivy. And stop dragging your feet. *Move.*"

She closed the gate behind us, but she left the key ring dangling from the padlock. Because she didn't want to carry it, I supposed. She needed both hands for other things.

We started up the pathway. Moonlight and the yard light blotched the trail with light and shadows. As I'd pointed out, the trail was still littered with debris from the windstorm. Broken branches, twigs, vines, dead leaves. The dinosaurs looked different in the moonlight, less like deteriorating statues and more like predatory monsters poised for attack.

"You had this all planned when you invited us to dinner?" I asked. The condemned prisoner gets a last meal. And it was, I had to admit, a great meal.

"Of course not. I had no idea until the middle of dinner, when you were looking at Duke's keys, that you'd figured it out." She stepped over a fallen branch. "It's kind of like shopping. Sometimes you see something you hadn't planned to buy but suddenly you realize you just have to have it. Like I now have to do this."

She was comparing killing me—because that's what she had in mind, no doubt about it—with *shopping*? I stumbled over a branch, almost losing the carton of mango chunks in my hand. *Lord, I'd really like a chance to give the mango to Mac. He's very fond of it.*

"You know, this isn't going to work," I said when I paused for breath on a steeper section of trail. "You can't just shoot me in cold blood and hope no one ever finds my body out here."

"Oh, I don't think—" She broke off and paused behind me on the pathway. "Although you could be right about the body being found. I figured it would take a lot longer than it did for someone to find Renée's body out there in the burned cabin."

"You'll never get away with it."

"Oh, I think I will. I'm getting away with it on Renée, and this will be even easier," she pointed out. She looked over at the tyrannosaurus rex nearby and tilted her head as she sketched a scenario. "Such a tragic accident. We'd decided on this walk in the moonlight and then I mistook you for a predatory animal. A cougar has been seen around here, you know. Or perhaps I thought you were a dangerous prowler sneaking around out here, maybe the same one who killed Renée. I'll have to decide which will work best."

She'd come up with both those ideas within the few minutes between when we were sitting at the table and now? A quick thinker. A deadly thinker. Could she make either of them work?

I hastily presented the first argument that came to mind. "You could be in for *years* of legal complications, maybe even *conviction*, for killing an unarmed LOL."

That stopped her for a moment. "LOL?" she repeated

"You know. Little Old Lady."

"A mistake is a mistake." I heard a mental shrug in the statement. "I'll get a good lawyer."

I took a different approach. "If you kill me, won't that mess up your plan to frame Brian by planting the gun in his laundry room? Maybe they'll figure out you planted it there because you were the one who killed Renée."

She didn't bother to deny she'd killed Renée or that she'd planted the gun. Which I knew did not bode well for the length of my future earthly existence.

"This won't change anything," she said confidently. "They're totally unrelated incidents. I'm just relieved that those dumb cops actually found the gun in Brian's place. I was afraid they might be too incompetent to do even that."

I didn't think the local deputies were either dumb or incompetent. But, unless they showed up in the next few minutes, I did think I could be dead before they got everything squared away.

"You blew up Brian's Porsche too?"

"Don't be ridiculous. I don't know how to blow up anything. He did that himself."

I didn't think so, but arguing with Sheila wasn't really getting me anywhere. I had to *do* something.

Lord, help me think!

A weapon. I needed a weapon, something I could use to incapacitate her long enough for escape. A fallen branch? She'd shoot me before I could lift it high enough to do any good. A rock, something bigger than the one with the fingerprints that we'd sent Megalthorpe? I surreptitiously looked around. Lots of rocks, but all I could see were either too small to be effective or so big I'd need Incredible Hulk muscles to lift them.

Well, in an emergency, you make do with what you have.

251

Chapter 21

IVY

I bent over, pretending to struggle to move another branch out of the way. I waited until Sheila was just a step behind me in the moonlight. Then I straightened, did a muscle blast with every cell in this LOL body, and swung the carton of mango chunks. Wham! I got her in the nose. The lid flew off and Sheila screeched. Mango chunks and juice splattered her face and hair, filled her nose, dribbled into her eyes, ran down her cheeks. I wanted to run, but I determinedly stepped in closer and used both hands to mango-rub everywhere I could reach. Slippery, juicy, goopy mango! Mash, squish, squash, rub-a-dub-dub! Nose, eyebrows, ears.

Sorry, Mac. There isn't going to be any mango left for you. But it's for a good cause.

Swish, swash, smear. Hey, a little mango can go a long way!

The gun clattered to the ground as Sheila swiped at her mango-ed eyes. It skidded into the dense foliage off the trail. I heard a splash as it plunged into the creek somewhere down below. Sheila threw her head back and forth and flailed her arms at me. I dodged flying mango and flapping arms.

I wanted to run back down the trail, but Sheila stood between me and the gate. One eye was still closed with mango, but the other was open now, and, even one-eyed, an angry, shrieking Sheila was a formidable adversary. She advanced on me, bigger, stronger, and younger—

I took the only direction I could go. Uphill. Sheila thundered after me. This is the woman who sometimes bicycles or even jogs all the way over to Kate's Kabins. I'm the LOL who enjoys a leisurely stroll with husband, dog, and cat. She'd catch up with me here in about two shakes of a ghost goat's tail.

I had to get off the trail, get in the woods. Hide!

I wish I could say I took the picket fence in a flying, adrenalin-fueled leap. What I did was make a flying leap, get my sweatpants hung up on the sharp point of a picket, and hear a big r-r-i-p when I crashed to the ground. My head hit a dead log. A stick poked me in the ribs. My ankle smashed into a rock. I shook my head, trying to clear the haze. Behind me I heard Sheila clambering over the fence and saying words she hadn't learned on her occasional forays into church.

The yard light didn't reach here in the undergrowth, but scattered moonlight showed she was now on my side of the fence. *What now, Lord?* Get up and run? With my head feeling as if it had just collided with a tombstone? A foot caught in blackberry vines stopped any immediate notion of fleeing. *Hide, Ivy, hide!* I clutched the ground as if it were an old friend and scooched deeper into the brush. This was a good time for full-force invisibility.

I held my breath as Sheila crashed through the woods past me. Yes, invisible.

Cell phone! Now!

I frantically grabbed the phone out of my pocket and pushed the On button. Call Mac? 911? I didn't get a chance to decide. In the dark shadows of a hillside woods, a turned-on cell phone screen gives off enough light to be seen from outer space.

Well, maybe that's exaggerating, but it gave enough light for Sheila to look back and spot my hiding place. She floundered toward me. I tried to slither away. Except slithering doesn't work when you're tangled in blackberry vines and windstorm debris. My leg hung up on something, and Sheila slammed a broken branch down on me. She hit my most vital point—the cell phone. It tumbled out of my hand.

I reached for it, but she took another whack. And another.

Then I realized she thought the lit-up phone was still in my hand, and I scooted the other direction, leaving her to attack the defenseless phone.

Better the phone than me.

I managed to get out of whacking distance, got to my knees, and stumbled at a crouch through the trees. I glanced back and saw that the cell phone light had gone out.

Okay, Lord, I've used up the mango chunks and the cell phone. What's left?

I eased to an upright position and listened, trying to pinpoint Sheila's whereabouts, but now all I heard was the silence of the night. No crashes, no curses, no ominous crunches of foot. Where was she? Uphill from me? Downhill? Ahead? Behind?

Okay, I knew what she was doing. She'd gone into statue mode. Silent, motionless as one of the dinosaurs, biding her time, waiting for me to make some giveaway move so she could pounce on me.

I could play that game too.

I froze, also motionless and silent, barely breathing. Except, you know what happens when you're trying to remain motionless and silent. Your left leg itches. Your skin crawls with the need to scratch it. Your stick-poked ribs ache. You need to shift position to relieve the pain. Your chest feels ready to explode with the need. And then—what else could happen? Why, you sneeze, of course, from all that powdery stuff stirred up by your movements.

A sneeze strong enough to register on the Richter earthquake scale.

It seemed as if I could hear and feel the echoes of it all through the dinosaur park. But what I heard, of course, was Sheila on the move again. Coming a little more cautiously this time, but out of statue mode, advancing on me like some animated monster in leggings.

I moved too, retreating. Except now there was a downed tree behind me, and I edged up the hill to get around it. I floundered a step, paused to listen, extracted my leg from a thorny blackberry vine—ouch!—managed a few more steps. Okay, yes, I was getting away from her! All I had to do was stay hidden and silent, work my way downhill and out the gate.

Something touched my back. I turned—

Shining eyes! Teeth!

Something jumped and crashed through the brush. Big as a marauding tank! Noisy as an attacking army!

I screamed and plunged headlong into a tangle of brush and vines and branches. Which is not the way to make a silent escape. The tangle caught me like a bug in a spiderweb. Now my position must be as obvious to Sheila as a bonging buoy on a stormy sea.

In a shift of clouds and moonlight, I suddenly saw what I'd backed into. Sammy the Saber-Toothed Tiger. I tried to breathe easier. His teeth and eyes might look lethal, but he was actually no more dangerous than a stuffed tiger in a toy store.

Something, the something that had apparently been bedded down for the night beside Sammy until I rudely interrupted, was still crashing through the brush, but it was, blessedly, headed away from me. Hopefully, it, whatever it was, was as scared of me as I was of it. I hadn't time to worry about categorizing its identity now. I had bigger, closer worries. Sheila definitely wasn't bothering with stealth now. Sheila was all crashing speed, a destructive tornado bearing down on me. I caught a flash in the moonlight. Her silver concha belt. A killer with pizzazz. Only a few feet away.

No way could I outrun or outmaneuver her on this jungled hillside. My turn to go into statue mode. I scrunched my back against a tree, slid noiselessly to the ground, and tucked myself into a ball. A shifting shaft of moonlight lit the ground a couple feet away, but the light only darkened the shadows at the base of my tree. I hoped.

I pulled my jacket up over my head to keep any gray hair from showing in the dark. I willed my muscles to relax. A turtle probably relaxes within the safety of its shell, doesn't it? *Shrink, Ivy. Shrink and relax.* I reminded myself of how often I'd felt invisible in a crowd. An invisible LOL. I pulled that cloak of invisibility around me now. Sheila couldn't wander around in the dark forever. She'd have to give up and leave. I'd wait her out, sneak back to the gate, and escape.

Hey, Ivy, you know any other good bedtime stories?

Because two eternities later—though I suppose in real time it wasn't more than a minute or two—I peeked out from under my jacket and there she was. My eyes were on the level of her knees. A rip in her leggings exposed a knee bone. It shone like a lethal weapon in that shaft of moonlight. The scarf was gone. So was the turquoise clip in her hair. No pizzazz now.

Maybe she hadn't seen me—

Then I saw my foot sticking out from under the shroud I'd tried to make of my jacket. I groaned. White socks. Could I have chosen anything more visible? Not unless I'd painted a neon target on my chest.

She kicked me in the leg. "Get up, Ivy."

I couldn't think of any advantages to getting up, so I didn't.

I tensed, waiting for another bigger and better kick, but she vaulted to a different plan. She reached down and grabbed me, *oof*-ing a bit, but there I was, slung over her shoulder like a sack of onions. I remembered something I'd thought the first time I met her, that she was strong enough to drag Duke to the church or the altar or anywhere else if she took a mind to. What she obviously had a mind now was to carry me somewhere.

I doubted it was a rescue carry.

MAC

I looked at my watch the moment I woke on the recliner. How long had I been asleep? Shouldn't Ivy be home by now? I hesitated only a minute before tapping the numbers into my cell phone to call Duke.

The phone on his end was ringing, ringing, ringing. But no answer. What did that mean? I remember he'd complained that the phone didn't ring louder than a mouse's squeak. Maybe they were having fun with a noisy game of cards or Monopoly or something.

I put the dinner Ivy had left for me in the microwave to heat. I ate it. I fed BoBandy and Koop. I listened to Miranda Lambert on the radio sing about her little red wagon.

Surely Ivy should be home by now. I called Duke's number again. Still no answer. Okay, enough. I slipped on a jacket and went down to the pickup. BoBandy came along.

When I reached the trailer, Duke opened the door before I even got to the walkway ramp. He immediately saw I was alone. "I heard the pickup. Where's Ivy? And Sheila?"

"I don't know. That's what I came over to find out."

"Ivy said she was going to walk home—"

"Walk!"

"And then Sheila heard something and got worried. She grabbed my gun and went out to make sure Ivy was okay."

Duke came outside and stood at the top of the ramp. We both faced outward.

No Ivy. No Sheila.

"Can your dog find her?"

I went to the pickup and let BoBandy out. He sniffed ground and trees, tail wagging.

"Find Ivy!" I said.

If this were a TV show, the dog would immediately race off and track her down. Lassie to the rescue! But that didn't happen here. BoBandy is a great dog. Good natured and friendly and affectionate. He listens. Often he seems to know what we're saying.

But right now he had no more clue what *Find Ivy* meant than if I'd asked him to find the square root of 127.

Then Duke said, "Do you hear someone screaming?"

IVY

I'm not particularly heavy, even if I have put on a few pounds since the wedding, and Sheila is definitely in good shape from jogging and bicycling, but hauling me uphill through brush and branches was enough to make her puff. She finally had to set me down—dump me down was more like it—and rest for a moment. A time to escape? Not with her big foot planted in the middle of my back.

I managed to turn my face out of the dead leaves and pine needles covering the ground. "Where are you taking me?"

"Since you eliminated the gun, I had to come up with another solution." She sounded aggrieved that I'd unfairly sabotaged her plans, but she had a *solution*. "This will work better anyway."

What kind of solution was up here?

The cliff.

The *cliff*. It wasn't a hundred-foot drop. More like fifteen or twenty, maybe. But, with jagged rocks at the bottom, more than enough to mangle LOL bones. I gulped.

"In this moonlight, no one will believe I just *fell* off the cliff. And you'll never going to convince anyone that I took a moonlight stroll up here and purposely dove off the cliff. "

She considered that and rewrote her earlier scenario. "You acted really strange down there outside Duke's trailer. Like you were all disoriented. Mentally confused. You started mumbling something about finding Mac and ran off into the park."

258

"The park gate is always locked."

A bothersome extra problem, but she was up to the challenge of solving it. "It was standing open. I'd been inside earlier because I was wondering if Brian had ever done anything to clean up the debris from the storm. I forgot to lock it when I came out. You could see that the gate was open and headed straight toward it."

"But why would I—" I clamped my teeth. *Shut up, Ivy,* I chided myself. All I was doing was helping her get her story straight so it would sound convincing when my body was found down there on the rocks below the cliff. I switched tactics.

"Why'd you do it?" I asked.

"Do what?"

"Kill Renée, of course."

"What difference does it make now?"

"What difference will it make if you tell me?" I countered.

"You're a nosy, interfering little old lady, aren't you? Okay, why not? Renée knew what I was doing, and I knew she'd turn me in sooner or later."

"You killed her just because she was going to get your garage sale business in trouble for not having the right permits?" I asked indignantly. "Why didn't you just, oh, slash her tires or something?"

"You think I should have slashed her tires?" She actually chuckled. "Ivy, I'm surprised at you. Shocked, even. I'd never have guessed you were a slashing-tires kind of woman."

"It would have been better than killing her."

"Of course I wouldn't kill her for her threat to turn my garage sale in for lack of permits."

So Sheila had done—or was still doing—something bigger and more illegal than running a not-legally-authorized secondhand store. What? Did Renée know Sheila had bought and perhaps sold a few guns? Selling a gun to a friend wasn't illegal but *dealing* in gun sales was no doubt a different situation. Then I remembered Sheila's unfinished remark when I'd semi-identified Ric Echol outside her garage. *So that's how*— How what? How Renée had found out something incriminating about Sheila. She'd heard it through ex-husband Ric.

I took a wild and totally uneducated guess. "She knew about your sales of Golden Temple?"

Sheila looked as if she might kick me again, but I took another wild guess. "Because Golden Temple isn't really incense, is it? That's just kind of a code name. Something a customer can ask for instead of saying 'I wanna buy some cocaine or meth' or something. Is that what you're giving Duke too? Drugs?"

"I'd never give Duke cocaine or meth." Now she sounded indignant. "But he *needs* the pain pills. His knees really hurt him."

"Opioids? OxyContin? Hydrocodone? Fentanyl?"

She didn't specify the exact identity of Golden Temple. "I took them myself when I hurt my back a couple years ago. I had some left over, so I sold them. When I realized how much they were worth on the market, I found a foreign source for them."

"People overdose on opioids! Haven't you heard all the uproar about the danger of using them? People *die* from them! They're a national problem."

"I only sell to a few people, a *very* few people, and they're people who need them for pain but have doctors who don't care." Now she was righteous. The dealer in deadly drugs doing humanity a good deed.

"But you know how illegal that is, or you wouldn't have a code name for them."

No wonder she'd been nervous when she suspected the biker I thought was Ric had inquired about Golden Temple for his buddy. Getting caught selling illegal opioids meant big-time consequences. Big enough that Sheila was willing to murder to escape them.

"It doesn't look as if I can get any more of them anyway. I'll save what I have for Duke. So shut up, Ivy. Just *shut up*. We're wasting time." She leaned down and did the ol' onion-sack-over-her-shoulder thing again.

I knew a lot more now than I did before. I knew Sheila had killed Renée and why. I knew she had a lucrative business selling opioids to a few select customers.

How much good was all that knowledge going to do me or anyone else? About as much as Koop knowing the secrets of quantum theory and worm holes.

When we first arrived at the dinosaur park, I remember thinking it would be a great place to hide a dead body.

Unfortunately, it appeared that dead body was going to be mine.

Chapter 22

IVY

My arms dangled down Sheila's back. My face flopped against her black sweater. It was rougher than it looked. I might even be getting a rash.

Like that was going to matter.

Branches brushed against my back and shoulders. One from a dead tree caught on my jacket and broke off. I grabbed it before it fell. A couple feet long, a few dead leaves on the end. A weapon? Yeah, right. Maybe I could give her a rash with those dead leaves.

We flopped along. I had time, if not exactly a comfortable setting, to think. I decided I might as well try to add another bit of knowledge to my useless supply. A mutant curiosity gene apparently keeps on going no matter what dire straits you're in.

"How'd you get Renée out to the Kabins so you could kill her?"

She stopped for a moment's rest. I really must be putting on weight. "Let it go, Ivy. Is this how you want to spend your final minutes, fussing about Renée? Think about Mac. Or eternity. Whatever."

Yeah, eternity. Would I be meeting the Lord soon? I look forward to that, eventually. *But maybe a different time and place, Lord? I know Mac will be in that eternity sometime too, but I'd really like to have a few more years here on earth with him.*

"Humor me." I swiped a bit of sweater fuzz out of my mouth. We came out of the trees onto bare ground as we neared the cliff. The moonlight seemed almost unnaturally brilliant, though all I could actually see was the ground below my dangling head. "I just can't figure how you got her to meet you there. You must have been very clever."

It isn't easy carrying on a conversation when you're dangling over a shoulder. I had to lift my head or I'd just be mumbling into her sweater. Flattery is even harder in a situation where you're feeling as hostile as I was. But Sheila fell for the flattery and couldn't resist telling me how cleverly she'd manipulated Renée. She'd never been able to tell anyone before, of course. She even paused in her hill climb to jump right into it.

"I called Renée and told her my husband and I were retired and just passing through the area, and we'd just found this wonderful piece of property with some burned-out old cabins. That a friend in Crescent City had told us she was the very best real estate agent in the area, and we wondered if she could find out if this place was for sale. We just loved it, I told her, and price was no obstacle."

"So what did she say?"

"She said that particular place wasn't for sale, that the owner had plans for it, but she had other great coastal properties available and she'd be glad to come out and talk to us." Carrying on a conversation with a soon-to-be-dead body slung over her shoulder apparently was no problem for Sheila.

"She'd really do that, drive all the way out here?" I asked.

"If enough bucks were involved, Renée would hike from here to Frisco and back. She couldn't resist 'price is no obstacle.'"

"Didn't she recognize your voice?"

"I put crumpled-up toilet tissue over the phone." She sounded gleeful, proud of her inventiveness.

I've heard of covering a phone to disguise your voice, of course. It's on some old TV show every once in a while. Though it's usually a handkerchief, so using crumpled toilet paper was rather creative. Well, maybe that's what it takes to be an effective crook. Creative thinking.

"Of course, a little flattery, telling her she was the greatest real estate agent ever, probably helped. She rushed right out to meet 'us.'"

Sheila might not recognize a bit of king-sized flattery used on herself, but she certainly knew how to use it.

"How'd you get her all the way out to the end cabin? Carry her like you're doing me?"

"Of course not. I just pointed the gun at her and told her to walk." Yes, elementary but effective. It had worked with me, at least for a while.

"Weren't you concerned your phone number would show up on her phone after she was dead?"

"I used a cheap burner phone and threw it in the ocean a couple days later." Triumphant now. The invincible killer. She'd thought of everything.

"So then she drove out to the Kabins to meet you. But her car wasn't there when we found her body."

"That turned out to be the hardest part."

"Harder than *killing* her?"

"Well, you know, more complicated. I was hoping her body wouldn't be found for a long time, but if her vehicle was there, I knew it would be. So, after she was—" She paused, apparently finding the straightforward word *dead* distasteful. "After she was *gone*, I drove my car home from the Kabins and rode my bicycle back out there. I put it in Renée's SUV and drove to her office after dark. Wearing gloves, of course. No fingerprints! Then I parked the SUV there, got out my bicycle, and just rode it home." Again, she sounded victorious and triumphant. "I had it all figured out ahead of time. Although it would have been better if you two hadn't stumbled around out there and found her body so soon."

Was I supposed to apologize for that? I didn't. After all, even if I was hanging upside down across her shoulder, I still had my dignity. More or less.

Unexpectedly, she laughed. "You're trying to keep me

talking, aren't you? Like something out of a mystery novel. Clever sleuth keeps villain talking until help arrives. Right?"

I didn't respond. Unless help appeared in the form of an alien invasion or at least a lone flying saucer swooping in over the sea, I didn't see how help could show up here. But the Lord had parted the Red Sea for the Israelites. Maybe he'd do a miracle for me here? *Maybe a pair of wings, Lord? That would be nice.* Although one small flaw in her perfectly planned murder, one point that might trip her up, suddenly occurred to me.

Too bad I was never going to get to tell anyone about it. But that didn't stop my curiosity.

"So, how'd you get the sheriff's department to get a search warrant on Brian and Kathy's apartment? I don't think they'll get a search warrant on an anonymous call."

"Oh, that was easy. I called them on my way down to Vegas and told them my name was Tiffany and I was sixteen years old—"

"They believed that?"

"I can sound sixteen if I want to!" At this point she also sounded indignant that I doubted her ability to sound so youthful. "I said I'd been Brian's girlfriend for a while but I got scared when he threatened me with a gun and I was pretty sure he'd used it to kill his girlfriend at the old cabins, and I thought the gun was still there at his place."

She shifted me on her shoulder and started walking again. We seemed to be out in the open now, beyond the trees, but the ground was rough. She stumbled a couple of times. Could I hope that would somehow work in my favor? We couldn't be far from the edge of the cliff. Maybe she'd stumble and fall over. Although if that happened, she'd undoubtedly take me with her. Not exactly a win-win situation. She was probably trying to get up to the highest point where I'd have farther to fall when she flung me over.

Finally she stopped and took a deep breath. "You're heavier

than you look, you know?"

She's grumbling about *my* weight? Wasn't *I* the one who had a right to complain? After all, the worst she'd get out of this was a sore back. And I—

I yanked my mind away from the messy details. "Are we there yet? Wherever you're headed?"

"Yes, I'm glad to say, we're here. And such a spectacular view!" She shifted me on her shoulder again. "Have you ever been up here before? I should do it more often. It's such an *inspiring* view, well worth the climb. The moonlight on the sea, the waves churning around the rocks beyond the cove. The stars like jewels in the sky. It's almost like a glimpse into eternity."

I wouldn't know. While she was rhapsodizing about the view, all I could see was the ground and her backside. And yes, as Duke had once remarked, that backside was indeed, in spite of all her jogging and bicycling, quite generously sized. Definitely not a fat-free zone.

"And the scent of sea. Isn't it fantastic, so fresh and sharp and clean?"

I wouldn't know about fantastic scents either. Right now, the scent of Sheila's usual perfume was overwhelmed by the smell of Sheila herself. She'd worked up quite a sweat lugging me up the hill.

But she'd be through enthusing about view and scent of sea any minute now. *Think, Ivy, think!*

The Lord didn't send a UFO to help, but he did send me a smidgen of an idea. I still had the piece of dead branch in my hand. A spindly thing. Not more than a couple feet long. Dead leaves on the end. As a weapon, about as effective as a feather duster.

But the other end, the end where it had splintered off the bigger branch . . . I ran a fingertip across it. Not as sharp as the pocketknife I'd bought at her garage sale, which I wished I had

266

now. But you make do with what you have.

I squirmed around, got a good grip on the stick, gritted my teeth, and closed my eyes.

No, no, my eyes had to be *open*, so I wouldn't miss. I forced them open, carefully picked my target in the moonlight—and it was, blessedly, a good-sized target—and jabbed the sharp end of the stick at the target, jabbed as if I were trying to hit the center of the earth. Nothing vital in there. Maybe the stick wouldn't even go through the sweater. But if it would just incapacitate her long enough for me to—

She howled and hopped and grabbed her backside. I tumbled to the ground. Maybe the jab went deeper than I expected? She shrieked and screamed and screeched. I was mere inches from the edge of the cliff. She wasn't going to have to fling me over. I was going to do it for her and just fall over the edge—

I frantically tried to scramble away but I was all tangled up in her hopping feet. We floundered together. I grunted when a flailing foot slammed my hip. I couldn't see the stick stuck in her backside now. Had it fallen out? Or maybe it had broken off and the broken end was still embedded, like a big sliver? She was howling as if I'd stuck a champagne saber in her backside. I scrabbled with fingernails and toes at the rocky ground, doing some shrieking myself. And then my toes were kicking in empty space—

She stomped me on the hand. Accidental, I think, but effective. Kneed me in the back when she fell.

And over she went. I scrambled back to safety. Her shriek didn't fade away. The fall wasn't that far. But then the shriek abruptly ended and, except for the roar of surf in the distance, there was only silence from below. Profound silence.

I just lay there for a moment, disbelieving. Then, flat on my stomach, I squirmed around and leaned my head over the edge. Moonlight hadn't yet reached this side of the hill. Only a pit of

267

darkness lay below me.

"Sheila?" I called tentatively.

Silence.

I raised the tentative call to a yell. "Sheila?"

Silence.

Was she unconscious down there? Injured? *Dead?*

I stumbled to my feet. I'd only wanted to incapacitate her and make my escape, not *kill* her!

I took one more look into the dark pit. Still silence. Still blackness. No way could I get to her, much less rescue her by myself.

There was no trail, and I fought my way through brush and blackberry vines and trees. I ran into a downed tree. I stumbled over a broken stump. A branch whapped me in the face. I passed Sammy the Saber-Toothed Tiger. He didn't scare me now, but that hole Duke had dug was around here somewhere—

Lord, keep me from falling into it!

My own noisy descent obscured any other sounds, but just past the toothy tiger something moved—something live!

Cougar?

No, goats! A whole herd of them. Well, maybe not a herd, but at least three or four. They split to go around me, separating as if I were a rock in a stream. Not ghost goats. Live goats, noisy, *smelly* goats. A big, cranky billy goat swung his horns in my direction.

I was no goat-fighting toreador, and I just dodged him and kept going, lurching and floundering and stumbling.

Finally I slammed right into the picket fence. I took a breath to gather strength and then backed up a few steps and made a run at the fence. I didn't think I had it in me, but this time I did it. I vaulted right over the pickets. Ivy, the late-blooming Superwoman?

On down the trail. Somewhere along in there I started

yelling for help.

And when I reached the parking lot, a small crowd came running to meet me. Mac. Duke. Brian. Kathy. BoBandy danced around my feet.

Mac wrapped his arms around me. "Ivy, what's wrong?"

"Sheila . . . she was trying to throw me over the cliff . . . but she fell over herself!"

"Why—" Mac broke off as if deciding an explanation wasn't the most important need at the moment.

"I'm already calling nine-one-one," Duke said. "I've got this new cell phone, if I can make it work—"

"Tell them we need search and rescue. An ambulance. And the police."

Even in my breathless state, I sensed a certain irony in that. Sheila provides Duke with a new cell phone. He uses it to call the police on her.

"What do you mean, Sheila tried to throw you over the cliff? Why?" Brian demanded.

"Because she killed Renée! Because she planted the gun in your laundry room! And she realized that I'd figured it out!"

"Stop asking questions," Mac commanded roughly. He picked me up in his arms. It felt a lot different than being hauled around by Sheila. Safe. Sheltered. Secure. I closed my eyes and let everything go limp.

Home is where the heart is, and I was *home*.

"Bring her over to the trailer," Duke said.

"No, our place," Kathy said. "Oh, poor Ivy. Her face is all scratched and her clothes torn. All because of that awful woman."

She kept a hand on my arm as Mac carried me across the parking lot. My new BFF. Someone opened the door. I smelled cinnamon and vanilla. Kathy had been baking cookies again. I wasn't exactly hungry, but the homey scent was reassuring. Mac set me on the sofa. Kathy draped a blanket over me.

269

"Ivy, honey, are you okay?" Mac ran his hands over everything from my arms and legs to my feet and head. "The ambulance is coming. Duke called for one."

"I don't need an ambulance. But Sheila does. If she isn't already dead."

"I'll go try to find her—"

"She's on the rocks at the bottom of the cliff. I didn't mean to *kill* her when I jabbed her with a stick. I didn't think about her going *over*." I tried to struggle to my feet. "I'll have to show you—"

Mac pushed me back on the sofa. "You stay here. I'll grab a flashlight out of the pickup." He gave me a quick kiss on the forehead. "I'll leave BoBandy with you. Brian, you got a rope we can take along?"

"There's one hanging out in the carport."

Then they were both gone. I gave Kathy a quick look. I'd just escaped one killer and now here I was, trapped with another. Except she didn't know that I knew she was a killer too. She was, in fact, gushing thanks even as Duke grumbled about his bad knees that kept him from rushing up the hill with Mac and Brian. He dropped into a chair nearby.

"Ivy, you're so brave. And I'm so grateful to you!" Kathy kept patting me appreciatively. "Now you can tell those deputies what really happened. That they were all wrong and Brian didn't do *anything* to that woman. That it was Sheila who did everything. You've saved him, Ivy! You've saved *us*."

Lying there flat on my back, BoBandy's nose pressed into my hand, I wasn't about to point out that she and Brian weren't exactly *saved*, because some unpleasant facts about the past were very soon going to emerge.

Kathy gave my shoulder another pat. "I'll go make some tea."

I started to protest. I wasn't inclined to eat cookies or drink tea or consume anything Kathy's killer hands had touched.

Then I reminded myself she didn't know that I knew about a dead husband who wasn't really a husband, so I surely hadn't anything to worry about from her. *Yet.* "That would be nice. Thank you."

Kathy bustled off to the kitchen, and Duke gave me a morose look. "You sure about Sheila?"

"I'm sure."

"I knew Sheila had her . . . flaws. I didn't want to marry her. But I never would have guessed she was a *killer.*" He didn't sound doubtful, just a little forlorn.

"I'm sorry. She told me all about how she'd tricked Renée into coming out to the burned cabins and why she did it. She used your keys to get in here to plant the gun she killed Renée with."

"But why *did* she do it?"

"It had to do with some pills she was secretly selling to a few people. A very serious crime, and Renée found out about it."

I thought he might connect that with the pain pills she was giving him, but at the moment he didn't seem to. "Did she blow up Brian's Porsche too?"

"No, someone else did that."

"Crooks everywhere," Duke muttered gloomily. "The whole world's full of crooks and outlaws."

It was beginning to seem that way, and Duke didn't know the full extent of the crook population. There was Killer Sheila, also illegally selling opioids. Somebody blowing up an expensive car. Killers Kathy and Brian, getting rid of an old man back in Missouri so they could collect on Brian's life insurance. More crimes in the offing. Brian and Renée planning some scheme with the Kate's Kabins and the dinosaur park properties, maybe eventually getting rid of Duke if he stood in the way.

Crooks and outlaws everywhere.

271

But I was, as always, comforted by the knowledge that, no matter what the situation or how many crooks gathered, God is in final control.

Kathy returned with a cup of fragrant tea and a cookie. At the same time, the first screaming siren arrived. I struggled to my feet and trooped outside with Kathy and Duke to direct the first responders up the hill to the cliff. A deputy leaped out of the driver's side of the sheriff's department vehicle and Deputy Hardishan jumped out the other side. He confronted me at the door.

"What's going on?" he demanded.

Kathy answered before I could. "Sheila Weekson! She killed Renée Echol and planted the gun *here*. She was trying to kill Ivy, but she fell over the cliff herself. Mac and Brian are up there looking for her!" She lifted her hand toward the hill in a dramatic, they-went-thataway gesture.

I was impressed. Kathy had managed to capture the essence of this evening's activities in a minimum of sentences.

More vehicles roared up, sirens screaming. An ambulance. Another police car. Another vehicle with Search and Rescue emblazoned on the side. Deputy Hardishan did not immediately head for the hill, however. He gave me a hard look, maybe even a suspicious look. He wasn't necessarily accepting that Sheila had just *fallen* over the cliff, not with *me* here.

"I can give you all the details later." I glanced at Kathy. Lots of details. "But it's true. Sheila killed Renée and tried to kill me. But Mac and Brian are up there now, trying to rescue her."

He hesitated momentarily, but apparently he decided they could sort all this out later. He and the other deputy headed for the gate, several guys from the search and rescue vehicle following. The men from the ambulance also followed with a folding stretcher.

Kathy, Duke, and I went back inside to wait. Nothing else

we could do. I drank my tea and ate the cookie. Duke just sat there, still not disbelieving, just sad.

After an hour or so, maybe longer—time had gotten a bit muddled—we heard noise out in the parking lot. We all went outside and watched the EMTs load a stretcher into the ambulance. Two deputies and the search and rescue guys grouped together around their cars for some kind of discussion. I didn't see Deputy Hardishan or the deputy who'd been with him. Mac and Brian crossed the parking lot.

"Is she—" I didn't know how to end the question, so I put a positive spin on it. "Okay?"

"She has broken bones and a bad head injury," Mac said. "But she's alive. She was unconscious when they got her up to the top of the cliff, but she was mumbling something on the way down here on the stretcher."

Yeah, Sheila might have a lot to mumble about. If she was up to thinking, she might even be concocting a story of how she was trying to rescue me in my disoriented mental state and I pushed her over.

The ambulance left the parking lot with siren wailing, confirming that Sheila was still alive. No need for a siren if she was dead. In spite of all I knew she'd done, even what she'd tried to do, I was relieved. Though, guiltily, maybe that was more because I didn't want me and my jabbing stick to be responsible for her death.

"Deputy Hardishan and another deputy are still up there," Mac added.

"What are they doing?"

"He might be trying to arrest a goat. We ran into a bunch of them up there. He tried to shoo them off, but one old billy goat with horns took offense and butted him."

"Where?"

I meant where did it happen, but Mac gave a different answer. "On the backside, I believe."

273

Deputy Hardishan looked to be limping a bit when he came across the parking lot a minute later.

A bad night for backsides.

Kathy said, "You're a good woman, Ivy." Another pat. "Wanting Sheila to be rescued, even after what she tried to do to you. And thank you again, thank you for what you've done for *us*. You've cleared Brian's name."

I hadn't done it yet, but yes, I could clear Brian of any guilt in Renée's death. He hadn't killed her, and the gun in their laundry room belonged to Sheila, not Brian. But Kathy wasn't going to be nominating me for LOL Do-Gooder of the Year after she found out I'd contacted PI Megalthorpe in Missouri.

Which might not be long.

Another car pulled into the parking lot, and through the window I could see a head with a familiar comb-over hairstyle. Megalthorpe had proved his worth as an investigator and found Brian and Kathy on his own.

Megalthorpe didn't get out of his car, but Deputy Hardishan motioned and said he wanted to talk to me out there in the cruiser. Mac wasn't invited, but he came along. I sat in the car. Mac and Hardishan stayed standing. Apparently the deputy didn't feel like sitting yet. He took notes about what I said Sheila had told me. I'd rather not tell him about my jabbing stick, let him think Sheila just stumbled over the cliff, but honesty made me tell it all.

"I think the stick went in . . . fairly deep. And that's why she started jumping around and finally fell over."

Deputy Hardishan didn't comment, but I saw him add that to his notes. I realized what Sheila had told me might be considered unacceptable "hearsay" evidence and not hold up in court, but I had one bit of information the deputy might be able to check out.

"Do you still have Renée's SUV?"

"Yes, we do."

"I was thinking—I've heard that whenever two objects come in contact, there's always some kind of exchange."

"Every contact leaves a trace," Hardishan agreed. "Locard's exchange principle, it's called."

"Sheila's bicycle was in Renée's SUV, but the lab or whoever hasn't known that. If they've come across any scratches or bits of paint or anything they haven't so far been able to identify . . ."

Hardishan didn't jump up and down with glee, but I thought his nod held a hint of victory. "We'll check it out." He closed his notebook. "You folks probably want to get on home. I'll be in touch."

I slid out of the cruiser. Mac got a hold on my arm and stopped me. "We came across a little information about Ric Echol, if you're still interested," Mac said to Hardishan.

The deputy gave Mac a sharp look. "We're interested. We know he's in the area, but he's kept his nose clean and so far we haven't been able to nail him down."

So Mac told him we'd learned Ric had a good buddy known as Bowser, and Bowser occasionally worked at a plant nursery near the airport. "He might know Ric's whereabouts."

"We're familiar with Bowser. We'll check it out."

"You also might want to talk to the man in the car out in the parking lot. Over there," Mac added, nodding that direction. "He's a private investigator named Megalthorpe from Missouri."

The deputy managed an expressive lift of eyebrow in spite of his encounter with the goat. Of course, it wasn't the eyebrow that had made close contact with the goat. "Missouri?" he repeated.

"He has information about a crime you've never even heard of, but I think a connection with our local residents will interest you."

"Well, thank you. You two are just full of information."

That sounded a little snarky, but friendly snarky.

And then Mac took me back to the motorhome. We didn't move everything into it, but we didn't have to discuss it to know we wanted to spend the night in our very own bed.

There's something a little creepy about sleeping in a bed belonging to someone who's just tried to kill you.

Chapter 23

IVY

"Get out!"

Mac and I both stared at the woman screaming at us when I opened the motorhome in response to the hammering on the door. It was a week after my encounter with Sheila at the cliff, and she was still in the hospital under guard twenty-four seven. Her head injury was more severe than they'd originally thought. Sheila's daughter, Vivian, had seemed distraught but friendly enough when she'd arrived earlier in the day, before she'd gone in to the hospital to see Sheila. She'd said her mother's attorney had called and suggested she come up and take care of Sheila's home and any business affairs that might need attention. Vivian thought the implication was that Sheila might not be free to do anything herself in the near future.

Vivian had also said she wanted to use up perishables in her mother's refrigerator and planned to make chicken soup for dinner. And why didn't we come over and share the soup with her that evening? I said I'd bring some garlic bread to accompany the soup.

It looked as if we were now uninvited.

At least we wouldn't have to be on the lookout for paper clips among the carrots and onions.

"We're planning to leave in another day or two," Mac said. "If we could—"

"No, you're leaving *now*." Both Vivian's red hair and blue eyes practically shot sparks. The red hair was the same shade as Sheila's, which probably meant I'd been mistaken in my assumption that Sheila's was bottle-red. Unless they bought the same brand bottle. "Mom told me all about how you told the authorities some wacko story about murder and selling pain

277

pills and how you pushed her over a cliff!"

So that was Sheila's story. No doubt the same one she was telling law enforcement. Were they believing it? I doubted it. A couple of days ago Hardishan and another deputy had come out and removed Sheila's bicycle from the patio by her double-wide.

"If you're not out of here in half an hour, I'm calling the cops!"

A half hour? Could we do that? Actually, we beat that and were pulling out of the driveway in twenty minutes. Without confronting Vivian again, we'd rubber-banded an envelope to the doorknob of the double-wide. In it was money sufficient to pay for the electricity we'd used in the over-the-garage room with some extra for Sheila's hospitality in letting us stay in the room.

We headed over to Duke's trailer to tell him goodbye and give him the gift we'd ordered off the internet for him, which had arrived a couple days ago.

I wasn't really angry about our rushed departure. I could understand Vivian's antagonism, although she was mistaken about the facts. Whatever Sheila had done, she was Vivian's *mother*. We were planning to leave soon anyway.

But even if we weren't angry at Vivian about the abrupt eviction, I felt . . . disconcerted. I've never been kicked out before, and it's the kind of thing that makes you feel guilty even if you haven't done anything.

Some unknowns had been cleared up.

We knew through Deputy Hardishan that Ric Echol was in custody. They'd talked to Bowser. They were suspicious of him on a possible hit-and-run case, and he'd tried to bargain his way out of his own problems by offering a flood of information on Ric. Including that Ric had been responsible for the explosion of a certain Porsche, even going so far as to supply a reason for why he'd done it. Ric thought Brian Morrison had killed ex-wife Renée, and when Ric's anonymous call to the sheriff's office about Brian's involvement with Renée hadn't gotten Brian charged with her murder, he'd turned to do-it-yourself justice. He'd planned to blow up Brian in the Porsche, but he didn't want to kill or hurt Kathy—crooks can apparently have their own version of a conscience—so he'd done a fairly sophisticated job of wiring in a timer to explode the Porsche several minutes after the engine was started, when Brian would be well away from the house. Except he hadn't counted on Brian leaving the engine running while he went back into the house, so it was empty when it exploded out in the parking lot.

Deputy Hardishan didn't say whether this gush of information had helped Bowser with his own problems.

Mac had sent in his article about the old tales of treasure in the dinosaur park to the magazine and received enthusiastic approval on it.

Kathy and Brian were also in custody now. Deputy Hardishan was closemouthed about their conversations with authorities in Missouri, but something else turned up when a man in Idaho contacted the local newspaper about what he was now thinking was a scam of some kind. It concerned a Brian Morrison soliciting investments in a proposed resort with ocean frontage and an extravagant theme park with moving dinosaurs and elaborate rides. Brian and Renée's scheme? After showing up with another search warrant, they'd taken Brian's computer and various other records.

After doing that, they'd decided they were finished with the apartment and gave Duke permission to go in and clean up. We'd helped him with that. And in the process we'd found something unexpected. It was a box with two urns in it, both full of ashes. One had "Mother" worked into the construction of the fancy urn, the other plain urn was unmarked. The ashes of Kathy's "husband"? Why had she kept them? Guilt? Some sense of responsibility? Could any information be obtained from cremated ashes? We turned the urn over to Deputy Hardishan.

Megalthorpe had stopped in to see us before going back to Missouri. I asked how he'd located Brian and Kathy's place on his own, and he said he'd used old-fashioned detective legwork and showed the photos he had to numerous people in the local area. Brian's old newspaper photo hadn't been any help, but a couple of people identified Kathy's photo as being the woman who made those good cookies at the dinosaur park. By now I'd concluded that Kathy had originally been so determined about not acknowledging she knew me back in Missouri because she was even more afraid I might recognize her current husband as the same husband she had back in Missouri, who was supposed to be dead.

We'd gone into the Hideaway one day for lunch. Ron Sweeney was working there again, but we weren't in his section of tables and didn't talk to him.

Sheila was facing charges of the murder of Renée Echol, attempted murder of me, and various other charges. Hardishan had said they might need us to come back and testify at her trial, but that could be some time yet. He thought, with the contact evidence that Sheila's bicycle had been in Renée's SUV, that they had a strong case.

We parked the motorhome at the dinosaur park and walked over to Duke's trailer. I wished I'd had time to make cookies for him. Kathy wouldn't be supplying cookies for him anymore. We already knew he'd been to see Sheila in the hospital and heard her stubborn story about my making up outrageous lies about her and almost killing her too. He didn't believe it, but he'd still seemed a little stunned when we helped him with the apartment cleanup. His girlfriend a killer; his friends running the dinosaur park and making cookies for him, also killers.

He opened the door and gave me a hug. I was relieved that,

although he was still sad and subdued, he wasn't holding any grudges against me.

We told him we were on our way south and just wanted to stop and tell him goodbye. We didn't tell him we were leaving a bit early because Sheila's daughter had kicked us out. In honor of the start of our honeymoon, I was wearing the jeans grandniece Sandy had sent me. The glittery design still looked like an octopus in a sparkly Christmas tree, but it would soon be a dark and moonless night anyway.

Now Duke had some news. His nephew was retiring in a few days and had decided to move out here within a month. He'd live in the apartment and maybe open the dinosaur park next summer. Duke hoped he'd spruce it up a bit. Duke said he'd decided to move the trailer into an RV park in town that took residents on a permanent basis. Close to Billie's Burgers? I wondered. But I didn't ask.

Then we gave him the gift. He recognized what it was immediately, of course.

"A champagne saber!"

Not the twenty-five-thousand-dollar version he'd seen in the magazine, but a rather nice stainless steel version. And a set of champagne flutes to go with it.

Duke gleefully wielded the saber in a few practice strokes. "How about we try it out right now? I still have that bottle of champagne in the refrigerator."

"No, you save your champagne for a really special occasion. Maybe one is coming soon."

MAC

Now we were on our way. As Duke had pointed out earlier, we'd run into an extraordinary number of crooks and outlaws here. But, as always, as I've learned from Ivy, the Lord is in final control.

It was almost dark, and the beam of the motorhome lights momentarily lit up the figure of Tricky the Triceratops in the parking lot. I hoped the nephew would spruce him up too.

It was, as Ivy had mentioned earlier, a bit disconcerting being kicked out of our temporary space in Sheila's pasture, but my spirits picked up as we headed down the road. We could stop at an RV park, park in a rest area, or drive all night. We could do whatever we wanted. We had food, heat, everything we needed. Our honeymoon had been somewhat delayed, due to this detour. But honeymoon is, as Ivy says, a state of mind.

And beside me Ivy looks . . . I've been uneasy with the word so much in use now, but right now it fits. Yep, Ivy may think those jeans are too glittery for an LOL, but I think they're fine.

There's no better to say it: Ivy MacPherson looks hot.

The End

E-BOOKS BY LORENA McCOURTNEY

THE MAC 'N' IVY MYSTERIES:
Something Buried, Something Blue (also available in print)
Detour (also available in print)

THE IVY MALONE MYSTERIES:
Invisible
In Plain Sight
On the Run
Stranded
Go, Ivy, Go!

THE JULESBURG MYSTERIES:
Whirlpool
Riptide
Undertow

THE ANDI McCONNELL MYSTERIES:
Your Chariot Awaits
Here Comes the Ride
For Whom the Limo Rolls

THE CATE KINKAID FILES MYSTERIES (Available in
both paperback and e-book):
Dying to Read
Dolled Up to Die
Death Takes a Ride

CHRISTIAN ROMANCES
Three Secrets (Novella)
Searching for Stardust
Yesterday Lost (Mystery/Romance)
Canyon

Betrayed
Dear Silver

The author is always delighted to hear from readers.
Contact her through e-mail at: lorenamcc@centurylink.net
Or connect with her on Facebook at:
http://www.facebook.com/lorenamccourtney

Happy Reading!

CPSIA information can be obtained
at www.ICGtesting.com
Printed in the USA
LVHW011633070820
662641LV00001B/151